CLAN

David P Elliot

MOORHEN PUBLISHING LLP

First published in Great Britain in 2008 by
Moorhen Publishing LLP
1 Hazelwood Close, Windmill Hill, Brixham, Devon, TQ5 9SE
www.moorhenpublishing.co.uk

Distributed by David P Elliot
30 West Quay, Abingdon, Oxfordshire, OX14 5TL
Mobile: +44 (0) 7775 858322
email: david@davidelliot.plus.com

A CIP catalogue record for this book is available
from the British Library.

ISBN   978-1-905856-03-9

Cover design by Deep Red Designs
Cover images by Jeff Elliott

Printed and bound in Great Britain by
SRP Limited, Exeter, Devon

Dedication

Here's to all Elliots and Elliot bairns
And them that lie in Elliots' arms.

To Alan
Best wishes &
enjoy the read!

David P E...

25th July 2008
"Yorketter of Reetin"

Author's Foreword

William de Soulis is not an invention.

No more than William Wallace or Robert the Bruce, legends of Scottish history, are inventions.

Unlike modern leaders, these men faced their enemies personally.

Not for them the luxury of sending young men and women, with incredible weapons of mass destruction, thousands of miles to fight a remote enemy.

These warriors, for warriors they were, stood their ground, fought hand to hand, giving no quarter and asking for none in return.

They risked their own lives, not just the lives of their followers.

Some, like Wallace, had no personal ambition and sought, altruistically, to free his country from the domination of an English king.

The Bruce united a country under powerful leadership, defeating superior odds again and again.

William de Soulis however, fought for himself.

With his unflinching belief in his right to rule, he was prepared to take on anyone in his way, including The Bruce and William Wallace, to take what he believed to be his rightful inheritance – the Scottish Throne.

These men were fearless giants, physically and mentally. Who of our modern leaders would last more than a few seconds against them?

But unlike Wallace and Bruce, William de Soulis also had a reputation for evil – a reputation that will become clear as this tale unfolds.

If you would discover more, go to Hermitage Castle between the towns of Newcastleton and Hawick in the Scottish Borders. It still stands as a monument to dangerous and bloody times.

If you are brave, go at night, but I will not be there.

I believe it is haunted.

If you are an Armstrong, a Scott, a Kerr, a Robson, a Nixon or one of the many other famous Border families, I salute you today as a friend, even if our history, allegiances and blood feuds might suggest otherwise.

If you are an Elliot, I salute you as family.

We live in a time when politicians seek to keep us in fear in an effort to make us docile and controllable. They tell us much about how they will protect us, how they will deliver us from evil, if we are just prepared to put our faith, trust, but mostly our liberty, in their hands.

I have no belief in politicians – perhaps it is Border blood that makes me instinctively distrust those who seek power over others.

I believe in Family and Friends.

Ultimately, I believe in Clan...

Prologue

February 1298 – Hermitage

It was half scream and half roar.

Seconds earlier, the Great Hall, with its blazing wooden wall torches and man-high open log fires, was echoing with the clamour of dozens of warriors, some lounging at long trestle tables picking at huge platters of cooked meats consisting of whole roasted suckling pigs and poultry and massive sides of beef, as well as piles of coarse bread, fruits and large jugs of rough wine and ale.

Others wrestled with wenches, who seemed fair game to any groping hand as they squeezed between the jostling and boisterous men, struggling with large pitchers of ale as they refilled proffered cups. Still more sang bawdy songs, fought or feigned attack on each other as drunken men, fuelled by alcohol, have done since time began.

But suddenly there was only that almost supernatural sound, followed by instant silence, as the inhuman noise echoed from the stone walls and faded away, emphasising the sudden silence that had fallen on the assembly.

All eyes fell on the two giants in the glow of the huge log fire. One was dressed in black and stood six feet six inches tall, towering over the surrounding men, a good foot and a half taller than any other – with the exception of the giant who faced him. Dressed in green, this man stood an inch taller than the other and was equally powerfully built.

The scream had emanated from the giant in black, his face coloured with rage, wild eyed with flecks of foam at the mouth that suggested a loss of control approaching insanity. "You would deny me Wallace; you, a bastard second son of a worthless dead knight, would defy me my true birthright."

The surrounding assembly backed away, terrified, desperate to put distance between them and the reach of the huge broadsword that the black giant, William de Soulis had drawn.

William Wallace, the giant in green, stood his ground, a strange calmness in his eyes as he too drew his sword.

Soulis raised his weapon and swung viciously at the head of Wallace, a rain of sparks marked the huge clash as the blow was parried, deflected down, and the sword withdrawn to return a blow in the direction of the head of Soulis. This blow also was parried, but such was the power of it, Soulis staggered backwards, almost losing his footing, but managing to raise his sword once more, just in time to stop a second blow from severing his head from his shoulders.

Weakened by the second blow, he fell to one knee, once again raising his sword to block a third and crucial blow from the advancing Wallace.

This time however, so powerful was the strike from Wallace, that Soulis's own sword was driven back into the face of the kneeling giant. The blade smashed into bone, causing a wide wound from forehead to chin, diagonally across Soulis's face and he fell backwards, apparently mortally wounded.

Wallace stepped forward, raising his own sword, with both hands clasping the hilt, preparing for a stabbing movement to finish off the stricken warrior, but withdrew when he saw the helpless condition of his erstwhile attacker, who looked to be bleeding to death before him.

Turning away from the prostrate body, he eyed Soulis's men menacingly, silently daring any to avenge their stricken Lord.

None dared.

With one glance back at the stricken Soulis, William Wallace strode towards the exit of the great hall, a path opening before him as the terrified spectators gave way, his small entourage falling in behind him as he strode out of Hermitage Castle.

*

February 1972 – Hermitage

The young Egyptian threw open the door as the car he was driving bumped slowly to a stop against a large grey rock adjacent to the narrow burn outside the derelict castle, before rolling back slightly and coming to a rocking halt.

He pulled himself painfully, headfirst, out of the car, crawling on hands and knees, dragging himself slowly away from the vehicle, trailing blood from the now freely-flowing wound in his stomach. As if, somehow, it was his final lifeline, he clutched the blood-soaked bank notes crumpled in his right hand so tightly that his knuckles were white.

With one final effort, he dragged himself to the ditch leading down to the burn before collapsing face down in the dirt and stones. He lay there for a few seconds as he desperately tried to remain conscious, but realising he had no strength to move any further he began to scrape ineffectually with one hand at the dirt and stones until he had created a small indent in the hard earth and shingle. He pushed the bank notes into the small hole and scrabbled to cover them with loose stones and earth, desperate to hide his hard won money.

Suddenly, his wrist was gripped, vice-like and as he raised his head slightly to see what was gripping him, he saw razor sharp, yellow, hooked claws tightening around his wrist and slicing through his skin like a knife through butter. His heart was gripped with terror as he painfully turned his head and struggled to focus tear-stained eyes on the creature whose claw was gripping him effortlessly.

The boy began to call on a long forgotten God as he stared into a face of pure evil, which slowly lowered towards his face, sheer hatred in the jet black eyes that stared at him from grey, leathery skin. Strands of matted hair hung from a blood-soaked chin and mouth, dripping with foul-smelling saliva as the hooked and pointed yellow teeth clicked together, ready to tear out his throat.

His last view was of the strange, blood-matted bonnet pulled down tightly on the vile creature's head.

So this was death – the Egyptian, who had murdered and stolen the name of a young Italian boy, Andrea Dettori, just hours before, had seen death; had stared it in the face.

So this was what came in the end – this was the foul creature that would transport him into hell for eternity, where he would pay for his sins, which had been many.

He tried to turn away from the stench of the creature's breath as he fell, gratefully, into unconsciousness, just as he began to feel the sharp teeth slowly tightening around his throat.

*

February 2007 – Abingdon, Oxfordshire

David Elliot sat on the black leather couch, the television flickering but muted before him as he lay, head resting on the low back, his eyes closed. Opening his eyes lethargically, he rolled his head slowly, from side to side as he surveyed the room about him.

At fifty-seven, he was tired, overweight, unfit and frustrated and he looked with a sense of bemusement at his 'home'.

A pair of shoes and an open and discarded copy of the 'Appointments' section of the 'Sunday Times' lay on the floor, surrounded by the assortment of other sections and magazines that he would never read; a few books, CDs, DVDs and the odd family photograph. It occurred to him that apart from these insignificant items, there was almost nothing of him in the place.

Women had come and gone in Elliot's life; three he had married and three had divorced him. That was his experience of women, the one thing he could rely on in life – that women would leave.

As they came into his life, they filled the house with themselves; a picture here, a vase there, the things that turned a house into a home, that made it warm, comforting and welcoming. Equally, as they left, they took away those same things and the warmth and comfort went with them.

Repeating this cycle three times, he realised that almost nothing here was truly 'his'. The home had once again become a house, nothing more than a place to live in, if living was what it was called.

He sighed and leaning forward, he picked up the stapled wad of A4 pages before him on the coffee table and scanned it once more.

It was called a 'Compromise Agreement' apparently. A fancy name for a contract that acknowledged that the company wanted you out – but without the effort, (or more accurately the cost), of finding a justifiable reason for sacking you.

The 'Compromise' bit was that he promised not to cause trouble, to sue for wrongful dismissal or bad mouth the company to anyone – in return they would give him a few quid, tax-free, to go away.

Once he signed it he would be out of the door immediately; 'on gardening leave' was the expression – another euphemism for 'go home so we can forget about you as quickly as possible and get on with our own, more important, lives'.

"Sod it!" he said out loud to no one in particular.

At his age, the prospect of job hunting again was not an attractive one. Elliot threw the agreement back onto the coffee table and picked up his coffee, sipping the hot liquid. How did he get to this age, divorced three times and still not decided what he wanted to be when he grew up?

He told himself that the IT business was a young man's game now. How did you explain to some young kid that you really are dynamic, enthusiastic, driven, a 'self starter' (whatever that meant), but with no degree, no 'other language' and all the other clichés that really meant you needed to be young, malleable, compliant – but most of all young.

Was there no place any more for ability, experience, someone who could actually write a sentence grammatically and with all the words spelled correctly? Who could turn up at an appointment on time without ringing from a mobile phone three times, explaining that they were late because of a hold up on the M25? When wasn't there a hold up on the M25?

Apparently all was subsumed into an ongoing quest for quick money, short termism and youth, yes, you got that contract yesterday, but what have you done lately?

A comment made by Spencer Tracey, the veteran Hollywood star sprang to mind. Apparently when Marlon Brando appeared on the scene, heralding a whole new generation of so-called 'Method' actors, a journalist asked Tracey if he had ever considered Method acting.

Irritated, he had replied, "No, – I'm too old, too tired and too talented."

Elliot knew how he felt.

The fact was that he was a bad employee. He knew that. He was clearly bright but was seemingly unable to fit the norm apparently required in businesses today. Not that he was deliberately difficult, well, not all the time at least, although boredom sometimes led him to argue for the sheer hell of it.

More often it was because he had a quick brain and was not process driven, eventually getting frustrated by the time it took for people to catch up with decisions and conclusions that seemed to him self evident, his impatience bringing out an argumentative tendency.

In short, it seemed, people found him too clever by half and he didn't fit in.

Well at least I got out before I had to report to someone with gel in their hair, he thought.

Maybe it was time to do something else, something worthwhile, something that would survive him in this irritating world of short termism, when nothing counted except money, and then only if it came today rather than tomorrow.

He picked up the document again and signed and dated it.

"Sod it!" he said again, this time louder and with more venom.

CHAPTER ONE

The darkness hung damp and icy, in the bowels of the huge stone shell that was historically 'The Strength of Liddesdale'.

Hermitage Castle sat brooding on the edge of what was once the 'Debatable Lands', a three mile wide and twelve mile long strip of rough moorland, a few miles to the north of Carlisle, which marked the disputed border area between Scotland and England. So politically sensitive was this area, that the mere building of this powerful defensive icon in the 13th century, gave Henry III an excuse to invade Scotland, claiming it had been built too close to the border, which at that time was marked by the river Liddel.

Attack and counter attack followed between the warring factions on either side of the contested border, as the English and the Scots vied for territorial supremacy. So violent and contentious was this land in those desperate days that a joint declaration between Scotland and England was enacted to try and put an end to the constant factional bloodshed. Apparently contradicting its very purpose, the declaration ironically sanctioned killing, robbing and any other form of crime on anyone found in these debated lands, with the misguided hope it would discourage the settling of the land by occupants loyal to either side.

The actual consequence, however, was to attract a particular breed of so called 'broken men' to inhabit the area. They took full advantage of the lawless nature of the place to create their own laws and traditions, finally leading to the advent of the 'Border Reiver', clan or family-based factions, both English and Scottish, who raided, murdered, stole and kidnapped with relative impunity on both sides of the border, swearing allegiance to none except their own kin.

The valley that Hermitage guarded, as a consequence of its lawless state and daily mayhem, came to be known as the 'bloodiest valley in Britain' such was its reputation for murder and other forms of iniquity.

But now in this year of 2007 the castle had lain empty of human habitation for generations and the whole concept of the 'Debatable Lands', and its bloody reputation had been consigned to history.

Tonight however, in a cold forbidding February, close to seven hundred years of history was stirring and unravelling remorselessly in the cold darkness below the castle.

Outside, the wind howled across the moorlands and hills, twisting the rough grass and bending the black branches of the leafless trees in its relentless path. It drove icy rain horizontally; rain that would strike like so many razor cuts into the faces of any poor creature, human or animal, who might have ventured out on this night.

But should anyone be unwise enough to seek shelter in this place, they would have quickly turned to face the elements again, rather than stay a moment further within these dark, forbidding walls.

It was claimed that the screams of children could be heard in this place. Others said it was a trick of the wind. Either way, it was true that many children were imprisoned and sacrificed here, in the lust for power and influence that had driven William de Soulis, who in the late 13th and early 14th centuries, was the Lord of Hermitage. His family occupied the castle for some two hundred years until that fateful day in 1321 when the seeds of the events unfolding this night were sown.

Are places evil because people do evil there? Or can a place be inherently evil, driving the occupants remorselessly to acts of depravity?

Hermitage Castle would suggest the latter, as William de Soulis was not the first or last person to practise heinous crimes within its confines; but he was certainly the most depraved.

The legends said that the castle had sunk some ten feet into the ground with the weight of the sin and iniquity bearing down on it and with many other incidents of murder, drownings (a common form of execution in those days) and at least one person having been starved to death in the dungeons, it was claimed as one of the most haunted places in Britain.

On this particular night, almost seven hundred years after the events of 1321, a huge wooden chest sat in the centre of the windowless dungeon that extended below ground, underneath the castle proper.

Only wall mounted wooden torches which fired a phosphorescent glow within the stones of the walls themselves tempered the oppressive darkness within, casting a cold, eerie glow on the dank walls, the floor and the chest itself. This casket was ancient and made of aged oak, bound with rusting iron bands and its weight settled it two inches or so into the sodden, slime-covered, stone floor.

The torches guttered briefly as the temperature dropped further from its already bone-chilling level, and an eerie silence fell, as the distant howling of the wind and rain outside seemed to calm briefly.

Suddenly the silence was broken by nine loud knocks as a huge fist crashed down onto the lid of the chest. It was followed by a low guttural voice calling from the shadows: "Arise, dark spirit, arise. It is seven years since I last called you. Arise, I demand you attend me." The antiquated speech pattern was resonant of a much earlier time.

A groan came from the chest as if the wood panels themselves were creaking and stretching and it seemed to stir briefly.

Another nine knocks drummed out: "Spirit arise – I call thee," the voice came again.

This time the chest rocked violently back and forth and a crashing and scratching could be heard from inside.

A final nine knocks smashed down upon the lid, the voice became louder and more insistent, "I hear thee Sly Red Cap, come forth I command thee."

The chest stopped rocking and remained still for long seconds, and then rusted and ancient hinges rasped as the long-closed lid eased open inch by inch. An answering voice was heard from within.

"What is your wish, Lord Soulis?"

Suddenly, as if the hinges had given way, the lid crashed back, fully open. A scuffling could be heard inside and a foul smelling shape emerged, stretching, from the box.

The creature was short, around four feet tall, but basically humanoid, with disproportionately large hands and feet, tipped with vicious yellowed claws which curved inwards and scratched noisily against the wooden chest. The skinny neck and body, wrapped in filthy, matted rags, was topped by the face of an old man, cadaverous, and with grey, wrinkled skin.

Jet black, soulless eyes without irises, flickering with light from the torches, stared menacingly from sunken brows. Staring intently, head swaying from side to side like a snake hypnotising its prey before striking, the eyes searched the darkness for the source of the voice.

The creature's mouth was wide and large, and was unable to close on the rows of long, yellow teeth, with strings of saliva linking upper and lower jaws. A serpentine tongue, flicked from the mouth intermittently, as if testing the air, snake-like, for its next meal; the remnants of the creatures last one, hung in festering strips from the thin, bloodless lips and razor edged teeth.

A straggly long beard and moustache, matted and greasy, hung from the lower face and greasy strands of shoulder length, grey-black hair stuck out from under a stinking, dark-red, matted cap.

"Robin Red Cap at your service, Lord Soulis," the evil dwarf rasped, searching the darkness for the source of his calling.

CHAPTER TWO

Andrea Dettori was not his real name, but he had been using it for so long now that he had ceased to think of himself as anyone else and, despite his name, he was not Italian. Actually he was Egyptian, but dark hair and olive skin gave him a Latin appearance and Italian was one of seven languages he spoke fluently, so that had always been good enough for most people.

The real Andrea Dettori was the first man he had killed some thirty-five years ago now. There had been many more since.

The real Andrea Dettori had been born in Naples in 1949, the only child of Alex Dettori, a restaurant worker. Andrea's mother died in childbirth and after struggling to work and bring up a son without a mother, Alex emigrated to Glasgow, Scotland in 1955 with a six year old Andrea and an ageing Aunt. Seeking a better life, his dream was of opening his own Italian restaurant.

Unfortunately Alex was not a cook and whilst he could have been considered years ahead of his time in opening an ethnic restaurant, his public was not ready for what was universally described in Glasgow as 'foreign muck'. As a result the 'restaurant' quickly turned into a dirty, greasy, glorified fish and chip café that Alex ran with the Aunt until she died in 1966.

Thereafter, without the Aunt to help, business deteriorated almost as fast as Alex, who had taken to drink shortly after her death.

Unfortunately his skill at drinking was far in advance of his business acumen and culinary skills, and soon the young Andrea was fighting daily with a violent, drunk father.

Andrea left and became a child of the streets, stealing, fighting and living rough rather than stay with his violent father who he never saw again until he buried him in 1972. His father had died of sclerosis of the liver, leaving Andrea with nothing but bad memories and £50 in cash.

Andrea felt nothing. No sense of loss, just the elation of having £50 in his pocket, an amount that seemed to him a fortune at the time. Andrea had taken the money and gone back to his life on the streets, which is where only hours later he met the young Egyptian illegal immigrant in a Glasgow bar.

The two were not friends as such, more acquaintances who shared little except each other's company and a damp and filthy cellar that passed as living accommodation; somewhere to sleep out of the rain and wind and to hide the minimal and pathetic possessions that were all the more precious, given their limited nature. Occasionally they had fought together, viciously protecting each other and their personal possessions from other street people.

But that mutual self interest was not as strong as the desire to possess the £50 that Dettori kept close to him, and later that night the Egyptian boy killed Andrea with a knife to the kidneys in the cellar of the shared squat.

£50 was a fortune to him. He would have done the same for much less.

But the Egyptian had miscalculated. Thinking Dettori asleep, he had plunged the knife into him, not realising that his victim had taken to sleeping with an open knife in his hand, so determined was he to protect his inheritance.

In the ensuing struggle the Egyptian boy received a knife wound to the stomach. As they rolled in the filth of the cellar, biting and clawing at each other like the feral creatures they had become, a panting Egyptian eventually managed to subdue the mortally wounded Dettori who slowly stopped struggling as the blood loss from his kidney wound drove him to unconsciousness and a slow, twitching death.

Clamping a filthy rag to his stomach to staunch the blood loss, he poured paraffin from a stolen camp stove that they sometimes used when the damp and cold became unbearable, over the corpse and after setting fire to the body in an attempt at concealment, he took the money and the dead boy's identity – he had been Andrea Dettori ever since.

He had guessed, rightly as it turned out, that the police would not spend much time investigating the death of a homeless drunk. Without fingerprints and the luxury of dental records, (Andrea had never visited a dentist in his brief life), there was pretty much no way of identifying the body.

He had come a long way since then, and as he built up a history over thirty-plus years as Andrea Dettori, suspect and forged documents were subsequently replaced by reissued, apparently 'genuine' ones, and his identity became secure.

Today, all these years later, Dettori was still thin and wiry but now he was dressed in a smart, dark grey suit: very Italian, very expensive. A white linen shirt set off by a bright, red tie made him look the classic Italian businessman, although he had long since abandoned his fake Italian citizenship for an English one, an easy thing to do when you had the political connections he had.

His hand went to his stomach as he felt the slightly raised scar of the long-healed knife wound through the expensive, hand crafted shirt. It was a reassuring reminder of how far he had come in the intervening years. He had certainly come a long way from that squat in Glasgow.

He got up from the black, leather bound chair and the expensive, highly polished, mahogany desk and pressing a matching wood-panelled cupboard door on the far wall, slid it silently open, revealing the soft blue light of a hidden bar.

He threw a handful of ice cubes into a large crystal whisky glass and listened to the satisfying crack as he poured a generous measure of single malt over the ice. Leaving the bar open he walked to the floor-to-ceiling window of the apartment's office that looked out over the Thames and across the City of London, sipping the whisky appreciatively.

From his vantage point twenty stories up, he looked down at the black river, glistening with the evening lights and watched the white and red lights of the traffic leaving the City. The office was an air conditioned cocoon of luxurious silence in the heart of the bedlam below as workers struggled to get home.

That first killing had taught him a lot. It was random, unconsidered, driven by hunger and a desire to own the money. As a consequence of a lack of planning, he had killed inefficiently and received a serious wound himself from the dying Andrea, which had nearly killed him.

He had never taken an ill-considered move since. On that night he had been driven by hunger and desire, but never again was he to take any action without fully considering the options and outcomes.

He had been unable to go to the hospital, for fear of someone reporting the knife wound to the police, which would, no doubt, have lead to a connection with a still smouldering body with a knife wound a few streets away.

He had therefore run. Stealing a car, he tried to put as much distance between him and the murder scene as he could. On the basis that the safest place to hide a tree was in a forest, he headed south towards Carlisle and England, hoping to make his way to London and maybe even out of the country.

Keeping as far as possible to quiet roads he headed through Peebles, Selkirk and Hawick before turning off the main road, faint through loss of blood, desperately looking for a remote farmhouse where he could rest up. His journey, of not more than one hundred miles or so, had taken him well over three hours when he turned off the main road. But he was unable to find a farmhouse or any sign of civilisation, except for an old, unoccupied castle.

He fell, rather than climbed out of the car, clutching his wounded side, and was shocked to see how much blood he had lost. It soaked his clothes and pooled in the seat of the car he had vacated. Later experience taught him that a body held an awful lot of blood, and a relatively small amount lost could make a minor injury look like complete carnage. In his case, however, he was losing blood fast enough to know he was dying. As the effects of the blood loss took its toll, Andrea, who had acquired his name only four hours or so earlier, slipped into unconsciousness and to an almost certain, remote and lonely death.

Of course, he had no idea that on that cold February day in 1972, that it was exactly 651 years since 1321, a number divisible by seven, and therefore, the 92nd time William de Soulis had called upon Robin Red Cap. He also had no idea that the place he was dying outside was called Hermitage Castle.

He had worked many times since with the Red Cap, or one of its many associates, and he was aware of how close he must have come to being another victim of this vile little creature who had discovered his unconscious body.

His last memory before passing into blessed oblivion was of a foul-breathed monster, with huge yellow teeth and black soulless eyes so close that the serpentine tongue of the terrifying creature actually flicked against his cheek and eyes, slimy saliva dripping from the open mouth onto his face.

But he had been saved.

Saved by a powerful mentor, the Lord who had kept him safe, rescued him, nursed his wounds, taught him, advised him and ultimately brought him all the power, wealth, strength and influence he now possessed. A master eminently more powerful, and ultimately more frightening than the monstrous Red Cap that had found him.

Of course he had undertaken work for him ever since, unquestioning, obedient, never once hesitating to do anything he was ordered to do. He owed everything to this mentor, who he repaid by giving him his total loyalty.

William de Soulis was his guardian, he owed everything he had to him, not only his life on that first fateful day when he had been saved from the Red Cap, but all his influence, power, wealth and everything that was yet to come. He would die rather than betray him – but then he also knew that death, and a particularly horrible one, was certain if it had ever crossed his mind to do so.

As a consequence it never crossed his mind.

The silence of the air-conditioned office was broken by an intercom.

"Your car is ready Mr Dettori and the plane is fuelled and ready to take off."

Dettori swallowed the last of the whisky and took one last look across the City, a large part of which he controlled either directly or indirectly.

Soon the world would pay the same homage and respect to his mentor as he did, soon the world would be a better place and his role in it would be massive.

Placing the whisky glass on the desk, he strode purposefully out of the office.

CHAPTER THREE

"Six hundred and eighty-six years. Six hundred and eighty-six years, and I have called you every seven years.

"Ninety-eight times you have come to me, Red Cap, and you have been unable to grant me my wishes, but this time it will be different."

A giant shape emerged from out of the shadows, slowly moving towards the chest and the Red Cap. The figure was cloaked from head to foot in black and stood some six feet six inches tall with a large, muscular frame. He towered over the Red Cap as he reached out a huge powerful arm pointing down at the familiar.

"This time it will be different." His tone brooked no argument.

The Red Cap shuffled uncomfortably in the presence of the huge figure, whose full red beard was parted by a diagonal scar which extended halfway above his right eyebrow, across his right eye, the bridge of his nose and down the left-hand cheek to the chin, creating a wide, raised crease, where the hair did not grow. Shoulder-length red hair matching the beard was visible below the hood of the cloak.

This was a warrior – and one you would not wish to meet on any battlefield, especially close up. The battle wounds on face and forearms suggested that this man would not stop coming forward until he was physically unable to.

"I made you a great warrior," the Red Cap whined, unable to look into Soulis's eyes directly and attempting to ingratiate himself with the giant. "You were the greatest wizard of your time – except one, the greatest warrior – except one."

Soulis's hand went to his face and traced the line of the scar that disfigured it. "I should have been king," he said. "My claim was truer than that of The Bruce or Balliol. But that young fool Wallace would not support me. How can you trust a man who wants no reward?"

The Red Cap shuffled, "Ah – Wallace, the Guardian of Scotland. He trusted The Bruce over you, only Wallace could defeat you in combat – if you had accepted my gifts before you fought him, that blow would not have felled you."

Soulis flashed an angry glance at the Red Cap, who shuffled backwards, fearing the wrath of this unpredictable warrior.

Soulis recalled the night he had entertained William Wallace in this very castle asking him to support his claim to the Scottish Throne. That a Lord of Soulis's rank should be forced to seek the support of that outlaw, the landless second son of a minor knight, still rankled with him.

But Wallace was the greatest risk to Soulis's power because of his almost mythical reputation that commanded loyalty from the populace. Wallace was held in awe, like a god. He could inspire and attract to him armies willing to lay down their lives for him. All the more incredible as he could have taken power himself any time, such was his reputation and following, but he had no interest or desire in doing so.

Any aspiring King of Scotland at the time of Wallace's great victories, particularly after defeating the English Army at the Battle of Stirling Bridge, needed him on their side.

Incredibly, the higher ranking lords and nobles submitted themselves to the leadership of this minor knight, even Robert the Bruce himself bowed to Wallace's guardianship.

To fight for a crown one needed armies willing to die for you, and leaders who could inspire them. Soulis could handle those gutless barons who offered fealty to Edward, King of England, or The Bruce or his rival John Balliol – often they would change allegiance for any small political or financial advantage, but Wallace was different.

Wallace could not be bought or frightened. It was said that Wallace fought like a man who was already dead. Death was inevitable on his taking by the English. He knew that, and a man without options is a hard man to kill. If you are going to die anyway, you might as well die fighting.

In a time when the average height of a man was a little over five feet, Soulis was considered a giant at six feet six inches.

Wallace at six feet seven inches was even taller and equally powerfully built. Not that his size would normally have concerned Soulis, a sword between the shoulder blades whilst your enemy was turned away, was effective whatever height or weight your target. But anger – often Soulis's downfall – took over, and when Wallace refused to support his claim for the crown, Soulis, in his fury, had drawn his sword and attacked him.

In the short ensuing sword fight, Wallace had parried his blow and hit back with such power that Soulis's own sword, raised to protect his head, was smashed back into his face, causing the vicious wound evidenced by the huge scar. Despite the long weeks he spent recovering from this near fatal injury, he was fully aware that had Wallace's blow hit directly then his head would have been detached from his shoulders.

Soulis realised he had acted rashly in attacking Wallace directly, given that he could easily have waited until Wallace was distracted, like he had on an earlier occasion with Alexander Armstrong, the second Lord of Mangerton. Soulis recalled the time in this very castle when he despatched Alexander Armstrong in exactly the way he should have killed Wallace.

Alexander Armstrong, his victim, had intervened in a skirmish after Soulis had rode out bent on having a beautiful young Armstrong girl who had taken his fancy. Her fool of a father had tried to stand in his way and was killed with a single blow from his sword for the temerity of attempting to thwart the will of William de Soulis.

He found it unfathomable why these worthless people should consider this lowly girl's honour was worth dying for, given that she had nothing but her rough beauty to recommend her. If the fool of a father had let Soulis take the girl and not defied him, he would have lived and had one less hungry mouth to feed.

Nevertheless, this pathetic loyalty led to a rabble of Armstrongs surrounding Soulis, intent on exacting revenge for the father's death. Without the invulnerability later bestowed on him, Soulis would certainly have been killed, had he not been rescued by the rabble's Lord, Alexander Armstrong, who intervened and then escorted Soulis in safety back to Hermitage.

Of course, Soulis's pride would not allow him to be beholden to this minor Lord who was far below his own exalted station, so on the pretext of thanking him, a few days later he invited him to Hermitage, where Soulis had prepared a feast.

As the evening progressed, Armstrong, normally a man who was prepared for anything, began to relax in the convivial atmosphere and mellowed by drink he let down his guard. Without warning, as Armstrong turned his back on Soulis to recharge his drink, Soulis plunged a parrying dagger into the defenceless man's back, severing his spine and killing him instantly.

The small entourage of Armstrongs that had accompanied their lord to Hermitage drew swords, but realised the futility as fifty of Soulis's men appeared to surround them and they could do nothing but lift their murdered lord's body and carry it away from Hermitage, leaving Soulis laughing at their loss.

Today, Milnholm Cross still marks the place where the mourning Armstrongs rested for the night, with their murdered lord's body, on route to the clan burial site in Ettleton Cemetery, where Alexander's body was finally interred.

Soulis would never understand the loyalty of these clansmen to their kin. Only strength was important to him, strength and power, and you didn't show either by weeping over one, or a thousand, dead relatives, especially the worthless likes of the Armstrongs.

Real power came from a single-minded focus on self. He would sacrifice anything or anyone for the power his rank and standing entitled him to, something, in fact, his rival Robert the Bruce, knew all to well.

From serving Wallace, Robert the Bruce and the rest of the Scottish aristocracy later deserted him as they bent their knee to the English king.

Being a true patriot, Wallace alone refused to submit to the English and was, as a result, declared an outlaw.

With the connivance of his erstwhile friends, he was eventually captured and hung, drawn and quartered in Smithfield, London in 1305. In the face of an incredibly violent death, Wallace was defiant to the end. When accused of treason he answered by saying he had never, unlike so many others, sworn allegiance to the English king and therefore could not be a traitor to him.

The warrior was dragged by horses through the streets, wrapped in a leather hide to protect him from mortal injury. A quick death was not sufficient punishment for this man. He was hung and then cut down still alive, and emasculated and disembowelled. His heart and other internal organs were cut out and burned.

In a final insult he was beheaded, his head placed on a pike and displayed on London Bridge, whilst the rest of his body was quartered and a piece sent to Newcastle, Berwick, Aberdeen and Perth, as a warning to others who would defy the English king.

So much for heroes, so much for loyalty, only self interest was worth fighting for, Soulis knew.

But there was another clan that Soulis held in more contempt than the Armstrongs, and that was the Elliots.

If Edward, King of England had hoped that the inhuman slaughter of Wallace would warn others from following his path, he seriously miscalculated. He had turned Wallace from hero into martyr and it was Robert the Bruce who eventually took the throne of Scotland from Balliol, Edward's stooge, and after suffering several defeats, reclaimed Scotland for the Scots, culminating in his historic victory over the English at Bannockburn.

Throughout this time, Soulis plotted and planned to take the Crown from The Bruce, but a final attempt to kill him in 1321 failed, and as a result his lands and properties were confiscated.

The Elliots were the scum that The Bruce brought down from Angus to occupy his lands. Not only occupy but hold, defend and fight for – including his beloved Hermitage.

Other, more famous clan chiefs, such as the chief of the Douglas clan, were the Keepers of Hermitage on behalf of The Bruce, who passed the castle on to his son, but the Elliots were the militia who fought and held the castle and the lands that surrounded it. Their military efficiency was the source of Soulis's hatred of the clan.

It was as a result of his many attempts to win the Crown of Scotland, through the guardianship of Wallace, the short, ineffectual reign of John Balliol and the eventual ascent to the throne of Robert the Bruce, reinforced by his near death experience in the fight with Wallace and his near miss with the Armstrongs, that made him re-double his efforts to conjure supernatural help, spurring him to ever deeper iniquities in his lust for power.

The acts that followed sunk an already cruel and vicious tyrant to even greater levels of depravity.

CHAPTER FOUR

"Holmrig Cottage," Kate Ralstone said as she re-arranged eight month old Thomas on her hip as she spoke on the telephone, turning her head to one side to move the phone out of the reach of the small grasping hands.

A small and beautiful ex-dancer, Kate had taken to motherhood with all the energy that she had previously given to her ballet and contemporary dance, although she sometimes felt parenthood took far more physical effort than any amount of dancing. Full of passion, Elliot's dark haired and beautiful eldest daughter was difficult to resist with her flashing smile and her enthusiasm for everything she did.

"It's a few miles outside Newcastleton," she continued. "It looks beautiful and it's not far from Hermitage Castle. Is that the area?"

"That's the area sweetheart," Elliot answered his daughter, "but..."

"But what Dad? Look I know you feel you should be job hunting, but you also need a break and a week in the middle of nowhere, away from mobiles, email and work will do you good. You know you have been promising yourself a trip to follow up on your family history. You need to do this Dad."

"Well, I suppose..."

"Great," Kate's voice brooked no further discussion, "I'll email you the details and you can look for yourself. Simon will take a few days off and we can spend a bit of time together relaxing. Don't worry, I'll organise it all. All you have to do is turn up and decide where you want to visit.

"Got to go now Dad. I'm meeting Simon at the leisure centre. He's promising to get Thomas used to the water, but we'll probably end up watching him swimming up and down again. I'm sure he still thinks he's going to make the Olympics."

Elliot hung up the phone. He realised again that he had been out-manoeuvred by his eldest daughter and he was now committed to the trip, especially as her engineer husband, Simon, was taking time off from his contract work, so would not be being paid whilst away.

He had to admit that a few days away sounded great and would probably restore some of his flagging energy, maybe even recharge the batteries and give him time to think.

He flicked on the computer to check for Kate's email and to load up the family tree going back seven generations. He began to think about the last known locations of his direct ancestors. He knew the Elliots in Scotland were now mainly concentrated around the Newcastleton area, and that was why Kate had picked that as a base.

The current clan chief was resident at Redheugh just outside Newcastleton and that was also the location of the 'clan room', a small museum kept by the Elliot Clan Society for memorabilia on the history of the family. It was a good place to start.

Some seventy miles away from Newcastleton though, in Hutton and Whitsome near Berwick, on the east coast, were the last known locations of the earliest ancestors he had traced so far.

This was still some way from Newcastleton and the area around Hermitage Castle where Elliots were located around 1321. So he still needed to trace back another 150 or so years to make the connection with the area surrounding Hermitage Castle, at the height of Reiver times and the 'Debatable Lands', and then back a further three hundred years to their original arrival in the famous Elliot areas to the north of Carlisle, near Langholm, Newcastleton, Hawick and Jedburgh.

There were many famous Elliot centres, including the better known ones of Redheugh, Larriston, Wolfelee and Stobs, but he had discovered William Elliot, his fifth great grandfather (seventh great grandfather of his beloved grandson, Thomas), and William had a son called Andrew, born in 1758. He knew nothing else about William except for the birth date of his son. But that in itself was so significant in Elliot's eyes. It meant that William must have been alive in 1746 during the last great land battle fought on British soil, the final demise of the Jacobite rebellion at Culloden.

He knew it was a common misconception that the Battle of Culloden was between the English and the Scottish forces, but there were as many, if not more, Scots on the English side supporting the Hanovarians, as there were supporting the Stuarts, and the 'Young Pretender', Bonnie Prince Charlie.

The Elliots along with the Armstrongs, their closest neighbours, were also probably the pre-eminent (if pre-eminent is the right word for such a blood-thirsty bunch) so called 'Border Reivers' who mounted nightly raids against other homesteads, both Scottish and English, in a region where law was almost non-existent or corrupt.

Borders took second place to clan. Alliances were made and broken, with the same regularity that deadly feuds broke out. People were killed, or often kidnapped for ransom; cattle and sheep, food and other goods stolen. In a time when clan was everything, the only real allegiance, nothing could be taken for granted as to who a clan or family might support, or indeed that that allegiance might not change as necessity dictated.

Three hundred years before Chicago was founded, long before anyone had ever heard of Al Capone, these Border Reivers had perfected the 'protection racket'. The modern term 'bereaved', Elliot knew to be derived from the term to 'be-reived', or to be raided and robbed.

Even the term 'blackmail' was derived from the practices of the Border Reivers. In the days when tenants paid rent in the form of oats or barley, so-called 'Green or White Miel', Reivers would offer immunity and protection from raiding for a similar payment, known as 'Black Miel'.

Elliot found himself becoming enthused again by the fascination for the history that surrounded his ancestors – he needed to get back those additional 150 years, hopefully joining up his genealogy with those in the area of Hermitage Castle. The castle fascinated him, it was drawing him in. Why did he feel the need to go to this place so strongly?

He started planning the places they would go and forgot for a short while concerns about the future.

CHAPTER FIVE

Simon Ralstone plunged into a tumble turn as he reached the deeper end of the swimming pool and kicked powerfully against the wall to propel himself forward underwater, stretching, his legs locked together in a butterfly kick until he broke the surface once more and stroked into a rhythmic front crawl. Breathing to one side, he was beginning to tire rapidly as he gasped for air at least three strokes earlier than he should have needed to.

The final five lengths were really going to hurt. At thirty-six, the effects of too many cigarettes and lagers were taking their toll and he realised that the sedentary life he had lived of late was affecting his exercise recovery rate and he was beginning to feel his age.

Born and brought up in Middlesborough in the northeast of England, Simon had trained as an engineer and now spent his time contracting in the oil industry; most of his day spent sitting at a computer, designing and refining pipelines.

Still highly competitive, it irked him that he had never quite reached the standard of competition swimming he felt he had been capable of. Some of this was physical no doubt. He still had the powerful arms, legs and shoulders of the swimmer, but he was probably, at five feet ten inches, a good six inches too short to have been the perfect build. This, he realised, was more an excuse than a justification; his unwillingness to curtail his social life he knew was the real reason. The stomach, once a classic 'six-pack' was now showing distinct signs of middle age spread.

But now, what he lacked in physical fitness, he strove to make up for by driving himself a little harder and a little longer. As he reached the end of his fifty lengths, he rested his arms on the edge of the pool and buried his face in them, panting hard as he slowly recovered.

Raising his head and looking up he saw Kate, sitting on the edge of the pool, legs kicking slowly in the water, a chuckling Thomas, resplendent in bright orange arm floats, on her lap.

Both his wife and son seemed highly amused at his exhausted state.

"Old age and treachery," Kate said with a laugh and then, climbing to her feet, "See you in the coffee bar," before carrying Thomas off to the changing rooms.

Simon buried his head again in his arms breathing deeply, building up the strength to hoist himself out of the pool. His pride would not let him use the ladder; equally he didn't want to suffer the indignation of being too tired to pull himself out of the pool.

"Old age and treachery," he thought and smiled. He knew exactly what Kate meant. She, like a lot of women, found this hugely competitive instinct of men, even when it couldn't possibly matter, quite bemusing.

He recalled the evening a week or so back when he and Kate's father David, had turned a game of pool in the local pub, into something akin to the Olympics, as they struggled for dominance, with cries of foul, endless discussions on the finer rules of the game and accusations of cheating and luck as her father ultimately won the titanic struggle, three games to two.

As Simon had acknowledged defeat finally by buying the drinks, her father had raised his glass to Simon. "Old age and treachery will always overcome youth and skill."

Simon pulled himself out of the pool, his legs feeling distinctly unsteady as he walked wearily to the changing rooms.

Kate sat in the bar of the leisure centre drinking coffee; Thomas, exhausted by his splashing in the pool, asleep peacefully in the pushchair.

Simon arrived, dropping wearily into the chair beside her and smiled. Kate reached across and ran her hand across the severe crew cut head of her husband and down around his unshaven chin, the dark, black stubble now heavily tinged with grey.

"Maybe you should borrow Thomas's water wings next time." she mocked gently.

"Is everything set for Scotland?" he said.

"Yes, all booked," Kate said, then quietly, "I'm really worried about Dad, he has so much on his plate at the moment. I want him to enjoy this break and forget about everything for a few days."

"Don't worry," Simon said gently in his soft 'Boro accent, "I'll let him beat me at pool again, that'll cheer him up.

"So, where's my coffee?" he said brightly.

CHAPTER SIX

Soulis watched the Red Cap shuffling and snivelling impatiently. The creature was obviously completely unable to comprehend the enormity of what the wizard had planned.

To this foul familiar, the future was the next opportunity to 'blood his cap', the foul practice of all Red Caps to kill and then to drink the blood of his victim before soaking his cap in the wounds and add to the centuries of gore stinking and decaying on the disgusting bonnet that was pulled tight around his head.

Robin Red Cap was his own particular familiar, sent to him by the Dark Spirits to whom he had long since mortgaged his soul. But this Red Cap was one of a breed that haunted castles and other places renowned for acts of evil.

Victims of these creatures were typically killed either by rolling rocks down from cliffs onto their unsuspecting prey, or by ripping them to pieces with their razor-sharp claws.

Robin Red Cap initially held sway over Soulis, but as the wizard's powers grew, he eventually became his slave.

Sly, rather than intelligent, still the vicious dwarf had been useful. Before the confiscation of his lands and property and the coming of the Elliots to settle there, they had done much work together.

In return for the blood of innocents, the Red Cap, working as an intermediary with the Dark Forces Soulis sought to conjure, had granted him much.

The more depraved the act, the stronger became the dark powers that Soulis possessed.

He recalled the first tentative steps following the black arts. He had learned how handfuls of salt, scattered around this chamber as he chanted arcane rituals, bound the dungeon to the Dark Spirits.

The cat he buried alive in that very dungeon, the dog he smashed against the wall and left to die in agony for days. The calf, throat cut and buried, feet up, still alive as Soulis sprinkled its blood around the place. Blood he captured in his bare hands, from the poor creature's spurting artery, all the time invoking the Dark Spirits to grant him power.

The answer to these early invocations came in the form of this foul creature before him, who, following those first tentative steps into the dark arts, had granted him powers; powers in the form of near invulnerability in battle.

He remembered the words of the Red Cap familiar as he was rewarded for his crimes:

'Steel shall not wound thee, cords bind thee, hemp hang thee or water drown thee.'

With the granting of this mysterious reward to Soulis for his service to the Dark Spirits the Red Cap had disappeared with a warning that he should not be called for another seven years.

But as Soulis mulled over the gifts he had been granted he realised that the protection was incomplete. The Red Cap had not mentioned protection against fire which could still kill him. If he could be killed by fire he needed to recall the spirit to rectify the error, and recall him he did.

No breach of a contract with the Dark Spirits goes unpunished, and for the sin of calling the Red Cap again before seven years had passed, the Red Cap was bound to refuse the request and disappeared again, after first leaving Soulis with a solemn warning:

'Beware a coming wood and triple binds of sifted sand.'

Such was the later consequence of the warning, Soulis had never again tried to call the Red Cap before the passing of seven years. His failure to obey was the reason that, close to seven centuries later, he was still seeking his final reward; the power to rule, unchallenged forever.

With the powers granted through the Red Cap from the Dark Spirits, Soulis had become emboldened and, determined to gain his rightful place on the throne of Scotland, he took to ever increasing cruel and abhorrent activity, growing stronger and more powerful in the black arts. Whilst other claimants fought, battled, cheated and connived for influence, Soulis worked steadfastly, year after year, to perfect his art.

But each added ability came at the cost of more vile crimes. Not content to sacrifice animals, he soon discovered that the more innocent the focus of his cruel attentions, the more obscene the crime, the greater the power he was granted.

So Soulis turned his attention to the children.Kidnapping children, even babes in arms, for use in his rituals blackened his soul but strengthened his mastery of the occult.

Even Soulis could not number the children kidnapped and slaughtered in his quest. Those not directly sacrificed in his disturbed rituals were fed to the Red Cap.

As his strength grew, so did the stories of the haunted screams of children heard by passing travellers on dark nights as they journeyed north or south past the castle.

No one camped near this edifice and no local would approach during the night when the aura of evil was at its strongest.

The thought of the children brought Soulis's mind back to the present and the matter in hand and he turned towards the Red Cap.

"They are coming soon, I can feel them getting closer – and you will bring them to me." He commanded the Red Cap's attention with his sudden outcry. "There will be four of them – your reward will be the three adults, but the child is mine. Your gift will be the blood of them all, save the child.

"Remember Red Cap – the child is mine."

He turned from the Red Cap and slowly disappeared into the shadows.

"The child is mine," he repeated almost inaudibly; as if to himself.

CHAPTER SEVEN

Elliot suddenly jerked to an upright position in bed and a familiar panic shot through him like an electric shock as he struggled to breathe in and found himself, for a second or two, unable to do so. After a terrifying moment, he was able to gasp air noisily into his grateful lungs and he breathed in deeply through his mouth, at the same time swinging his legs out of the bed and sitting, leaning forward, he allowed the air sucking into his lungs to reduce his racing heartbeat and with it the panic attack.

His body was soaked in sweat. He stood up and throwing the bedroom window wide open, he leaned out breathing in the icy air and feeling the strange comfort of it on his damp skin.

It appeared to him that once again he had stopped breathing in his sleep, something that seemed to happen with a frequency in line with his stress levels.

He closed his eyes allowing his breathing to return to normal and he stood there silently until the cold air on his naked skin began to feel uncomfortable and he sat down on the edge of the bed, leaving the window wide open, allowing a reassuring draught of cold fresh air into the room.

Not wishing to lie down for fear of a repeat attack, he bunched up the duvet and wrapped it around his shoulders, slowly warming himself.

Eventually, exhausted, but unwilling to lie down and risk a further attack, he inserted the earphones of his iPod and once again sought solace in music, which was the one thing that usually stilled his racing mind. As the familiar music washed over him, he eventually lay back and stared up at the ceiling, wondering, not for the first time, what he could do to stop these panic attacks, whether there was any physical cause for them, or whether, as he suspected, they were a consequence of his mental state.

He was, he knew, very conscious of his mortality. Perhaps this was something that happened to all middle-aged men. With many it seemed to him to manifest itself in a desire to return to their youth: buying a sports car or more often a motorbike; a hunt for younger women; clubbing and generally behaving like an old fool.

With Elliot it was a recognition that he was rushing towards death without having achieved anything meaningful in his life.

After three marriages and several other short-lived relationships, it seemed he was, for some reason, incapable of forming a stable relationship, caught permanently somewhere between loneliness and a desire to be alone, never really understanding which was the more dominant.

He had tried many times to be the person his partner of the moment had apparently wanted him to be, but this had just led to a feeling of panic. He really felt his mind worked in an entirely different way to other people, and communicating for what he considered to be 'the sake of it', he found difficult and exhausting.

Some had advised him to 'Be yourself'. Good advice on the face of it, but it seemed to Elliot what they really meant was, be the 'yourself' that I imagine you to be; which was ultimately the same thing as trying to be as others would like.

Frankly, he did not know how to be anything other than the way he was, so he had come to the conclusion that the best he could hope for was to be a good friend and not to spoil a perfectly good relationship by trying to live with someone.

He did not hold anyone responsible for this. Perhaps psychologists would say there were some deep issues relating to his upbringing that made him the way he was and maybe that was true.

To him, he was sure it was about his feelings of self worth, or more accurately, the lack of it. That was it in a nutshell. He was, in his terms, too talented not to try, but not talented enough to succeed. Nothing he did was quite good enough for him, it seemed. He was his own biggest critic, in fact his own worst enemy, and this led to a constant feeling of frustration.

Fundamentally, despite having had a succession of well paid jobs, they all seemed to him to amount to nothing. So being bright, he faked it. He gave the impression that he was committed;

that he was part of their stupid games, their silly meetings, their reports, their earnest conversations about nothing at all.

But in reality he was always aloof, always apart, his head and his heart were always somewhere else, searching for something he could be proud of.

In short, after over forty years of work he had done nothing that he personally considered worthwhile, nothing he was proud of, and that hurt him more than he could ever explain.

To others it seemed he was just restless and difficult, not a team player, unable to focus on anything for long, until it seemed he could stand the games no longer and self-destructed.

Now at fifty-seven, without putting too fine a point on it, he felt death closing in on him and he still had left no mark on life, left nothing that he would be remembered for.

Except of course, his children.

Kate, Emily and David had grown up pretty well, despite him. But even that he felt guilty about. Where had he been when they were growing up? What did he contribute? Was it really enough when all he could really say was that he loved them and hadn't damaged them too much?

The reality was that in his formative years he spent most of his time wanting to be somebody else, somebody who, despite the faults he could see intellectually, seemed to have everything he did not have, and that was an apparent total lack of fear.

That person was his father.

Intellectually he knew of course this could not be true, but no matter how many times he told himself that his father must have been frightened at sometime, of something, it seemed to him that he could not recall when that might have been, and a lack of fear seemed to Elliot to be the touchstone of a happy life.

His father came from a real working class background and left home to live alone at fourteen. He volunteered as a tail gunner in Lancaster bombers during the second World War and when made redundant at forty-five years of age, took a job as a store man, despite being an experienced engineer, rather than sign on the dole.

Within two years, he became Managing Director of that same company, by sheer intelligence and strength of will.

Then he died.

40

At the ridiculously young age of fifty-three, he died – and Elliot had lost his best friend and his mentor. Before he had time to see him grow old and frail, to lose some of his strength of will, his sheer cantankerous attitude to life diminish a little, he was gone.

Perhaps if he had seen his father decline as most others did, he would have had time to see him more objectively, to see him as something less than perfect and thereby develop a real personality of his own, rather than living constantly in his shadow.

Now he was left, struggling to find his own place in the world and he was not equipped for it.

As Henry Thoreau said, 'Most people lead lives of quiet desperation, and go to their graves with the song still in their heart.'

Elliot was terrified of dying, not because of any inherent fear of death, but of dying having achieved nothing that he felt was worthwhile in his life.

He dreaded the thought of dying with the 'song still in his heart'; somehow he had to find a way of singing it.

As he listened to the music he realised – was it coincidence or some deeper meaning – that the song playing was 'Father & Son' by Cat Stevens.

Once again fate seemed to be quietly mocking him as he listened to the lyrics that resonated to the depths of his heart:

Take your time
Think a lot
Think of everything you've got.
For you will still be here tomorrow
Though your dreams may not.

He had taken his time, nearly thirty years since his father died, and he had thought an awful lot, but actually felt he had precisely nothing in his life, nothing he could be remembered for.

Tears welled in his eyes.

He was still here…

…but his dreams were not.

CHAPTER EIGHT

Gregori Romanski sat back in the comfortable seat of the Gulfstream executive jet, owned ostensibly by his company, STATOL, but at his exclusive disposal. Romanski liked to travel, and when he did, he liked to travel in style.

A dark, thick set man in his sixties, he was an archetypal Russian, who at the height of the Cold War would not have looked out of place taking the salute outside the Kremlin in Moscow as the blatant expression of Soviet military power paraded passed on May Day.

But now, this twenty-five stone, six feet two inches man, with the crumpled face of a boxer who had won more fights through sheer strength than any technical ability, and hence had taken an awful lot of unnecessary punches to the head, knocked back yet another ice cold, straight vodka and immediately poured another.

The small shot glasses seemed lost in the huge, stubby fingered hands of this Russian, who now was built like a man of huge appetites with the money and the inclination to indulge them all.

A broad, pudgy nose, broken so many times that it seemed to have no cartilage left in it, was covered with the tell-tale broken capillaries of the heavy drinker. Looking like a haphazard red road map, they extended out across both upper cheeks.

The dark eyes peered from deep set eye sockets; his forehead protruded outwards, giving him a slightly Neanderthal look. The eyes seemed deeper still, given the thick, bushy brown eyebrows that sat above his heavily-jowled face.

He had done well out of the collapse of the Soviet system, having been perfectly equipped with the right combination of ruthless violence, ambition and low animal cunning to secure for himself a large part of the break up of the Siberian oil fields.

Bribing those who needed bribing, killing those who could not be bribed, he had built a huge and powerful empire that encompassed not only a significant part of the Soviets' erstwhile natural resources but also extended to a profitable trade in ex-Soviet military equipment and arms, that he sold without compunction to anyone with the one qualifying criteria he demanded: sufficient money.

He was en route to Scotland for a meeting to discuss the future of the Soulis Foundation. He would be landing at Edinburgh, knowing Dettori had arranged for two private helicopters to meet him and the other four associates of the Foundation, who, along with Dettori himself, made up the six executives of this highly secretive trust.

For safety, never more than three of the associates travelled in the same transport at the same time; hence the two helicopters.

The meeting was to be held at Dettori's Scottish residence, a huge private stone castle known as 'Branxholm'. It had exactly what one would expect from a man of Dettori's wealth: a beautifully maintained castle dating back to the 13th century that had been extensively, and expensively, maintained, renovated and enhanced with every possible modern convenience.

The castle sat in one hundred acres of forest and landscaped gardens, with manicured lawns and perfectly-raked gravel paths with hidden and subdued lighting for evening walks. A wide gravel drive swept up to the front of the castle, circling a perfectly-mown, dark green oval lawn, uncluttered, except for a three feet tall stone monolith directly at the lawn's centre, which was, in essence, a large bird bath.

The gravel paths meandered past pergolas and water features and fountains of various kinds. Clipped topiary and the immaculate condition of the grounds, surrounded by ancient woodlands, evidenced the extent of the money that had been invested in its upkeep.

The imposing building of grey stone was huge, with a central three-storey building between two matching rounded wings. What had once been defensive steps across the front had been manicured into lawns and the building looked out across an extensive and beautiful valley, with a wide set of stone steps leading down from the large entrance to the grounds below.

Hidden well away from the house was an aircraft runway capable of landing jets at least the size of the imposing, some might say somewhat ostentatious, Gulfwing that Romanski favoured.

It also had its own helicopter landing pad. Dettori preferred that jets landed at a commercial airport, like Edinburgh or Glasgow, as multiple jet landings were more likely to attract attention than a couple of helicopters – and Dettori liked his privacy.

The rooms and facilities were as opulent and extensive as one might find in the finest hotels. Sporting two swimming pools, a fully equipped gym, and luxurious bedrooms, comfort was assured.

Office facilities included secure satellite and Internet connections, protected by industrial strength firewalls and a completely secure computer room, where banks of servers blinked constantly. All were protected by un-interruptible power supplies and their own generators and surge protection equipment.

The house itself also had its own emergency electrical back up systems and the accommodation was five-star, in every sense of the word.

The rather more down to earth Russian had to admit the place was impressive and classy. Romanski's tastes were far less bourgeois, coming as he had from abject poverty where he had found it necessary to fight for every scrap of food as he clawed his way up from street urchin to a leading player in the Russian Mafia. He was proud of his humble roots.

It would have surprised him to find that Dettori himself, whom he had always assumed came from some ancient Italian nobility, had equally underprivileged antecedents.

Yes, the place was certainly impressive, and Romanski had visited many times, but there was one thing the place lacked and it had been the first thing that he had noticed and the first thing he would have expended money on.

Security.

Of course the doors had good quality locks and a few closed-circuit television cameras, enough to keep out your average burglar. But where was the real security – the electric fences, the razor wire discreetly laid back from the external fences, the electronic alarms throughout the grounds, the trip wires, the dogs, the floodlights in the woods, that could be turned on at a second's notice?

Above all, where were the men? If he had been equipping this place there would have been at least fifty trained ex-Russian special forces soldiers, all armed to the teeth with machine pistols, knives and their own very special ways of killing.

Against the kind of enemies that had access to the level of finance that Romanski, Dettori and the other associates moved in, this place was wide open to a well-funded professional attack.

Unless the talks concluded the way Romanski intended, sooner than Dettori expected, he would learn this lesson.

Romanski smiled to himself, and settled back to doze as the jet hummed towards its destination.

CHAPTER NINE

"I think you should go." Caroline felt the urge to place a comforting hand on Elliot's as he sat opposite her in the busy coffee bar in the famous Covered Market in the centre of Oxford, but resisted the urge to do so.

Their relationship was complicated enough and she was anxious that her desire to help was not misinterpreted by too obvious a sign of affection. After all they had known each other for almost thirty-five years, twenty-three of which they had spent married to each other and their children bound them inexorably together despite the fact that they had been divorced for many years and she had long since remarried, as had he.

The main difference was that her marriage had lasted, whereas Elliot's had failed yet again.

They had both long since realised that whatever they had felt about each other then, traces of which might still remain in weaker moments, soon disappeared when they were in each other's company again. It seemed that within minutes, old wounds began to re-open and soon the old arguments, blame and counter blame, began to surface.

But Kate had mentioned to Caroline that she was worried about her father and told her about the proposed trip to Scotland to research family history. Having now met him again, she shared her daughter's concern. He looked drawn and pale, a sense of almost resignation about him, as if he had given up.

She had become a counsellor soon after their marriage broke up. She had seemed unable to reconcile her feelings of guilt and it had been as much to understand her own feelings as her desire to help others.

Of course one of the first things she had learned was that you could not effectively counsel people you were emotionally involved with and the history between them made her entirely the wrong person to help him. But the concerns of her children and her absolute knowledge that Elliot would never open up to anyone else, left her half feeling she should walk away and half telling her that if she did not help, nobody else would.

His demeanour had worried her however.

But her training had taught her that an individual's strengths were also their greatest weakness, when overplayed – and Elliot could be irritatingly logical, instinctive and analytical. Coupled with a keen intellect and a love of debate, Elliot was often aggressively certain, and dogmatic almost to the point of rudeness. What was even more irritating of course was that more often than not, his apparently thoughtless and instant decisions proved to be accurate. She was certain this was what made him so difficult to work with.

Work? They should try living with him, she thought, a familiar frustration rising within her. But his certainty and confidence was also one of the most attractive things about him and to see him so lethargic, so vulnerable, worried her.

"Maybe the trip will help you to reconcile the death of you father," she said, and then regretted putting it so bluntly as she saw the look on his face which said without words, 'Here we go again!'

It had been she who had taken the phone call that morning in 1978 from his brother to say that Elliot's father had died and she had witnessed at first the incredulity and then the complete emotional collapse. She had often thought since, that people who lived with ailing loved ones, who saw them decline steadily towards death until eventually their passing came as a blessed relief were, in some respects, lucky.

Elliot's father was at the peak of his powers, and a problem that had given him pain for years had been diagnosed as an ulcer. It was only after having dragged himself in the space of two short years from storeman to managing director of the European arm of an American computer company, that he had the money and inclination to have the operation that his doctors had been advising for years. He had booked himself into a private hospital – and he had never come out.

Nobody was fully sure what had caused him to suffer a massive heart attack which killed him instantly as he lay, apparently recuperating, in the private hospital in Reading.

Elliot had struggled ever since and rather than let the real grief out, to mourn and to come to terms with his loss, he had reacted by internalising everything. He had been seriously damaged and responded by concealing his feelings. He became completely sure that there was no God, no heaven, nothing in life except random chaos and cruelty and he shut out the world – including her.

She understood that this hard external shell he presented was misinterpreted by people who thought he was cold and didn't care, whereas the truth was he cared too much. But the accumulation of little hurts, which seemed to most people to run like water off a duck's back, he simply sealed up within himself, growing and attacking him like some malignant tumour from within.

"I don't need another lecture on my father," Elliot responded, and Caroline felt a familiar pain as she found herself once again in danger of responding in anger.

"Look," she said her voice breaking with emotion, "I will not – cannot – go through this again. I left you because the arguments and coldness hurt me so much. I will not allow you to continue to hurt me after all these years." She felt herself trembling as she continued, "You are a good man, David. You are kind, thoughtful and have a good heart, but you seem determined that nobody should ever find that out. You think you are being fearless and strong, like your father. But you are not your father, with him it was natural – you are just acting – acting a part. You are *not* your father!"

Caroline struggled to control herself but tears were beginning, once more, to well in her eyes.

She shook her head in despair, "Why oh why do I do this to myself?" she said. "Go to Scotland, David. Find out about your family, about your father and where he came from. And realise they are all dead – as you will be one day! Don't go with all this bitterness in your heart. Your father is alive as long as you remember him. You cannot bring him back by trying to be him."

She searched angrily in her handbag for a tissue to wipe her tears away. "I never learn do I? I think I can control my feelings, to be adult, and as soon as I am with you, it all comes back. Go to Scotland and then come back; start your life over, not as your father, but as you. You are worth it you know."

She stood up, looked as if to make a passing comment and then held back. Frustrated, she turned and walked away, leaving Elliot watching her back disappear into the crowds of passing strangers.

He peered down into his now cold coffee. Then a memory came to him, a memory of a comment his father had made to him one evening. They were both drunk and arguing about something as they often did. He could not for the life of him remember what it was about, but he said at one point that he wished he could be like his father and be so certain about everything. His father had stopped smiling and his face had become very serious.

"Don't be like me son," he had said quietly. "Be better than me."

Elliot had never understood what his father had meant, but was it possible that he was not quite as certain about everything as he seemed?

CHAPTER TEN

The company car and his fuel card he would keep for another month, another part of his compromise agreement, so using their fuel and their vehicle for the trip was another good reason for taking it now.

Kate, Simon and little Thomas had driven from their home in London and stayed overnight before they set off from Elliot's flat in Abingdon, Oxfordshire, a little after nine on that Saturday morning.

It was gone four in the afternoon when they arrived in Newcastleton, an unprepossessing little town that had been redesigned and re-planned by the Victorians when the railways arrived. One long straight road dissected the town and the streets off the main thoroughfare to the right as the road headed north were equidistant. The street network was planned in neat squares and the roads on the right all headed down to the focus of the valley, the river Liddel.

Previously known as Copyhaugh then Copshaw Holm, the town was renamed Newcastleton by the Duke of Buccleuch as a centre for the hand weaving industry, but it had a far more historic background as the main centre on the river Liddel that ran through the debatable lands, and was notorious in Reiver times as a home to the Elliots and the Armstrongs.

It was difficult to imagine the area's bloody history looking at this unremarkable little town, but its own Castle Liddel, named after the river running through the valley, was destroyed in the 1300s and Hermitage then dominated the area.

Elliot pulled slowly into Douglas Square, presumably named after the Douglas family who were keepers of Hermitage on behalf of Robert the Bruce when the Elliots moved into the area around 1321 at the invitation of the great man. He recalled the fact that it was a Douglas who took the heart of Robert the Bruce at his request after his death, on the crusades to Jerusalem.

Elliot stretched wearily.

"Maybe we can get coffee here before we drive on out to the cottage." Elliot indicated the Grapes Hotel in the square as Simon studied the map that had come with the directions to Holmrig Cottage.

Ordering coffee they settled themselves in the comfortable settees of the lounge bar. Thomas sat in the centre of a pile of toys examining them one at a time. Kate was again fascinated by her son's apparent close attention to anything he picked up – the minute attention he seemed to give to everything.

Simon spread the map out on the low table in front of them, pushing coffee cups and jugs to one side as he and Elliot studied the map.

"Looks like there are two roads out to the north just over the bridge outside the town. We can take either. One heads out to Hawick, the other to Jedburgh, but the cottage is off this road which runs between the two." He indicated a single track that meandered between the two roads about five miles out of town.

Elliot looked at the place names, Larriston, Wolfelee, Redheugh indicated on the map, all centres of Elliot settlement and he recalled the poem he had read about the multiple spellings of the Elliot name:

Double L and single T
The Elliots of Minto and Wolfelee;
Double T and single L
The Eliotts that in Stobs do dwell;
Single L and single T
The Eliots of St Germains be;
But double L and double T
The de'l may ken wha' they may be.

Of course Elliot assumed the insult inherent in the final line for the 'double L and double T' was because of its association with England, being the prevalent spelling south of the border.

"What are you doing?"

Kate's sudden exclamation immediately shook the two men from their focus on the map before them and they looked across the lounge bar to see Kate moving towards a little old man. Standing with Thomas held before him, he was staring intently into Thomas's eyes and was muttering quietly, his face inches from Thomas.

Kate clasped Thomas around the waist and pulled him from the old man's grasp as Elliot and Simon rose to their feet and moved towards the old man.

"Is he alright?" Simon threw a glance at Kate who was intently studying Thomas, before turning his attention again to the old man.

Thomas seemed fine and was watching the adults from the protective embrace of his mother, large brown eyes moving from one to the other as they spoke.

"What were you doing?" Kate's face flushed with protective anger as she clutched Thomas tightly to her.

"Forgive me I meant no harm, he is a lovely child, a very special child."

"What were you doing?" Simon reinforced Kate's question as he moved menacingly towards the old man.

Kate placed a gentle, but restraining hand on Simon's arm as she looked at the old man, who seemed a little embarrassed. He looked about eighty years old, with soft, white hair that curled to below his ears. He stooped and was terribly frail and thin, wearing a dark open-necked shirt under an ancient bottle-green waistcoat beneath a crumpled old tweed jacket with leather patches at the elbows. His trousers, brown cords, seemed several sizes too big, and on his feet were large brown boots.

"I'm sorry," the old man said, "I sometimes forget what a very cruel world it can be. I meant no harm. You know the very old and the very young have a special bond. They understand each other," he continued quietly.

Kate studied the old man's face and seemed more reassured by his gentle blue eyes.

"Perhaps I am in my second childhood. You know there was a time when old people and children could spend time together without fear. What have we done to our world?" The old man looked wistful, as if recalling earlier and happier times.

"Well, you know what they say, 'Nostalgia is not what it used to be'," Elliot moved forward towards the old man.

Kate turned to her father and then back to the old man. "This is my father David and my husband Simon. We're here for Dad really, he is studying our family history.

"And this little fellow is Thomas," she snuggled him into her neck, rocking him gently in her arms.

Elliot moved forward and held out his hand to the old man, "David Elliot, and you?"

The old man took Elliot's hand and shook it with a strength that belied his frail appearance. "Everyone around here calls me Old Tom, but I prefer Thomas, just like your grandson – my name is Thomas Truman.

"So you are an Elliot and you have come home." He smiled. "I have lived here a long time." The old man stared intently into Elliot's eyes, his own pale blue eyes seemed to see into his soul. "If you need any help or anything at all, I am here most evenings. I prefer the lounge, I'm sure your ancestors would have preferred the 'Reivers Bar' at the back, with the pool tables and darts. They played as hard as they fought you know."

"Truman doesn't seem to be a Border name, did you move here from somewhere else?" Elliot mentally paged through the famous border names, but Truman seemed to be missing from his mental list.

"We are ancient," and with this strange comment he tickled Thomas under the chin, staring intently into the child's eyes, smiling when he responded with a giggle.

Truman turned and walked slowly from the bar and Kate watched and smiled as Thomas waved to the old man's back, cuddling him again tightly into her neck.

The three adults stood together for a few seconds staring at the door that the old man had passed through, a little puzzled by something, but none of them was quite sure what it was.

"Well, I guess we'd better find this cottage," Elliot said at last.

CHAPTER ELEVEN

This was painful for Soulis. Astral projection required massive effort and all the power Soulis possessed.

Unlike the Red Cap and similar demons who were never human but the creations of the Dark Spirits, Soulis was held within the confines of the Hermitage until he could free himself, which would need an adept of incredible power to achieve and Soulis had spent centuries honing those powers.

For seven hundred years Soulis had been waiting, waiting for the moment mostly beyond his control when fate brought the right conjunction of circumstance that might only happen once in an eternity.

But he had been patient, and his patience was soon to be rewarded as the Fates brought him the opportunity in the guise of these four people, whose presence he could feel. They were not far away now, in range of his ability to project.

Of course he could send out the Red Cap who, since Soulis had become progressively more powerful, was his slave rather than his master now. The Red Cap could travel, even by day if necessary although he preferred the cover of night. He, on the other hand, could project his mind a few miles, and despite the physical pain and the huge effort this took – you never got anything from the Dark Spirits without some form of payback – he needed to see these people for himself, to observe, to ensure nothing was left to chance.

The Red Cap, though useful, particularly when killing was needed, was unreliable. He could never see beyond his own lust for blood. Though cunning and deceitful, he rarely planned ahead.

He felt a surge of energy as he caught sight of the visitors arriving at the cottage. It amused him that they were not even aware of who they were, what their fate would be at the hands of Soulis and how close they were to death.

But he cautioned himself against complacency, it could be another seven hundred years or seven thousand years before the opportunity arose again, he must not allow anything to interfere with his release.

He was ready – but was the world ready for him? This thought also amused him.

He felt the searing pain in his head as he stared into the darkness and he felt himself on top of a hill, a high grassy hill looking down into the valley below at a grey stone cottage set by a small loch, fed by a stream.

He watched...

CHAPTER TWELVE

They took the right-hand turn over the bridge out of the town heading towards Jedburgh, passing a large dark building on the right that had once been a church but was now boarded up.

The road wound up the hill out of the town and soon Elliot slowed as they passed a cemetery on the left surrounded by a rough stone wall broken by two gates. The first gave access to what was clearly the newer part of the cemetery as the headstones were obviously recent additions. The second gate led into the older part of the cemetery where ancient tombs and headstones had been weathered by decades of wind and rain blowing across the exposed hill, the low wall providing scant protection from the ravages of the elements.

"Do you mind if I stop for a couple of minutes?" he looked at Kate who sat beside him and then into the back where Thomas was fast asleep in the car seat. Simon was also dozing, holding onto the chubby hand of his son, the hand looking tiny in his grasp.

"Looks like they're okay," Kate smiled, nodding in the direction of her husband and son.

Elliot pulled into a small gravel parking area alongside the wall of the cemetery and he and Kate climbed out of the car, to be greeted by a chill blast of icy wind that blew across the exposed hillside. Opening the boot the pair pulled on waterproof jackets. Elliot pulled a checked cap from the pocket and smiling, handed it to Kate.

"Most heat loss is through the head," he laughed as she pulled the cap on, which folded down the side of her head, covering the tops of her ears. Actually, it suited her and Elliot could not resist pulling out the small digital camera he was carrying and taking a picture of her.

Pulling on a wide-brimmed brown felt hat he closed the boot and checking that Thomas and Simon were still dozing, they walked to the green-painted iron gate that broke the wall, which was around four and a half feet high. The cemetery was completely surrounded by the wall and sloped downwards away from the road.

They stopped inside the gate, breathing in the cold fresh air, and admiring the sweep of the valley which extended right and left before them as it wound between hills, devoid of any buildings and any sign of occupation apart from the ubiquitous flocks of hardy sheep munching lazily at the tough moorland grass.

Kate wandered off to the left, inspecting the ancient, weathered headstones. Most were worn and difficult to read, others were completely worn away, but two names seemed to predominate on those still readable: Elliot and Armstrong.

In the meantime, Elliot was walking down the hill towards the bottom wall. When he reached the bottom he leant on the wall taking in the full beauty of the surroundings and enjoying the cold wind that seemed to be driving the fears and tension from his body as he breathed in air, totally unpolluted, for the first time in years.

Across to his right were stepped, grass-covered earth ramparts, which indicated the one-time presence of some kind of defensive position. Probably an old wooden pele tower, popular in the area in its more turbulent history, had once stood there. If it had been stone, typically there would have been some ruins, but there seemed to be nothing but the earth steps left.

Elliot smiled, he felt at home here and he turned to find Kate coming up to him. "Lots of Elliots here," she said, smiling and she put her arms around him hugging him close.

"Maybe that's why I feel so at home here." He hugged her back.

"Thomas is awake," they turned to see Simon calling to them over the gate. "Think he's getting hungry."

Taking a last look around, Elliot and Kate walked, her arm tucked in his, back up the hill to the car.

Elliot drove on, making a mental note to return when they had more time and more daylight to explore the cemetery. The road wound its way through farmland and moorland until, after about five miles, they turned left onto the quiet single track that led to the cottage. As they rounded a bend, the road dropped sharply into a valley of coarse moor grass. A small burn meandered at right angles to the road feeding a small loch surrounded by leafless trees that stood like guardians on the bank.

To the left stood the cottage down a dirt track about five hundred yards from the road and surrounded by its own grounds. It was a grey stone, two-storey building, with a green porch and a low, rough stone wall around the front of the cottage creating a quaint stone-flagged front yard.

"Apparently we are supposed to keep the gates round the front shut, especially if the door is open, otherwise the sheep come in," Kate remarked. "It's beautiful," she added.

A single-storey extension ran at right angles from the back of the original cottage, where extra bedrooms and a bathroom had been added to increase the living space.

A watery sun was beginning to set behind a steep hill to their left. Hardy sheep, apparently impervious to the bitter winds, seemed to cling precariously to the side of the hill as the light rapidly faded. The group bustled around the vehicle unloading before the last of the daylight was lost completely.

With his back to the road, Elliot felt the hairs bristle on the back of his neck. He turned to look behind him, his eyes scanning the rim of the hill.

Silhouetted against the skyline, about a mile away, he thought he made out a small black figure, too far away to make out clearly. He screwed up his eyes but could not make out the detail. Reaching into the glove compartment he found the small pair of binoculars there and raised them to his eyes, sweeping them across the brim of the hill. He saw nothing.

He shuddered suddenly as it seemed to him a cold draught passed across the back of his neck.

"Someone has just walked over my grave," he said, to no one in particular, before turning back to the car and hauling out bags. He followed Simon and Kate into the cottage, Kate carrying Thomas ahead of Simon, who struggled behind loaded with luggage.

The cottage was comfortable and warm. The lounge contained a television but no telephone and of course mobile phone coverage was non-existent. Central-heating warmed the cottage and a wood-burning stove was set in the fireplace. Simon immediately set about lighting a fire, not strictly necessary for comfort, but it would add cosiness to the place.

Three windows looked out; one to the front which looked up towards a working farm on the top of a hill, the only other building in view, another looked out towards the road and across to the hill where Elliot had thought he had seen the figure earlier. The third looked from the back of the cottage out across the moor.

Elliot took the front bedroom on the ground floor, a lovely old fashioned en-suite bathroom with a huge enamel bath led off from it.

Running down the centre of the ground floor into the extension was a corridor, with a little square hall halfway down, with a side door. An interesting selection of mostly historical books stood on a table, and pictures and a map hung on the walls of the hall.

Elliot studied the old pictures on the hall wall, beside a large scale Ordnance Survey map of the area surrounding the cottage. The map showed the local points of interest, and his eyes settled with a strange excitement as it was noticeable how close Hermitage Castle was to the cottage. Further down the Hawick road, not far from the turn to Hermitage, stood the markings for an old druid stone circle called 'Nine Stane Rig', or 'Nine Stone Rig', which Elliot realised also bore relevance to the history of the castle. In the past few months he had read a lot about the history surrounding the area and he remembered some relationship existed between this site and Hermitage Castle.

The corridor continued away from the original building and ended outside a large double bedroom in the extension that Simon and Kate took and Thomas had his own single room separated from this master bedroom by another bathroom.

Stairs went up from the front hall to a small landing from which two further bedrooms were accessed with sloping ceilings under the eaves of the cottage.

"What shall we do about food this evening?" Elliot asked, returning to the living room having half-heartedly unpacked his bag and hung shirts from the mantle piece above the open fireplace in his bedroom.

"Why don't you and Simon drive into Hawick and get something for tonight and maybe breakfast? I'll stay here, look after Thomas and finish unpacking."

Simon had finished laying the fire and it was burning cosily, casting a warm glow around the room. With the curtains now drawn against the darkness, the room was warm and comfortable.

"Won't be long," Simon said as he and Elliot donned coats and went back out into the night.

"Look up there." Elliot pointed at the sky. Being in one of the few places left in Britain not suffering from light pollution, the starlit sky was breathtaking.

'Won't be long' was a rather optimistic statement, for although Hawick was less than twenty miles away, on these windy and hilly narrow roads, devoid of cats eyes or other road markings, twenty miles was a long way.

They returned a couple of hours later, loaded with food from the supermarket, concerned at the time they had been away. If anything were to happen, without a phone, mobile signal or transport, how would Kate have alerted anybody? It would have been a good half-hour's walk to the only other civilisation, at the farm.

But then, out here, what could happen? Apart from the inconvenience of maybe a power cut. After all, this was not a place you came upon by accident. If you arrived here it was because here was where you were going.

Elliot cooked and he shared a bottle of red wine with Kate as Simon stuck to his customary lager. An hour and a half later they were enjoying a lamb casserole with dumplings and, feeling warmed and mellow from the alcohol, they sat at the kitchen table chatting and planning the following day.

"So where do we start, Dad?" Kate shared the last of the bottle between her father's and her glass.

"Well, I guess the most sensible thing is to go out to Hutton and Whitsome, they are the last known locations of Andrew and Elizabeth. Andrew Elliot, my fourth great grandfather, was born in Whitsome in 1758, married Elizabeth Inglis in 1791 in Coldstream, and died in Hutton a few miles away in 1833. Elizabeth was also buried in Hutton in 1841.

"I know Andrew's father was a William Elliot – but that is all I know. But I suppose it is a good bet they lived around that area – I guess we need to look in the graveyards."

"Well, I suppose it is technically possible that he might have been somewhere else when Andrew was born, but more than likely he was working in that area," Kate said.

"Yes, and if he had a son born in 1758, unless he had him at twelve years of age, William must have been alive during the

Battle of Culloden in 1746. Did you know that was the last great land battle fought on British soil?

"Okay, so Hutton and Whitsome it is then. Well I don't know about you but I'm going to bed." The combination of the long journey and the wine had taken their effect and Elliot was suddenly very tired.

No sooner had his head hit the pillow, despite the strange bed, Elliot fell into a deep sleep. As Elliot slept he could not know that the planned trip would never take place and it is unlikely that he would have slept quite so well, had he been aware of the odious little dwarf with the red cap, snuffling and flitting from window to window, trying to find a chink in the drawn curtains to observe the sleeping humans inside.

What the Red Cap could not see however, he could smell, and the promise of new blood drove him into a frenzy. Only one thing was more powerful than his lust for blood – the fear of his master, William de Soulis, who, trapped in the confines of Hermitage a few miles hence, still was aware of everything the familiar was doing.

Death was not a concept that the Red Cap fully understood or feared. But there were things much worse than death.

That much he did know.

CHAPTER THIRTEEN

"Would you like a drink, Mr Dettori?" the steward said as his boss took his seat in the Learjet and fastened his seat belt in preparation for take off.

"No, thank you," he replied as he settled back for the trip to Branxholm. He always enjoyed his visits to his Scottish holding, he felt more at home there than anywhere else in the world.

He closed his eyes and lay back in the comfortable leather seat, his mind returning to those early days as he turned from street urchin to international businessman with remarkable speed, thanks to the support of his master. During those first days as Dettori recovered from his near death experience, William de Soulis had talked and he had listened. He had learned much from this incredible man, who at first terrified him and then enthralled him. As he learned more, he again realised that terror was a helpful safety device when dealing with Soulis. Anyone foolish enough to take him for granted was risking more than just his life.

His master had insisted that the young man had been sent to him by the Dark Forces to be his conduit to the outside world.

Despite being from a different time, his master understood the way of the world and Dettori was amazed at how much he understood about modern day politics, although his mentor constantly reminded him that human nature never changed and power was exercised in the same way, in whatever century you lived.

In fact, in his view it was simpler to exercise power today than seven hundred years ago. Today, no one challenged you personally. Who of the current leaders of the world would have the courage or the ability to face a William Wallace, a Robert the Bruce or a William de Soulis in single combat?

Ultimately, people were sheep. They needed fearless leaders who blooded their hands personally, not those who cowered in rooms never facing their enemies. But he understood that his vehicle to power in this century would need to be different. After all, there was no longer a King of Scotland, although interestingly Soulis was determined that there would be one again in the future.

So they had discussed the vehicle they would use and the Soulis Foundation emerged as the mechanism. So Dettori had put the Foundation together carefully, over a number of years.

He had plenty of time after all. He could commune with his mentor for two weeks only, every seven years, and those fourteen short days were important. He had to show Soulis that he had made progress, that he had not wasted the previous seven years, and that their plans were moving, inexorably towards the day of enlightenment, when the world would welcome their new leader: William de Soulis.

The first seven years had been spent building his own power base. He had started with straightforward theft, murder and blackmail, often aided by Red Caps, sent to help him by his master.

He had found them difficult to control until his own powers under Soulis's guidance became strong enough, so in the early days he could only use them during the brief periods when Soulis himself was manifest in Hermitage and could directly control them. As his powers grew, progress accelerated as he was able to use them directly himself during the long years he was unable to seek guidance from the master.

He had invested his illegal gains, legitimately, in businesses, seeking minor shareholdings and a seat on the board in return. His influence grew within these organisations as he brought huge amounts of business to them vastly increasing the companies' net worth.

Colleagues saw him as a super salesman, with a huge network of the rich and powerful which enabled him to elicit massive contracts that otherwise would not have come to these small, underfunded companies.

The reality was that Dettori preyed on the weaknesses of these benefactors. Everyone had their price or weaknesses and he encouraged them. Facilitating whatever these rich and powerful people wanted, whether that was women, men, children, drugs or any perversion they could dream up. Of course, he kept scrupulous records, photographs, videos, voice recordings and witnesses that at any time could ruin these individuals.

Imagine their relief when the inevitable blackmail demand came in the form of authorising the placing of multi-million pound orders with Dettori's companies, orders that they had to place with someone anyway.

Of course, their relief turned to despair when the corrupt business practices and ever more degrading perversions just became further levers that Dettori could use against them and they fell inexorably further under his control.

Dettori however, exercised his power over them sparingly, often acting more as a trusted advisor and friend than their blackmailer. In the early days he had been too impatient, demanding too much, too quickly and early victims committed suicide, rather than risk exposure.

A dead blackmail victim was of no value to Dettori's cause at all. As he played his victims ever more cleverly, he became rich very quickly. From his positions of influence he could instigate rumours, depressing share prices, buying up stock at the bottom and profiting incredibly when the stock rose again as rumours appeared unfounded.

Very soon he became indispensable to all of these companies who knew that without him, they could quickly be destroyed by his implied threats to leave and take the contracts he influenced with him, destroying their businesses as he went.

His board colleagues were pragmatic enough to know that he had made them all rich and would continue to do so as long as he got his way. Slowly he took larger and larger stakes in the companies until effectively he controlled them all.

Soon he was rich enough to select his partners in the coalition from a position of equal wealth and power. He knew exactly what he wanted and Clemenza the Columbian drug lord had been the first recruit to the cause. He had used Clemenza many times to obtain drugs and prostitutes to subvert his blackmail victims, and had learned much from him about human frailty and the vast fortunes to be made from both.

But Clemenza's success was also his biggest problem and that was the huge amounts of cash generated from a business that did not recognise any other form of payment. Electronic transactions left audit trails, audit trails led to arrests or death, usually the latter. He laundered money for Clemenza, through his vast network of legitimate businesses, or more often through the businesses of his blackmail victims.

These were often huge global affairs, which did business in parts of the world where cash was not an unusual method of transacting business and untraceable bribes to state officials were common place. Even electronic transfers of huge amounts of cash were not questioned or accounted for with the same precision that might apply in the USA or UK.

Through government sponsored trade delegations and politically motivated international conferences, Dettori met Sir Ronald Robertson, a man in his early seventies and a career diplomat.

Dettori had never met one individual who had so many diverse political contacts, in both the Developed World as well as the Third World. He knew who had power in any given situation, regardless of the apparent hierarchy within any given state, who needed bribing, whose allegiance needed to be turned, who needed blackmailing or simply needed to disappear, either without trace, or openly as a lesson to others.

Robertson was invaluable in building the network of despotic presidents, ruthless generals, princes and petty officials who could facilitate not only money laundering but the allocation of huge civil engineering contracts for Dettori's empire.

The diplomat also had reason to be grateful personally to Dettori, when a particularly vicious African dictator by the name of Matubu, threatened his life after Robertson's usually flawless political antenna for once let him down. The dictator ruled a small African state, which he had modestly re-named Matubuland, by fear. Not merely through savage and brutal torture and murder, but by exploiting the local population's belief in the supernatural.

He had collected around himself a bodyguard of loyal tribe and family members, who, fuelled by a combination of drugs, alcohol and self-induced hypnosis and dressed in costumes and masks associated with local devils, slaughtered the dictator's enemies in particularly vicious ways. The population believed unquestioningly that these men were genuine devils and that Matubu was a powerful wizard.

A misguided meeting in New York with Matubu's exiled political rival, a Dr Sebastian Soloman, led to a curse and a death sentence being placed on Robertson who was to die for daring to challenge the dictator. Of course Robertson had no belief in the supernatural, but realised that Matubu's followers would track him down remorselessly, until they fulfilled the 'prophecy'. He would never be able to relax anywhere and particularly in Africa, which would certainly seriously curtail his activities on that continent.

He had spoken of his problem to Dettori, who at first Robertson felt had not taken the matter seriously as he mentioned the supernatural curse; in fact Dettori seemed highly amused by it. Despite Robertson's explanation that he also did not take the supernatural stories seriously, Matubu's followers did and would track him down anyway.

Dettori had said, 'We should not try to dissuade them from their beliefs, we should reinforce them,' and with this rather puzzling response, Dettori told Robertson that he would deal with it.

A few weeks later, deep in the wilderness of Matubuland the dictator had organised one of his mass rallies. Matubu's thugs ensured that people attended and chanted his name declaring him their hero, their saviour, their president forever. On this day, on a raised platform, surrounded by thirty of his frighteningly garbed personal guard, with other heavily armed soldiers watching the thousands of forced attendees, ensuring they sang Matubu's praises with sufficient gusto, Matubu embarked on one of his rambling and flowery denouncements of the West.

As he ranted at the captive crowd suddenly the dictator came into contact with real supernatural power. The thousands in the crowd fell to their knees in terror as a small army of vile looking dwarfs poured out from the bushes surrounding the open ground, slashing and tearing at the soldiers watching the crowd.

Machine guns barked intermittently as the terrified soldiers desperately tried to defend themselves and screams filled the area: some from the soldiers who were being mutilated horribly by these strange creatures, with razor sharp claws and teeth, wearing bizarre red caps. Other screams came from injured watchers, who were notably not attacked by the creatures, but lay injured and dying from the indiscriminate machine gun fire.

The crowd watched as several of the creatures mounted the platform, slicing the gruesomely dressed guards to pieces, before closing on the terrified Matubu. Slowly the screams and firing died away as all of the soldiers and guards lay dead. The semi-silence was broken only by the occasional scream of pain and a low moaning from the injured in the crowd.

But the loudest noise came from the platform, where the terrified Matubu still with a microphone around his neck begged for mercy from a kneeling position on the platform where he was surrounded by six of the snarling creatures. After a few terrifying seconds, as if tired of the begging from the kneeling dictator, one of the creatures violently pushed a claw into his mouth ripping out his tongue.

This was the signal for the others to attack and slowly and deliberately they began to slash and bite, ripping open the body of the dictator, who screamed in agony as they appeared to know exactly how to inflict the maximum pain without killing Matubu.

Finally, as he died one of the creatures pulled off its cap and dipped it into the slippery mess that had once been Matubu's stomach, and raised it overhead in a triumphant gesture to the watching masses, emitting at the same time an unearthly scream. Blood ran in rivulets down its arm, before it pulled the blood-soaked cap tightly back onto its head.

In a last act of butchery, the dictator's body was ripped to pieces and the bits hurled violently in all direction, some landing bloodily in the centre of the crowd, who were splattered with the gore from the slaughtered meat.

From then on, Dettori owned Matubuland and controlled the country's oil reserves through Soloman, who was installed and took control after Matubu's death.

Of course, Dr Sebastian Soloman was no better than Matubu and ruled just as ruthlessly, but he was loyal to his masters and the West and he controlled a terrified population, many of whom had experienced first hand his apparent supernatural powers, not knowing he was as much a slave to them as they were.

Now Dettori was beginning to own countries as well as businesses.

A grateful Robertson, who also grew rich through his position as intermediary between Dettori and the new dictator of his African asset, introduced him to Susan Coltrane.

This beautiful and rich daughter of old 'Boston Money' used her contacts with neo-conservatives in the USA to introduce Dettori to the oil-savvy power base behind the US Presidency.

She negotiated and facilitated the purchase of a small American oil company, taking a holding herself. This minor player in the trillion dollar oil industry passed into Dettori's control almost without notice until they suddenly became owners to the rights to exploit the oil reserves in the African state.

Overnight they became a 'player', still comparatively small but with access to one of the few untapped sources of new oil reserves.

As Clemenza grew stronger and richer through his association with Dettori, his empire generated so much cash that in the end, it could not all be siphoned through Third World countries. They needed access to Western banking institutions and private communication networks, networks that could not be hacked by interested rivals or politically motivated intelligence agencies in the USA.

Susan Coltrane's banking credentials were impeccable and she also managed the accounts of one of the fastest growing American communications networks, headed up by an American-naturalised ex-Swede called Stefan Erikson.

He offered a stake in his business in return for the largest single non-military communications order ever placed, to build a completely standalone worldwide communications network to link all of Dettori's global interests together.

This order alone doubled Erikson's company's share price.

Included within Erikson's empire were a number of small but highly influential newspapers and magazines, with some of the highest paid and influential political journalists stationed all over the world.

With unparalleled access to the political elite around the world through the political connections of Robertson and Susan Coltrane, a lucrative business selling exclusive news stories to the world's better known agencies, Reuters, the BBC, not only brought in considerable revenue, but also allowed Dettori to subtly influence the news itself.

They were also becoming leaders in the ever growing news media driven via the Internet.

Again, with Susan's help, Dettori bought banks which she fronted for him; these small banks also grew inexorably as the billions of dollars moving through Dettori's business interests passed through their coffers and began to shift through networks of blind trusts and legitimate and not so legitimate businesses.

Many times, powerful organisations, both commercial and political, sought to unravel the complex web which was the Dettori Empire.

Often small discrepancies or allegations appeared in the press but ultimately they came up against dead ends, blank walls. Occasionally a minor manager somewhere took a fall, or mysteriously committed suicide effectively cementing their guilt, becoming the scapegoat, thus avoiding further investigation.

But so deep were the tentacles of power controlled by Dettori that almost nothing that went on inside any of the Western security services went on without his knowing.

The effectiveness of Dettori's secrecy was evidenced by the fact that he had become, by the mid 1990s easily the richest man in the world, but so little could be directly linked to him, he did not even appear on the 'Rich List' in his own adopted country.

The final link in the chain had been Gregori Romanski, the ex-Russian Mafia boss who owned STATOL the huge Russian oil empire.

Clemenza was constantly under threat in South America, either by other drug lords or the combined efforts of American covert activity by the CIA and the DEA. Many attempts had been made on Clemenza's life but he had always been too strong, too clever and too well informed to allow his competitors to catch him unawares. But after several attempts to destroy him directly and break up his empire, the United States secret services had provided military experts, special services personnel and weapons to one of Clemenza's competitors, who under the guise of being a politician dedicated to 'cleaning up' the drug barons, was being financed to destroy him.

The Secret Services had failed so often to remove these drug barons due to the inherent corruption in the political systems, often the drug lords could out bid in cash any offer from the USA.

Clemenza's opponent on this occasion had been offered the opportunity, not only to make a lot of money by his destruction but the chance to continue the lucrative trade himself, but with the cooperation of the Secret Services, who could engineer and control not only the supply chain into the USA, but by sacrificing the occasional low-level players, appear to their political masters to be controlling an uncontrollable situation, by a succession of apparent successful 'wins' against the illegal traffic, without, for a moment, slowing the flow of illegal drugs into the West.

Clemenza needed arms, technical assistance and intelligence. Dettori needed to expand his oil interests.

Romanski wanted access to the US markets, but knew the protectionist attitude of the USA would not countenance a Russian owning a foothold in their market.

The answer was simple: Dettori would provide access to the US markets through his own oil company, providing Romanski with a significant stake in the company, hidden through his interest in the Soulis Foundation. Dettori would also place a significant order for ex-Russian military weapons and technical assistance via his contacts in the old Soviet Union military, and to show his good faith he would deposit $250 million in a bank account of Romanski's choosing, as soon as he delivered and accepted his place as a trustee of the Soulis Foundation.

Romanski of course accepted, and provided a team of experts under the command of an ex-special services colonel called Mikel Batnykov.

Now freelance, Batnykov had a loyal team of crack special forces personnel for hire. A real patriot until the collapse of the Soviet system, Batnykov also would relish the idea of pitting himself against his old enemy the USA.

By the time they had finished, Clemenza's protection force was at least as well armed and provisioned as that funded by the American Secret Service. They also had one other great advantage, better intelligence. Robertson's and Coltrane's contacts between them reached deep into the intelligence services as well as into the corridors of their political masters.

The attempt on Clemenza's life was the worst US intelligence disaster since the infamous 'Bay of Pigs' debacle in Cuba. Batnykov and his team were battle hardened and more than a match for the team put together against them.

For political reasons at the last moment the Americans, not wishing to compromise real special forces personnel given the political embarrassment that would be generated if any US soldiers were captured or identified as such after being killed, weakened the plan with last minute changes. As so often was the case, at the last moment the whole plan was significantly compromised by the very late decision to use less reliable mercenaries.

The US agents in the field were identified and quietly killed in their hotel rooms, disrupting communications. But also they were left to be found with significant quantities of heroin in their rooms, planted there to discredit them and cause maximum political embarrassment.

Meanwhile Batnykov efficiently destroyed their troops by launching a pre-emptive missile strike on the ostensibly 'secret' jungle villa they were using as a headquarters, and hunting down the remains of the team leaving their bodies to be disposed of by the jungle animals where they fell.

The embarrassment of the US citizens linked to the Pentagon and the CIA, dead in a foreign land with huge stashes of drugs triggered so many questions that a Grand Jury was convened to investigate.

Of course the full story never surfaced, resignations and sackings followed that reassured Clemenza that no serious challenge to him would be forthcoming for a long, long time.

More recently, with the invasion of Afghanistan and Iraq, arms were supplied to the various warring warlords and insurgents propagating the war and ensuring that lucrative oil contracts and civil reconstruction contracts were secured.

Dettori was amused by the fact that he was being paid for the arms that destroyed these countries' infrastructures and being paid again for rebuilding them through the political influence so close to the US Government.

One after another, each of the trustees of the foundation became richer and more powerful through their alliance with Dettori and each accepted the 'good faith' payment of $250 million he made to them all to show his commitment.

Dettori had come a long way in thirty-five years, but what excited him more than all the power and the wealth was the knowledge that his mentor, Lord Soulis, would soon arrive to take control of this empire and take it to a level that even he could not comprehend: a new World Order.

This was the sign of his loyalty and devotion.

71

CHAPTER FOURTEEN

Susan Coltrane had flown in from New York via London Heathrow the day before, combining the meeting of the Soulis Foundation tonight, with the opportunity to attend some meetings in the City of London, prior to flying up to Edinburgh. She was irritated that once again having been delayed by an unexpected dinner invitation from Andrea Dettori at her hotel, The Dorchester, in London, she had found it necessary to move one of her appointments to this morning which meant she was arriving much later in Edinburgh than she had hoped.

She realised this meant she would be alone with Gregori Romanski in the helicopter even though the trip to Branxholm was fairly brief.

The rules that stopped her and all her colleagues from travelling on the same flight together meant that as she was the penultimate to arrive in Edinburgh, the other three arrivals, Clemenza, Erikson and Robertson had already taken the first helicopter.

Romanski was always last. She thought he did it deliberately. The Russian was a natural showman and, full of his own self importance, he liked to make an entrance.

In the VIP lounge she ordered another large gin & tonic, heavy on the gin light on the tonic, lots of ice and lime not lemon. She had noticed that everywhere in the UK they seemed to automatically put a tired slice of pre-cut lemon into the drink unless you specifically requested otherwise.

At least the barman here made a good one.

She knew Romanski would be drunk. Maybe if she was a little drunk herself he would be slightly more tolerable, although she doubted it.

Susan Coltrane was thirty years of age. Born to a hugely influential Boston banking family, she had always been rich. But she was also beautiful, a natural asset that was accentuated by her ability never to take second best at anything.

Clothes, make up, hair, health regime was the best that East Coast old money could buy, so she was used to appreciative stares from both men and women.

At five feet eleven inches she was tall, with shoulder length blonde hair. Her height was accentuated by the high heeled shoes she invariably wore. If her height was a problem for men she considered that their problem not hers.

She was not overly thin either, so did not have the gaunt and bony appearance that seemed so fashionable nowadays, and she knew that most men didn't find it attractive. In fact she was a good size fourteen if not approaching sixteen, but had an hourglass figure, large hips above fabulous long legs, which she invariably showed off with short skirts, just long enough to be sophisticated but short enough to be interesting.

Susan did not have a problem with using her attractiveness to get her way. If men were shallow enough to fall for it then she considered that that was their problem, just like her height.

But anyone who treated Susan as nothing more than a beautiful and rich woman did so at their peril. Financially, she was brilliant. Her banking family taught her about money from the cradle and a First Class Honours degree in economics cemented her natural talent.

She was still a little shaken from the unexpected meeting with Dettori the night before and she sipped her drink slowly as she allowed her mind to drift back to the previous evening.

*

Dettori had met her at The Dorchester exactly on time at 8.00 pm. She knew from past experience he was never late.

Usually very formal and polite she had never detected in him any interest in anything approaching fun or pleasure. His exclusive conversation was business and although not an unattractive man he was definitely not Susan's type. She thought of him as a bit of a cold fish.

Her taste was far earthier. She took her pleasures as seriously as she took her business and never normally mixed the two. She had no full time partner, being totally focussed on her business and she, was not prepared to compromise any of her life to the needs of anyone else. She was however, a passionate woman who fulfilled her own physical desires with men she allowed to pick her up in clubs and bars – at least she allowed them to believe they were picking her up.

These men were usually of a type: tall, muscular, slightly arrogant, sexist and, mostly, not terribly bright.

She was not interested in intellectuals. Excruciatingly intelligent herself, these men had one purpose in life, to satisfy her sexually and she knew exactly what she liked. Spending most of her life in complete control, her release was through occasional but frenzied one-night stands with these pick-ups, who she allowed to dominate her for her own satisfaction, before sending them on their way the next day never to be seen again.

Of course, this behaviour was fraught with danger. This constant playing with complete strangers, sometimes in the most insalubrious cheap hotels and bars, was coupled with the kind of violent sex that so easily could lead to tragedy. But the danger was part of the excitement for her and in any event she felt confident enough in her own ability to control the situation. Even so she had on a number of occasions come close to being seriously hurt, but these incidents just seemed to drive her fantasy more.

But, last night against all precedent, Dettori had blatantly and completely unexpectedly come on to her.

Over dinner, his usual calm, polite and highly business-like demeanour had been replaced by a sense of ill-concealed agitation as he expounded on how exciting the next few days were going to be. How the world was going to wake up to a New Age, when she and he, under the guidance of William Soulis, would change the entire business dynamic of the world. He talked all through dinner, not pausing, apparently not interested in anything she had to say, as she nodded politely and hopefully, she thought, in the right places.

But as the evening progressed he seemed to be getting, if not drunk, certainly tipsy and she recognised in him an excitement that was almost sexual in character.

As they talked, or more accurately, she listened to him, until almost midnight, she began to feel the effects of the alcohol which she knew from the one-sided nature of the conversation, she was drinking too quickly.

She had no idea why she had done it, but when Dettori had suggested coffee in her room, despite her practised awareness of sexual tension in men, and her rules on mixing business with pleasure, she agreed. She ordered coffee to be sent to her room and when they sat in the lavish suite, having poured herself another gin and tonic, and Dettori a single malt, which she knew neither of them actually needed, she began to wonder how the matter was to resolve itself.

Predictably Dettori made the move she was expecting and putting down his drink he walked across to the settee she was sitting on and sat beside her, turning his mouth towards her. Slowly she detected the combination of discreet cologne and malt whisky as their lips met.

The kiss was gentle rather than passionate, and as she drew back she smiled kindly at him, which seemed to be the reassurance he was seeking as he kissed her again, more forcefully this time. She felt his hand rise to her shoulder, slipping the strap of her black evening dress down her arm, his hand progressing to cup her breast through the soft material. She did not resist until his hand moved from her breast to her lap and slowly slid along the side of her thigh, gently lifting the hem of her skirt as it went.

She put her hand on his to stop its progress, and pulled away looking deep into his eyes as if considering what to do next.

Finally, not sure she was making the right choice she said, "Let me go to the bathroom, Andrea. Why don't you get into bed? I will join you shortly."

As she prepared herself in the bathroom she wondered if she was doing the right thing; whether her unwritten rule of not mixing business with pleasure, which had served her so well in the past, should be broken this time. But, given what was at stake with the Soulis Foundation, the billions of dollars involved, she felt that if Dettori wanted sex with her, then she would give it to him, even though she still did not find him particularly attractive.

Susan was wearing a pale pink silk nightdress as she came out of the bathroom and into the bedroom. She sighed as she saw Dettori in the large round bed, silk sheets were pulled up to his shoulders, one tanned arm lay on top of the sheet as he lay on his side, fast asleep.

She climbed into the bed quietly and, after one more look in the direction of the sleeping Dettori, turned onto her side facing away from him and switched off the lights plunging the room into almost complete darkness.

She had no idea how long she had been sleeping; in fact she was not entirely sure whether she was fully awake or not when she felt a strong hand on her shoulder and she was pushed with some force face down onto the bed.

She tried to raise herself up, to turn her head towards Dettori, but the hand clasped the back of her neck and forced her face down into the pillow, preventing her from turning. His hand held her trapped as she felt his other hand slide under the nightdress at the top, and she gasped as the expensive silk material was ripped, effortlessly from her back, the silk sheet being pulled back at the same time, exposing her now naked body. At the same time she felt strong legs pinning her own to the bed and forcing hers roughly open.

As she lay helplessly exposed, pinned and unable to move, she felt a familiar excitement stirring in her as she was deliberately manhandled; sensing rather than feeling, the urgency of this man intent on taking her with no pretence of tenderness or consideration for what she wanted.

Susan groaned with desire as she struggled to turn herself, not to escape, but to increase the pleasure she felt from being taken, as the strong arms and legs held her effortlessly unable to move.

The hand that had been clasping the back of her neck, went to her hair, grabbing tightly and pulling her head back painfully as she felt the powerful hips driving forcefully between her spread-eagled legs and she tried desperately to raise her hips to accommodate the inevitable thrust her whole body ached for.

She arched her back and her entire body was racked with pleasure as he entered her violently and she screamed with a feeling that was halfway between pain and ecstasy as she shuddered to an orgasm so intense that she felt herself slipping into unconsciousness.

When she awoke, the sunlight was streaming in through the windows and she felt as if she was waking from a dream.

She looked beside her in the bed, but Dettori was not there and she caught sight of herself in the rows of mirrored walk in wardrobes that spanned one wall of the suite's bedroom.

Her hair was wild and cascaded over her face as she peered out between the sweat-streaked strands. The silk sheets were knotted into ropes and tangled tightly around her naked body shimmering with a glistening film of sweat. If this had been a dream, she wanted more of them.

She called out to the living room of the suite for Dettori but there was no reply, so she slid gingerly to the edge of the bed, rising to a sitting position and looked around for her nightdress. Seeing a shapeless pink piece of material on the floor by the bed, she leaned forward and picked it up, examining it to find that it had been torn from top to bottom.

She stood up unsteadily and raised the ripped piece of cloth that had once been an extremely expensive Paris purchase to her face, before throwing it in the general direction of the waste bin and staggering naked into the bathroom and turning on the shower. Climbing under the hot, powerful flow of the water, it forced the sleep from her aching body as she allowed the hot water to scald her into wakefulness.

After shampooing her hair she climbed out of the shower and pulling on a large, white bathrobe, she walked into the living room, picked up the telephone, and dialled room service.

As she waited she looked around the room, Dettori was gone, and the only sign of his ever having been there was his empty whisky glass on the table.

"Can I help you Madam?" room service responded.

"Coffee please, make it double espresso, and croissants," she looked around the room again, "...for one," she said hanging up the receiver.

She had not belted the bathrobe and she caught sight of her body in the mirror, spotting a mark on her upper thigh. She walked over and stood before the full length mirror, allowing the robe to drop from her shoulders and crumple at her feet. At the top of her thighs she saw the beginnings of several large bruises, another was beginning to appear above her right breast and she lifted her hair to reveal bruises from strong fingers around her neck.

Susan knew that bruises were an occupational hazard if you indulged in the kind of sexual encounters she favoured.

She stared at herself directly in the mirror, "Well, Andrea," she said quietly, "what a surprise you turned out to be."

*

So why was it that she was now having dream-like flashes in her head of hands, covered with scars, much stronger, rougher and larger than Dettori's small, manicured, almost feminine hands? Why had the body that had pinned her to the bed seemed far bigger, more muscular than his?

And why, why did she have the unerring feeling that she had felt the scratch of a coarse, full beard on the back of her neck?

Susan was jolted back from her reverie by one of Dettori's men who had approached without her noticing and informed her that Romanski's jet had landed and the helicopter was ready to leave. They would be airborne shortly.

Susan sighed and swallowed back her drink as she saw the intrusive bulk of Romanski approaching her from across the lounge, a huge smile on his face and arms outstretched.

One day this vile Russian was going to look her in the face rather than at her breasts and legs she thought as she put on a brilliant and practised, but completely false, smile.

Gregori, as usual, ignored the outstretched hand and took Susan in a huge bear hug, crushing her breasts to his chest and bracing one leg against her pelvic bone. She felt like retching as the foul combination of vodka and cheap tobacco on his fat lips were crushed against hers.

"My beautiful, beautiful Susan, it is so good to meet you again."

"You too, Gregori," Susan said, not meaning it at all.

Fortunately the short flight was occupied mainly by Gregori berating Dettori's man for having the wrong vodka, at the wrong temperature, in the helicopter. At least, Susan thought, his attentions were directed at someone else, although it didn't stop him blatantly attempting to look up Susan's skirt as he talked.

CHAPTER FIFTEEN

Elliot awoke at around 8.00 am and after pulling on his bathrobe, made his way to the kitchen to make tea, only to find Kate already up, tea made, and a full English breakfast under way.

"Have I time for a bath before breakfast? I can't wait to try out that bath." Elliot was not a small man and the prospect of a hot bath that he could actually submerge himself in was attractive.

"Of course," Kate replied, "about half an hour?"

Elliot took his tea and ran his bath. Sinking slowly into the warmth of the water, Elliot closed his eyes and allowed the heat to relax his tired muscles.

By the time he returned to the kitchen, breakfast was on the table, with fresh tea and orange juice. Simon and Kate were seated and had already started. Kate poured tea and orange juice for Elliot and retrieved his breakfast from the oven where it was keeping warm.

Having placed the breakfast on the table before him, Kate handed something to Elliot, "What do you make of this?"

Elliot took from Kate a grey metal band that looked like some kind of bracelet. It was of an indeterminate base metal and consisted of a plain circular band, around which two snakes made of the same metal, wound, one clockwise the other anticlockwise. The tails were interwoven and at the other end, one snake held the other in its mouth, the jaws gripping just behind the head. It seemed very old, and there was some engraving on the central band and upon the backs of each of the entwined snakes.

"What is this – is it pewter?" he said to nobody in particular. "I need my glasses." Elliot went to the bedroom to retrieve them and returned with them perched on the end of his nose, turning the bracelet in his hand to read the engraving.

"Whoever engraved it couldn't spell," Simon pointed at the central band. "They've missed the 'i' out of Elliot."

As he studied the engraving, Elliot recognised the words instantly.

"No, not misspelled, just old; 'Ellot' was an early spelling of the name. The 'i' was introduced in the mid 17th century, about 1650, if I remember correctly."

He turned the bracelet excitedly in his hand.

"I understand some people still pronounce it Ellot in the borders today – although I have no personal experience of that. The name was derived, it is thought, from Elwald or Elwold, which literally means, 'Ruler of the Elves'. The introduction of the 'i' was not a good idea. It immediately confused the clan with the West Country and South Wales 'Eliots' derived from an entirely different Norman family of St Germains, whose name was derived from 'Alyot'. The current Head of the Clan's father, Sir Arthur Eliott, the 11th Baronet of Stobs talks of the derivation in his book: *The Elliots – The Story of a Border Clan*."

"What about the other words, on the back of the snakes?"

"Easy. '*Fortiter*' and '*Recte*' – Latin. They are from the Elliot, or Ellot, Clan motto – '*Fortiter et Recte*' – translated as either 'Boldly and Rightly' or 'With Strength and Right'. Where did you get this?" Elliot said, holding out the bracelet towards Kate.

"Thomas was playing with it, on the bed this morning. Not sure where it came from."

"Could he have found it in the house?" Elliot noticed that it was well worn; either it was very old or it was an expert attempt by someone to make it look old; 'distressing' he thought shady antique dealers called it.

"I don't see how; he was asleep in his room all night. I got him out of his cot this morning and he has been with me ever since, playing on the bed – he hasn't been anywhere to pick it up."

"Well, maybe we can ask the house owners. I'm sure if it belongs here they will tell us." Elliot continued studying the bracelet. "I'd like to get a picture of it though, would be a great little item for the family history record."

"Or it could have come from the pub," Simon said. "Maybe it was in with the pile of toys Thomas was playing with."

"Do you think it's valuable?" Kate was a little concerned; she recalled the medals and other military memorabilia that adorned the walls in the Grapes Hotel.

Elliot turned the bracelet slowly in his hand, "I'm not an expert, but it certainly is of historic interest if nothing else. Actually, that's probably it, I spoke to the landlord of the Grapes yesterday, he was in the antique business in Andover or Aldershot or some such place. He told me he specialised in medals. Don't know whether you noticed the bronze medallions on the wall, they were given to the families of those who fell in the First World War. Depressing things, I told him my dad had a couple. Two of his great uncles were killed on the Somme. He told me they were worth £250 each, haven't seen them for years, not sure what happened to them."

"Well, I think we'd better check with the landlord, I don't want us getting arrested for theft or something if it's valuable. Would you mind if we went to Hutton and Whitsome another day? I'd be happier if we sorted this out first," Kate asked.

"Looks like it's the Grapes this evening then," Elliot said.

"What a shame," Simon smiled. "You mean I've got to drink more beer?"

"What now then? If we're not going to Berwick."

"Well, we can go somewhere local. et's go up to Hermitage Castle."

"Do you mind if I don't come this morning? Actually I'm not feeling too great, I have a terrible headache." Kate looked rather pale.

"We can go another time if you're not up to it today," Simon said.

"No – you guys go. Thomas could do with a nap and I'll be fine if I have a lie down. You go and I'll look after Thomas. Save you dragging him around an old castle. I'll see you lunch time."

"Well, if you're sure, darling."

"Go on, go and look at your castle, I'll see you later."

Driving out of the drive, Elliot turned right then right again on to the Hawick road. In a few miles they saw the sign and took the turning to the left to Hermitage Castle. A half mile or so down the single track road the car took a sharp left bend and there, grey and forbidding in front of them, was Hermitage Castle.

"Wow," Simon's outburst was quite spontaneous. "That is something else!"

"It certainly is." Elliot couldn't put his finger on it, but somehow he felt drawn and repulsed at the same time. He drove parallel with the shallow burn that was Hermitage Water and separated the road from the castle.

On the other side of the burn a new fence had been built to prevent uncontrolled access, but this did not detract from the aura of this place as it rose majestically atop the ancient grassed and stepped defensive embankments.

They were similar to those they had seen yesterday, near the cemetery, but on top of them, instead of sheep, stood the most forbidding stone edifice Elliot had ever seen.

Of course he had seen pictures and read about its history, but none of that had fully prepared him for the sense of threat and menace that emanated from this formidable structure.

The castle consisted of two huge, rectangular, four-storey stone buildings, joined through the centre by another, indented, block, creating a truncated 'H' shape. The southern facing block sported triangular turrets; the rest of the building was flat, although at one time it was probable that they would have supported sharply sloping roofs. This southern face had a huge vaulted arch which extended to a height equivalent to three of the four storeys, and it looked for all the world like the entrance for a giant.

No wonder there were so many rumours of giants in the mythology of the area. Now blocked, this arched entrance was mirrored on the northern side, and this now represented the approach for visitors.

As they drove slowly past, a small wooden door in the indented side of the edifice sat alongside what seemed to be the top of an arch protruding a few feet above the ground. Was this some kind of sunken doorway? Were the rumours of the castle sinking into the ground true?

Elliot pulled up in a small parking area alongside a small bridge that crossed the burn to the castle entrance. A row of leafless trees stood guard along the far side of the burn between the road and castle.

As they got out of the car, Elliot noticed that the entrance was gated and padlocked, and he walked across the footbridge and read the sign on the locked gate indicating the castle was only open to visitors between April and September.

"Sorry Simon, looks like I've cocked up – all this research and I didn't remember to check the opening times."

"Well, let's take a walk back along the road and take a look anyway. I guess we'll have to come back in the summer and take a proper look."

*

Meanwhile, unknown to the two visitors, inside the castle the Red Cap was in a frenzy as he rushed between Soulis and the outer wall of the subterranean chamber, keeping track of the men he could smell outside.

"Let me take them now, they are outside, let me take them now."

"The child is not with them, I must have the child. You must bring him to me."

The Red Cap did not appear to be listening as he shuffled backwards and forwards, head swinging from side to side, alternately sniffing, snuffling and then pausing and listening at the wall, like a dog that could sense someone outside.

Soulis stepped forward grasping the Red Cap around the scrawny neck with one hugely powerful hand, squeezing and lifting at the same time, he hoisted the Red Cap from the ground and pulled the choking and violently thrashing dwarf to his face.

Ignoring the foul breath of the creature, he stared directly into the black soulless eyes. "You will bring the child to me," he bellowed directly into the creature's face.

The Red Cap ceased to struggle as the breath was squeezed out of him. Seconds before passing into unconsciousness, Soulis cast him away, crashing him violently against the damp, slimy dungeon wall, where the creature lay, choking and whining like a whipped dog.

"Leave the adults, you will have them later. Bring me the child."

*

Elliot had left Simon up on the road as he gingerly picked his way down the bank of the shallow burn, assessing the standing rocks on the bed of the stream as possible stepping stones to the other side.

Looking across at the castle, he scanned the high windows looking out from what was once the fourth floor of the building. Windows anywhere in reasonable reach of a potential raider were an oddity in any building from the period, whether a defensive pele tower or castle, a tower house or the slightly less formidable, but eminently defendable farmhouses, known as 'bastells' or 'bastles' of more modest landowners. At ground level, a defensive gun slit was usually the only opening, if one existed at all. Even the door was often built high off the ground and could only be accessed via a ladder that typically was pulled into the dwelling at night.

In later less turbulent years, many of the bastles that still existed had added steps leading up to the door.

Hermitage was no exception. This was a significant and highly defendable castle. Windows looked down only from the level of the fourth floor, and these dark apertures stared out like soulless eyes across the approaches to the castle, standing as it did on what in the 13th century would have been the main north/south road.

These more formidable towers were known as 'strenghes' or 'strengths'. It was immediately apparent why this tower was given the name of 'The Strength of Liddesdale.'

Suddenly Elliot shuddered, just as he had when they first arrived at the cottage, but this time the temperature drop was accompanied by a strong feeling of nausea and a feeling that something was clenching at his heart. His vision was blurred and he felt faint. Suddenly his body was soaked, as he broke out in a cold sweat, reminiscent of his night terrors. Sweat ran from his hairline into his eyes and through his blurred vision he saw a hooded face looking at him from one of the windows.

Staggering, he fell forward onto his knees and passed into unconsciousness. When he awoke, he found himself lying on the grass with Simon kneeling beside him, serious concern on his face.

"Are you okay? Maybe we should get you to a doctor, I was going to call an ambulance but there is no signal here at all."

"Was I out for long?" Elliot was checking his breathing. The pain in his chest had gone as had the nausea and the double vision, in fact he felt remarkably well, apart from where his cold, soaking jeans were clinging to his lower legs as he had collapsed to his knees in the shallow, icy water.

Fortunately, he had fallen backwards onto the grass bank, rather than pitching forward head first into the burn, where it would have been a miracle to avoid cracking his head on the rocks he had been assessing as possible stepping stones.

He also had a bruise on the right knee where he had landed on a rock, but apart from this he felt fine.

"You were only out for a few seconds," Simon was looking a little less worried now. "What happened?"

"I don't know. I felt ill, my vision was very blurred, but I thought I saw someone watching me from one of the windows."

"Maybe it was a worker or caretaker or something, they must do maintenance work, probably out of season. Perhaps they are working inside."

Elliot climbed gingerly to his feet leaning heavily on Simon's shoulder and looking up at the castle windows.

"It couldn't be," he said quietly.

"Why not?" Simon took Elliot's arm and helped him back up the bank to the road.

"I've seen photographs of the inside of the castle on the Net, the inside is a ruin." Elliot paused, and turned to look back at the castle behind him. "Nobody could have been standing at that window unless he was forty feet tall."

His voice quietened as he stared up at the windows. "There are no floors inside for anyone to stand on."

CHAPTER SIXTEEN

Elliot felt fine and really didn't want to spend the afternoon in some hospital accident & emergency department, but Kate had convinced him to visit a local doctor, the contact details for which the owners of the cottage had thoughtfully left on the mantlepiece, with other emergency numbers that might be required in such an isolated spot.

The doctor had indicated he could not find anything seriously wrong with him, apart from a few comments about weight and blood pressure, which Elliot could have anticipated before he went. With a suggestion that he should see his own GP on his return home he could only suggest that it might be the effects of a virus, after all there were a lot of them about and they had different effects on different people.

So you have no idea then? Elliot thought, but frankly was grateful not to have been referred to the local hospital for a scan. Like most men of his age, chest pains immediately brought fears of something far more frightening than a virus.

As they left the Hawick GP surgery, Simon was still thinking about the person Elliot had seen at the window in the castle.

"Maybe they're doing some renovation work They may have scaffolding or something inside."

"Perhaps." Elliot wasn't convinced. "The thing that is troubling me is that I thought I saw somebody watching us when we first arrived at the cottage, and I've been feeling drawn to that place from before we even left Oxford. Well, maybe Truman can throw some light on it." Elliot checked his watch which was showing a little after 4.00 pm. "Let's get back to the cottage and maybe we can book a table for dinner at the Grapes. If we get down there early evening, perhaps we can see him first."

"I'll ring and book now while we still have a mobile signal." Simon called directory enquiries and asked for the number for the Grapes in Newcastleton.

Elliot, Kate, Simon and Thomas arrived at the Grapes at 7.00 pm having booked dinner for 8.30. The landlord, used to families touring in the area, was happy to allow Thomas in the restaurant.

Entering the Lounge Bar they saw Thomas Truman sitting quietly in the corner. Elliot had anticipated they might need to track him down, maybe phone him, but there he was – waiting, as if they were expected.

He declined Simon's offer of a drink. A three-quarters full half-pint of bitter stood on the table before him, it looked very flat as if he had been taking a very long time over it. Simon went to the bar while Kate, Elliot and Thomas settled onto the settee, opposite the armchair where Truman was sitting. Simon returned a few minutes later and, settling two glasses of red wine in front of Kate and Elliot, he sat in another armchair sipping his customary lager.

Kate lifted the small felt fire engine, a favourite toy, from Thomas's pushchair, much to his disgust. Unzipping it she took out the bracelet and handed it to Truman.

"I wonder, have you ever seen this before? I am afraid Thomas might have picked it up from here while we were talking the other day. We were going to see if it belonged to the landlord."

Truman took the bracelet, inspected it briefly and then handed it to little Thomas. "It belongs to him, I gave it to him." Thomas grasped it joyfully, turning slightly away from Kate obviously concerned she was going to take it from him again.

"I'm not sure I can..." Kate was not comfortable but didn't want to appear rude to this obviously lonely old man.

Elliot was rather less restrained. "Look, something is not right here. I've just fainted like a sixteen-year-old groupie. I've been having hallucinations and you seem to know all about us, when I know we have never met before. What is going on here? Why are you so interested in us?"

"Dad!" Kate placed her hand on her father's arm. "You see Mr Truman, we are just a little confused..."

"I understand." Truman sipped his beer, "Tell me about these hallucinations."

Elliot briefly outlined the dark figure on the hilltop he had seen and then, in slightly more detail, the incident at the castle. Did Truman know if they were doing any renovation work that might involve scaffolding, ladders or some other mechanism to lift someone to the window?

"Hermitage has more sightings and more ghosts than any other building in Britain. Only three months ago a builder saw an almost identical vision, a face at the window."

"You mean alleged ghosts?" Simon said.

Truman glanced briefly at Simon, but without answering the question directly said, "How much do you know about what happened here nearly seven hundred years ago?"

Elliot answered. "I know a little: the fact that the lands were confiscated by Robert the Bruce from William de Soulis after a failed plot, wasn't he charged with treason? I know there were all sorts of stories about him practising black magic or something – I understand he was not a very pleasant landlord. But I guess these myths are easy to understand in an uneducated and subservient underclass, and the Church often used the fear of the supernatural to keep the populace in line.

"The Elliots and the Armstrongs were far from subservient. Neither were they great ones for religion. Back in the 16th century a visiting bishop once asked why there were so few churches in the area. 'They are all Elliots and Armstrongs here' was the response – which apparently was sufficient explanation for the noticeable lack of piety in the region.

"Not that they were entirely irreligious. When these Reivers were baptised, they deliberately left unblessed the child's favoured arm, as they were fully aware that when they grew to manhood that arm would be required to undertake some distinctly unholy acts."

Truman seemed to consider for a moment or two and then said, "Let me tell you about William de Soulis and his downfall seven centuries ago, you can make of it what you will.

"It is true he was a cruel and violent landlord, that was not particularly unusual for the time, but Soulis was particularly vengeful and unpleasant, especially when his own power or prestige was threatened; and he felt threatened most of the time.

"During the struggles for the right to sit on the Scottish throne, a struggle eventually won by Robert the Bruce, it is not generally known that William de Soulis had been one of fifteen or so contenders for the Crown, some say with a stronger claim through his bloodline. Actually his grandmother was the daughter of Alexander II, King of Scotland between 1214 and 1249. His claim was rejected, but there was much bad blood and he refused ever to accept that the final two contenders, Robert the Bruce and John Balliol, had a better claim.

"Of course, Edward, King of England wanted ultimate control over Scotland, so looked for fealty from one or other of them before giving his blessing, he finally gave it to Balliol, as someone who was likely to be more controllable and amenable to Edward's wishes than Robert the Bruce.

"Anyway, Balliol was crowned, but as anticipated he fell completely under the control of Edward and was, as a result, despised by many Scots. He was known as 'Toom Tabard' meaning 'empty coat' – such was his reputation for weakness in the face of the demands of Edward.

"As he grew weaker, the Bruce arranged a meeting with Balliol's representative, Comyn, in Greyfriars Kirk, in Dumfries, where a fight broke out and Bruce killed Comyn, an act that put him immediately at odds with not only Edward but with the Pope in Rome, who took exception to a murder inside a church, and, for this sacrilege the Pope excommunicated him.

"Edward and the Comyns fought back and defeated Bruce, but as every schoolboy knows, he was inspired by a spider building a web in a cave on a deserted island where Robert was hiding. The spider taught him to persevere, and try again."

Kate had, of course, heard the story of Bruce and the Spider. "Is that story not just a myth?"

"Actually, yes it is," Truman smiled warmly at Kate. "However, that is the only thing you will hear from me that is actually untrue, and there are more things you will hear shortly, that you will find far harder to believe.

"The Bruce fought back against Edward and the Comyns and after building his reputation with many small victories, patriotic Scots joined him in droves and then came Bruce's ultimate victory, when he destroyed the English army at Bannockburn, securing the Throne, despite Edward III not finally acknowledging it, until the Treaty of Northampton, in 1327, the year before The Bruce died."

"So what has this to do with William de Soulis?" Elliot was fascinated by the history, but failed to see the relevance to Hermitage, the Elliots and Soulis.

Truman took another sip of his beer before continuing. "Whilst all this political intrigue was going on, Soulis, who really cared nothing about the politics, but was interested only in his own power, continued to plot to take over the Throne.

"He had attempted, rather naively, early in his plotting to enlist the help of William Wallace, probably the only Scot with a greater reputation than The Bruce himself, after all The Bruce had become part of Wallace's campaign in the early days, although more of a politician than Wallace, who really was only interested in keeping Scotland free from the English. It is inconceivable that he would have considered Soulis a suitable candidate as King.

"Even after Wallace was captured and executed on Smithfield in 1305, even after Bruce was crowned in Scone in 1306, even after Bruce's great victory at Bannockburn in 1314, Soulis continued his plotting until 1321, precisely 686 years ago.

"Soulis nearly died in a fight with Wallace when he lost his temper and attacked him after he refused to back his claim for the Throne.

"He had also almost died in a similar way when he rode out after a young Armstrong girl, killing her father and only being saved from slaughter by an enraged group of the dead man's kin, by their own Lord, Alexander Armstrong the Lord of Mangerton.

"He rewarded Alexander, by stabbing him in the back a few days later in Hermitage. That will give you some idea of the type of man Soulis was, to murder in cold blood a man who had saved his life.

"These are historical facts; you can visit Milnholm Cross where Alexander's kin rested with his body overnight, on route for burial. After these two incidents, Soulis greatly accelerated his activity in the black arts."

Truman paused to smile quietly at Thomas before continuing.

"Robert the Bruce had a trusted knight who was the first to swear allegiance to him before he ultimately won power, and also fulfilled The Bruce's death-bed wish to carry the King's heart, after his death, into the Crusades against 'the heathen' the Muslims led by Mohammed IV.

"That knight was James Douglas, known by the English as 'The Black Douglas' and by the Scots as 'Sir James the Good'; he was Robert's second in command at their triumphant victory over the English at Bannockburn.

"William de Soulis brought Robert to the end of his tether during the 1321 plot to kill him and replace him on the Throne.

"Douglas discovered the plot through a lady known as the Countess of Strathern who confessed her part and named the conspirators including Gilbert Malherbe, John of Logie, Richard Brown and Sir David of Brechin.

"The Countess was imprisoned for life and each of the other conspirators, with the exception of Soulis, were tried at the Assizes for treason, and hung, drawn and quartered before being beheaded.

"Soulis was convicted of treason and his lands and titles, including Hermitage Castle, were ordered confiscated. However, so powerful was he as an adversary, and so influential both in Scotland and England, the political ramifications of putting him to death blatantly were not clear.

"Robert had spent years consolidating his position and had eventually entered a period when his Kingdom was not under constant threat, especially from the English who had suffered many defeats at his hand. He was unsure as to how King Edward in England would react to Soulis's death; he was a powerful landlord in England as well as Scotland. He decided to order his detention for life in Dumbarton Prison, but was fully aware that, whilst alive, he would always remain a threat to Robert and his descendants.

"They therefore hatched a plot which was very reminiscent of the way Thomas Becket, the Archbishop of Canterbury was disposed of, when Henry II apparently asked, 'Who will rid me of this turbulent priest?' an outburst which was taken as an order by some loyalists who promptly killed him.

"Whilst discussing Soulis's arrest and the confiscation of his properties a delegation arrived from the Lord of Branxholm complaining that Soulis had kidnapped the betrothed of the heir of Branxholm, a Lady Marion.

"The King was immediately able to put the plan into action by feigning a loss of temper to the crowded chamber and shouted in anger, 'I will hear no more of this Soulis, do what thou will with him, boil his bones if that be your pleasure, but let me hear no more of him'.

"Of course, as with Henry II there was always someone who wished to ingratiate themselves by carrying out his 'orders'.

"Sir James Douglas let the King's words be known to the appropriate people, notably the Clan Elliot who immediately left to carry out his bidding. After Sir James' emissaries had left, the King feigned remorse for his outbreak of anger and ordered Sir James to ensure that no harm came to Soulis. The chamber was full of witnesses of the highest reputation, to attest to the King's orders that Soulis was not to be harmed, but of course the King knew full well that the train of events that were to end Soulis's life had been set in motion."

Elliot was beginning to become confused. He knew from his studies that much of what Truman was saying was true, particularly the politics of the time, but much of the rest seemed fanciful. Either way however, he found it fascinating, and whoever this Thomas Truman was, he knew his history and was a great storyteller to boot.

"I will not sicken you with details of William de Soulis's depravities with animals and children but he got his reward, if reward you can call anything won from such crimes. He was granted near invulnerability by a creature called a Red Cap, we know them also as 'Dunters' or 'Powries', and they haunt evil places – not many places can be considered more evil than Hermitage."

Simon was now getting fascinated by the tale from this old man. "What do you mean by 'near invulnerability'?"

"The Red Cap granted him immunity from, let me see, what were the words exactly, 'Steel shall not wound thee, cords bind thee, hemp hang thee or water drown thee'."

Elliot was beginning to look incredulous. "Why is it these so-called predictions are always so inscrutable?"

"You must remember the old saying, 'When you sup with the Devil you should use a long spoon'? The Dark Spirits are by their very nature, deceitful and duplicitous, no matter how faithful their followers, they always speak in riddles, leaving them opportunity to renege on any deal they make.

"Soulis understood this, and having been told that he should not call the Red Cap for a further seven years, he immediately called him back as he feared death by burning which seemed conspicuously absent from the list of his invulnerabilities. For the sin of calling the spirit again too early, the request was denied, but also a warning was given: 'Beware a coming wood and triple binds of sifted sand'.

"Soulis, like so many of his ilk, could not control his physical lusts, and in an incident similar to that with the Armstrong girl, he had kidnapped a woman called Marion, who was betrothed to Walter of Branxholm, the heir to the lands of Branxholm to the north of Hawick.

"Soulis kidnapped the young woman whilst she was out hunting deer with her friends, and carried her back to Hermitage; clearly he had learned from the Armstrong experience that it was better to be on home ground when you set out to kidnap women.

"At first he wooed the young woman as he wanted her to agree to marry him, but such was her resistance, he locked her in his foul dungeon aiming to frighten her into submitting.

"Of course young Branxholm was a renowned warrior himself, and though younger and less experienced than the seasoned warrior Soulis, he was no less determined to recover his bride to be.

"Walter rode out to Hermitage with twenty riders to release Marion, but was met by more than one hundred of Soulis's men who set about them, driving them to flight. Most of Soulis's men pursued the fleeing Branxholme contingent leaving Walter to face Soulis and three of his men who had stayed behind.

"To give Soulis his due, or maybe it was another example of his blind arrogance, he faced Branxholm alone at first, being confident not only in his own swordsmanship, but in the invulnerability granted by the Red Cap, and whilst they were very well matched, Branxholm was unable to injure Soulis, as his blows seemed to have no effect.

"The battle raged until one of Soulis's men speared Branxholm's horse and as he fell to the ground he was captured and bound by Soulis who dragged him and chained him in the dungeon with his betrothed Marion."

Kate looked down at young Thomas, fearing he would be getting bored by all this lack of attention, but he seemed happy enough.

In fact as he talked, Old Thomas held out his hand to the child, to allow him to place the Ellot bracelet over his hand onto his wrist. Taking it from his wrist he handed it back to the child who immediately placed it back on Truman's wrist, in the kind of repetitive game that children enjoy.

Far from being annoyed by it, Truman seemed to enjoy the game as much as young Thomas, smiling at him warmly.

"Soulis gave Marion an ultimatum," Truman continued. "She could marry him, or be given Walter's head as a plaything, but all the time Walter told her to hold fast, he was not afraid to die and would rather be hewn to pieces than see Soulis possess Marion. Soulis left them together, chained against opposite walls, giving Marion until midnight to decide; marry him or see her beloved Walter die.

"As the hours passed Soulis began to worry about the fact that his men had not returned from their pursuit of the fleeing Branxholm men, but sometime later, a solitary rider returned, to tell Soulis that his men had become trapped in a bog in their pursuit and Branxholm's men had turned on them and put them to the sword. Soulis was not a man who accepted bad news well, and the returning rider was beaten almost to death for not dying with the others.

"At exactly midnight Soulis returned to his captives, he asked Marion for her decision. At Walter's bidding she again refused to succumb. Soulis turned to Walter and asked the young man, if the shoe was on the other foot and Soulis was his captive what would he do?

"I would hang you from the highest tree in the wood," was the young Branxholm's brave response, to which Soulis replied, that being the case, he would show how reasonable he was by taking Branxholm into the woods and allowing him to pick whichever tree he would like to be hanged from, and his betrothed Marion would hang from the next tree. Whereupon the two were bound with ropes and led by Soulis and his men out of the castle and then on horseback towards the woods.

"As they mounted and started towards the woods a rescue party rode up to release Walter and Marion, but instead of swords they were carrying long branches of rowan wood. Soulis knew the meaning immediately, 'Beware a coming wood', the warning issued by the Red Cap for the sin of re-calling him too early. Also, rowan has a long history as a defence against the supernatural; you will find references to rowan frequently around the area.

"Despite this, some of the rescuers, more familiar with the sword than the club, attempted to bind and kill Soulis, who fought like a man possessed, which arguably he was, but the steel of their sword had no effect and the bindings would not hold him, although the clubs of rowan certainly hurt and subdued Soulis, killing him was another matter.

"As the battle continued, Sir James Douglas, ostensibly there to ensure no harm came to Soulis sat astride his horse, silently watching the proceedings from a concealed position in the nearby trees. Soulis knew that someone, an adept of at least his capability, must have been advising these men. He also realised that these men attacking him were not from Branxholm, they were fighters of extraordinary skill.

"Later at the height of the age of the Border Reivers they, amongst others of the region, would earn the reputation as the 'Best light cavalry in Europe'. These men were Elliots.

"In the background not involved in the fighting, was a figure Soulis instinctively recognised as an adept. Clearly this was the person advising them.

"Soulis shouted at the figure, 'Who are you? Why do you hide behind these men? Face me you coward, face me alone!'"

"An adept?" Simon asked. "What is an adept?"

"Someone trained in the natural sciences," Truman replied.

"You mean witches, wizards, magic?" Simon smiled.

"They are called many things, I prefer adepts. Some use their powers for good, others, often referred to as 'Followers of the Left Hand Path', for evil. That is why being left-handed has always been associated with evil. It is only recently that left-handed school children have stopped being forced to write with their right hand.

"Anyway, the adept did not succumb to Soulis's challenge, but called from his position in the shadows for the Elliots to bring forward the lead. Men hurried from the rear carrying sheets of lead they had stripped from the roof of Soulis's own castle. As Soulis was clubbed to the ground they wrapped the lead tightly around his body and his struggling ceased as his legs and arms were pinned to his body by the sheets. Where bindings of rope were useless, the lead secured him firmly.

"In the end, Soulis realised the fruitlessness of further struggle. Eyes blazing, and foaming at the mouth he cursed the adept demanding the name of the hooded protagonist. 'My name is Thomas of Ercildoune,' came the reply, 'and your depravities, Lord Soulis, are at an end'.

"Soulis continued to scream his curses, both on Ercildoune and on the Elliots, calling on his familiar Robin Red Cap for help, but without his ritual and his chest he had no means to conjure him, so he was left to throw curses and threaten revenge, revenge that would not die with him and would threaten both Ercildoune and the Elliots from beyond the grave.

"Soulis was taken from Hermitage the few miles to Nine Stane Rig and there he was bent double in the lead and placed in his own cauldron, which had been dragged from his dungeon. The cauldron, so often used by Soulis in his dark rituals, was balanced on two of the nine stones of the ancient Druid circle. A huge fire was built under the cauldron and Soulis was boiled alive in the melting lead. In essence, boiling his bones as the King had apparently commanded.

"Sir James, who had been following at a distance waited until he heard the screams and curses from Soulis drown away and he was clearly dead, before galloping up to the group. He dismounted and approached the cauldron and, staring quietly at the dissolving remains within, said, 'I am here on the King's command to ensure no harm comes to Sir William Soulis. It seems I am a little late'."

The old man seemed to have finished his story, and Kate, Simon and Elliot sat in silence for a few minutes, staring at this strange old man with his incredible tale.

Elliot was the first to break the silence. As if waking from a kind of daydream, he suddenly shook his head and realised that he was in the 21st century, not the 13th.

"That is some story," he said. "Are you a historian or is this just a hobby of yours, studying the local mythology and legends of the area? Are you associated with the Heritage Centre?" Elliot knew there was a local museum a little further down the road, but, like Hermitage Castle, at this time of the year, it was closed.

"I am neither a historian nor a hobbyist, nor have I anything to do with the Heritage Centre. These things happened just as I have described," he replied firmly, "in 1321, exactly 686 years ago."

Simon had a question, "Did the King or Sir James Douglas call in Thomas of... where was it?"

"Ercildoune," Truman said.

"Ercildoune," Simon continued, "I don't see where he fits in – are you saying he worked for Robert the Bruce as well, like Merlin for King Arthur or something?"

"No. Thomas was concerned with keeping the balance. Soulis was originally just another ambitious and over privileged landowner. As he got more and more powerful his dark work at Hermitage was threatening the balance that exists between good and evil. Thomas had been seeking an opportunity to redress the balance for sometime. Neither The Bruce or Sir James knew he would be involved.

"Thomas of Ercildoune went to the Elliots and offered to help them defeat Soulis. Brilliant fighters though they were, it is unlikely they would have defeated Soulis in his own domain without help."

Elliot had been quiet for some time, trying to match what Truman was saying to the research he had done himself. He found the story fascinating, and much of the history seemed to match with what he knew – but the supernatural stuff? He couldn't believe any of it, but how could he expose this obvious nonsense for what it was?

But suddenly, from the depths of his memory he remembered something, something that proved all of this nonsense was just a fascinating work of fiction. He needed to check, and he pulled a PDA out of his jacket pocket.

Elliot carried the small, hand-held computer almost everywhere. It enabled him to keep information obtained from his research to hand, and to jot down any further data he might acquire while away from his computer. Searching through pages of documents he stored there from his Internet research, he found one that mentioned a Thomas of Ercildoune, a kind of Nostradamus type figure, and he smiled quietly to himself as he read the electronic pages.

Truman had risen to his feet explaining that he had to leave, but he seemed to be reluctant to leave little Thomas, who was still playing the game with the old man, passing the bracelet backwards and forwards.

Elliot savoured the moment as the old man headed slowly towards the door.

"Before you go, there is one thing I want to ask you." He held up the PDA, "I've just found the reason none of this can be true." He paused. "Thomas of Ercildoune was certainly a real historical figure, no doubt about that, I thought I'd come across him in my research," he smiled, savouring the moment.

"But according to my research, he died in 1297. None of this can be true because Thomas of Ercildoune died nearly twenty-five years before that night at Hermitage in 1321."

Truman turned slowly, looked into Elliot's eyes and shook his head, slowly, like a parent with a child who had disappointed. He looked down at little Thomas, before returning his gaze to Elliot, a warmth in his voice and a gentleness made Elliot immediately guilty for the pleasure he had taken in catching him out.

"Just because you don't believe in something, David, it doesn't mean it is not true."

The sudden use of Elliot's first name, for some reason, immediately put him in mind of his father, who died nearly thirty years earlier, and he felt a familiar burning at the back of his eyes as he recalled the loss he had never quite got over.

Truman continued quietly, "What do you think this is all about? Where do you think Soulis got the idea that he could come back; that he could return from the grave?

"Soulis knew exactly who Thomas of Ercildoune was. He new he was an adept and he also knew he had died years before."

"I'm sorry," Elliot was quieter now; he seemed confused by the obvious anomaly. "Either you are saying my research is wrong or...."

Truman looked at Elliot expectantly, as if encouraging a slow child.

"...or you are telling us that Thomas of Ercildoune was still walking the earth twenty-five years after his death?"

"No."

Truman turned and walked towards the door. He stopped and turned, before disappearing into the night.

"No," he said again. "I'm telling you Thomas of Ercildoune is walking the earth today, not twenty-five years after he died, but seven centuries after he died."

CHAPTER SEVENTEEN

Kate, Simon and Elliot stood silently, staring at the door that Truman had passed through, until a waiter from the restaurant came through to the lounge to tell them their table was ready and they filed through to it. A few minutes passed in silence as Simon settled Thomas into a high chair. He was still happily playing with Truman's bracelet which the adults had completely forgotten about during the fascinating tale that had been told them by Truman.

It was Simon who broke the silence, "Well, what the hell do you make of that? He's got to be mad hasn't he?"

Elliot shrugged, his mind still whirling with the implications of what Truman had told them.

Kate was busy removing the bracelet from Thomas, much to his disgust, but he seemed a little happier when he saw her zip it up into the little fire truck. This seemed to satisfy him that his new favourite toy was safe.

"We should have made him take the bracelet back. He seems a nice old man, but what if a relative accuses us of stealing it from him? If it's valuable they are probably expecting to get it when he dies." Kate looked concerned.

Wine and food were ordered but Elliot remained distracted. He seemed to be reading and re-reading pages of research on the PDA, which he had been constantly referring to since he had produced it to disprove, as he thought, Truman's story.

"What do you think, Dad?"

"I really don't know what to make of it, Kate." Elliot was still trying to find inconsistencies in Truman's story. "I've always prided myself on reading people. Usually I can tell when people are bullshitting, but this guy... I'm certain of one thing, whether this is a complete fantasy or not, Truman believes it."

Simon smiled, "There are people who believe what happens in their favourite soap opera is true."

100

Elliot returned the smile, "Agreed, but how many of them have studied something as deeply as Truman obviously has? He seems to know his subject very well."

"Are you sure? How much of what he says is accurate?"

"I'm not an expert," Elliot had maybe a slightly better understanding of the history than the average person, purely through his family history research. "From my reading at least though, it seems to me a lot of what he says is fact."

"Was there any connection between the Elliots and William Wallace for example?"

It was not unusual that Simon should focus on Wallace first. He was, at least south of the border, more familiar than most Scottish heroes; more so today even than Robert the Bruce, everyone it seemed had seen Mel Gibson in the film, 'Braveheart'.

"I know of no direct connection, but frankly it would seem extremely unlikely that Wallace had no contact with the clan. There was certainly a connection between The Bruce and the Elliots, that bit at least is clear. It seems the Elliots did come from Angus at the foot of Glenshie just as Truman says.

"They were invited down to the area around Hermitage following his confiscation of Soulis's lands. It seems to me that The Bruce was a politician first and a patriot second, he changed allegiances often to secure his place in history.

"Towards the end of the 13th century, Wallace was the dominant figure and Bruce followed him, rather than the other way around. It seems highly unlikely that if Bruce had dealings with the Elliots that Wallace would not."

"So how accurate was the film about Wallace?" Simon said.

"Not very, I'm afraid. Mel Gibson was not tall enough for a start. Do you know the real Wallace was supposed to be around six feet seven inches tall, and dressed habitually in green?

"He became an outlaw after killing some English bullies who picked him out of a crowd in Dundee; apparently they took exception to his fine clothes. He defended himself, killing most, maiming others. He stabbed the ringleader, someone by the name of Selby, through the heart with his dirk.

"Unfortunately Selby's father just happened to be the Constable of Dundee and had a taste for blood, especially that of the Scots whom he hated. Wallace became an outlaw, lived in a forest, robbed the rich and became a hero to the poor."

"Sounds like Robin Hood," Simon joked.

"Actually, that is not as stupid as it sounds. Wallace also travelled with a Benedictine monk. He was highly educated as the second son of a minor knight called Malcolm Wallace.

"His father Malcolm was killed in a skirmish by the English, it is thought that this led to Wallace's hatred of the English and his desire to keep Scotland free from English control. On his father's death, Malcolm's lands went to William's older brother, also named Malcolm.

"As is often the case the second son would go into the Church, where they were highly educated – the monk that travelled with him later as an outlaw, John Blair, was originally his teacher and recorded Wallace's later exploits.

"William also had a mistress, whom he never married because he believed war and marriage didn't mix. She was called Marion just like the so called Robin Hood. Another of his travelling companions was called Edward Little; and his younger brother who was also travelling with him was named John. If you have an older brother who is six foot seven inches tall it is perhaps not too much of a stretch to imagine you might be referred to as 'Little John'. Add to this the facts that Wallace habitually wore green, hid out in Selkirk forest and was the sworn enemy of the Dundee Constable; for Selkirk, read Nottingham, for Constable read Sheriff and you have an almost perfect match."

"Sounds a little fanciful," Simon said.

"Not really. Early propaganda. You have to remember what a heroic and frightening figure Wallace was. He inspired the Scots and frightened the English. It would make absolute sense for the English to invent their own 'English' version of their enemy.

"When he was captured and tried in London, the horrendous punishment he received was indicative of how much he was feared and how desperate the King was to make an example of him. Unfortunately for Edward, all he did was turn him into a martyr."

"So," Kate brought them back to the point, "what you seem to be saying is Wallace probably did know the Elliots."

"Almost certainly," Elliot continued, "and being one of the 'Guardian's of Scotland', he would certainly have known Soulis,

102

and, given his reputation, it is perfectly logical that Soulis would have tried to win his support for his claim to the Crown, at least in the late 13th century. Wallace's reputation would certainly have gone a long way to securing the crown for whomever he backed.

"It is equally certain, in my opinion, that he would have given pretty short shrift to someone of Soulis's reputation. Remember Wallace was a true patriot. He hated the English and wanted nothing for himself. He just wanted to keep Scotland free from the yoke of the English King. Soulis would have done a deal with the Devil himself to maintain power, much less the English King."

"So where does that leave us?" Simon recapped, "Wallace, the Elliots, Robert the Bruce, William de Soulis all of this is real history. What about the stories of Soulis and the kidnapping of local women and so on?"

"Well, it is also true that the local Lords often considered any attractive woman in his reach fair game. In fact they often considered it their right to take to their own bed any young woman about to be married. The story of wicked squires ravishing local girls is as old as recorded history and the problems caused by bastard descendants of royalty and the aristocracy are many.

"I can't vouch for the Branxholm story, but certainly the Armstrong story seems true, in fact one of the places I wanted to visit was Milnhom Cross, which is nearby, I have a photograph somewhere. We also know Nine Stane Rig exists, and it is close to Hermitage. I even located it on the map in the cottage."

"And all this supernatural stuff? Wizards, dark arts, what was the term Truman used, adepts?"

Elliot thought for a while before answering, "The belief in the supernatural is as old as man, sometimes as an explanation for the unexplainable. We have less belief now because we understand more through science. We no longer have to explain the sun rising each morning as the work of some god for example, but the belief in the supernatural is still within all of us to a greater or lesser degree. You just have to look at the interest in ghost stories and the like."

"So you think its all rubbish," Simon said.

Elliot sipped his wine. "Not all of it no; a lot of science today seems like magic to me. Can you imagine how someone in the 13th century would react to television for example?

"I'm sure people like Soulis genuinely believed they could do magic, invoke demons and so on. And reputation is a powerful thing. If you believe someone is invulnerable it would certainly impact on your ability to fight him, and if you believed yourself to be invulnerable then you would be a difficult person to defeat in a fight.

"A bit like Muhammad Ali, apart from his natural boxing ability, he also had a way of 'psyching out' his opponents. Often they were beaten before they got into the ring with him. Also because Ali had such confidence in his own ability he felt he couldn't be beaten and as a consequence rarely was."

"So it's mostly hysteria, ignorance and belief?"

"I think so; but then..." Elliot seemed to consider again before responding, "this Truman character seems to believe it and reading some of this stuff about Thomas of Ercildoune, well, there are a few, shall we say interesting coincidences that bear thinking about."

"Like what?" Kate asked.

"Well, we know, like all of the others, he was a real person. It appears he was a kind of Nostradamus-type figure. He made predictions and, like Nostradamus, people claimed they came true. There is also a stone to his memory in Melrose somewhere which honours him as a famous Scottish literary figure. He not only made predictions but also wrote ballads, at least one of which was about William Wallace.

"He was also linked to the Queen of Elfland," Elliot said, slightly embarrassed by the comment.

Simon laughed, "So we have wizards, what did Truman call that creature of Soulis's – a Red Cap? And now elves and fairies!"

"I know it sounds fanciful but it might explain some ancient link between him and the Elliots. Remember when I explained to you the derivation of Elliot being from Elwold or Elwald, meaning 'Ruler of the Elves?'"

"So Thomas controlled the fairies and your ancestors the Elves? You can't possibly believe that."

"No, of course not, but these stories come from somewhere. All I'm suggesting is that they may have been considered healers, wise men, seers, that kind of thing. Apart from Nostradamus type figures, you yourself mentioned Merlin, there is no shortage of these supernatural characters in history and many are based on real people."

"I suppose that makes some kind of sense, although there is still no evidence of a connection with the Elliots, other than the one Truman himself gave; with the story of Soulis boiling in lead and so on," Simon said.

"But there is with Wallace and The Bruce, and we have already established at least probable connection with the clan through them. Again it is unlikely such an important figure would be unknown to the Elliots or indeed to Soulis."

"Okay," Simon said, "I can buy most of this. These guys knew each other, they fought, they may have used the Elliots as foot soldiers. I can even believe they might have believed in magic and in Soulis's case at least he may have believed he was a magician."

He swallowed the last of his lager and indicated to the waiter that a refill would be welcome.

"But this stuff about coming back from the dead and this Ercildoune, being alive for seven hundred years, well, it is just ridiculous."

"I agree." Elliot knew Simon was right, but one thing was still bothering him. He was almost embarrassed to mention it.

"There is one other thing," Elliot said. "Thomas of Ercildoune had several other names he was known by. He was also known as Lord Learmont and sometimes Thomas the Rhymer as he was known for writing ballads of the times as well as his predictions.

"Ercildoune was the original name for Earlston, not far from Berwick, and in the hills there he is alleged to have met with the Queen of Elfland, who he went with and served for seven years. Maybe coincidence but seven years seemed to be important to Soulis as well."

"Not sure what that proves." Simon was not sure where his father-in-law was going with this.

"Of itself, nothing, but the legend continues that when he returned from Elfland after this seven years, the Queen granted him a gift. A gift that Thomas viewed more as a curse actually. She gave him a 'tongue that could not lie'. That's where he got his other name from. He was also known as 'True Thomas', because he couldn't lie."

Simon missed it for a moment, and then he realised what Elliot was saying.

"For 'True Thomas' read 'Thomas True Man', or 'Thomas Truman'. You have got to be kidding!" he said in disbelief.

CHAPTER EIGHTEEN

They drove out of the square in almost total silence and Elliot set off through the town heading north in the direction of the cottage.

Thomas had fallen asleep in his child seat in the back of the car and Kate sat beside him, her hand holding her son's small soft hand as she gazed at the sleeping child lost in her thoughts, her head resting against the back of the seat.

Elliot took the left-hand turn onto the Hawick road driving slowly as they passed over the bridge and out of the town parallel to the shallow burn that separated the road from the drive up to the current seat of the Elliot's where the Clan Chief, Margaret Eliott of Redheugh, lived, having inherited through her father Sir Arthur Eliott, the 11th Baronet of Stobs.

The single 'L' and double 'T' indicated their attachment to Stobs rather than Minto or Wolfelee, where the double 'L' and single 'T' of his spelling, prevailed.

Of course, he thought quietly, this spelling business seemed to have become somewhat arbitrary in the outside world, where through generations of birth, death and marriage records and an ever expanding State with its army of faceless bureaucrats who cared little as to whether the name they wrote down had one 'T' or two.

Having lived in England most of his life Elliot was used to people spelling his name incorrectly and whilst it still rankled somewhere in his subconscious, he had all but given up correcting people. Even the HR Director of the company he worked for could not manage to spell it correctly.

We lived, he thought, in a world where people constantly re-branded themselves.

Why did someone suddenly think that 'Personnel' should become 'Human Resources'? And who ever thought it was a reasonable use of somebody's time to actually define the apparent difference? And who actually gave a damn anyway? Apart of course from those people who *were* one of the army of administrators who worked full-time doing that very thing?

And why could they not be bothered about getting his name right? After all what else had they to do apart from spelling people's names correctly?

It was unlikely, he thought, that any such cavalier attitude to correct spelling would be tolerated around here.

Simon had been gazing out of the window from the front passenger seat, seeing very little in the deep darkness apart from the occasional glint of moonlight on the water breaking over the rocks in the burn. Slowly his head slumped forward onto his chest as, either from the effects of the alcohol, or the sheer hard work of looking after a rapidly developing son, he fell asleep.

Elliot smiled and looking in the rear view mirror he saw that Kate had also dozed off still holding the hand of little Thomas who had the ability to sleep anywhere. Sleep was a gift that Elliot envied pretty much above any other, given his own constant battle with insomnia.

As the others slept peacefully his mind returned to the conversation with Truman and he went over his story again in his mind. Looking up he saw a full moon shining brightly, silhouetting the hills and the leafless trees, which were leaning away from the relentless icy gales that had bent them over decades.

Clouds carried on the strong winds drifted like smoke across the face of the moon. It seemed to him like a scene from a bad horror film. *What was that one? 'An American Werewolf in London'!* He remembered the scene where the two young American boys were leaving the Slaughtered Lamb Inn to set off into the rain.

'Stick to the roads – stay off of the moors' was the dire warning of the unfriendly locals in the Inn as they left.

Of course they didn't 'stick to the roads' or 'stay off of the moors'. *But then if they had there would have been no story would there?*

As he turned off the Hawick road onto the narrow track leading down to the cottage he chuckled to himself openly. Of course that was it. It was the location.

He remembered a time in the '70s when he was driving back beside Loch Ness with his father in the early hours of the morning, after a nice meal and a few drinks. They decided to pull over and take a look at the Loch. The night was much like this; a full moon, clouds scudding across it, and a low mist hanging over the water. Elliot had scrambled down onto a pebbled area to get on a level with the Loch and looked out across the water. As he stared into the mist in the deathly silence, broken only by the lapping of the water near his feet, a few hundred yards out he saw what looked like something poking out of the water and travelling at speed across the Loch.

Calling his father they looked closely and as the clouds cleared and the moonlight brightened a little, they made out a fallen branch. It was the water rushing past the submerged branch that was moving, although an optical illusion was telling his brain the branch was moving, not the water.

A few more drinks and it would have been a confirmed sighting of Nessie, he thought, smiling to himself.

That was it of course; it was the location, the atmosphere and the almost obsessive interest he had been taking in the history surrounding the area.

Would he believe any of this whilst driving home from work down the M1 on a Friday night, along with thousands of other lemming-like wage slaves? Would he believe it whilst sitting on his sofa in his modern flat in Abingdon, flicking through television channels trying to find something to watch that didn't involve someone trying to get on an Easyjet flight back from Alicante or some such place, or watching some unknown so-called celebrity sleeping in semi-darkness, or some person who believed that all the problems of her sad little world would be solved if she had, slightly bigger, or slightly smaller, or slightly different shaped breasts?

Of course not.

He had given some credence to all this nonsense from Truman because he was in the perfect location. Miles from nowhere with no access to mobile phones, in just the kind of weather and situation that was necessary as a backdrop for any bad horror movie or supernatural claptrap.

Of course, some part of him wanted it all to be true: something beyond the mundane; the mere ordinary. As he pulled off the road and down the track towards the cottage he laughed at himself openly at the complete stupidity of giving even momentary credence to any of this.

It was then that Elliot saw the Red Cap.

CHAPTER NINETEEN

Dettori's guests had all arrived and they were currently in their rooms dressing for dinner, with the exception of Gregori Romanski who was in the bar drinking vodka and holding forth to anyone who would listen about how vodka had to be of the right quality and served at the right temperature.

Only Russians understood and appreciated decent vodka, he expounded. The pathetic French prattled on about how their wines and champagne must be at exactly the correct temperature. Bourgeois nonsense. Yet they would insult a true Russian by serving him warm vodka. He was pleased to note at least that Dettori kept a decent one at Branxholm and also kept it in the freezer: pity he wasn't as fastidious with the helicopters.

Dettori knew Romanski would leave it to the last minute before changing and he had already told the staff to delay serving dinner until 8.30 pm. Romanski was the only one who thought it was at 8.00 pm and therefore would inconvenience nobody when he arrived at 8.15.

Still, Dettori knew that after tonight this irritating Russian would have served his purpose and the executive board of the Soulis Foundation would come under the direct control of William de Soulis personally.

Already dressed for dinner, he decided he had earned another drink. He liked to keep a clear head at all times, particularly when conducting business, so unlike Romanski he had drunk nothing since he left his office in London five hours or so earlier. He poured himself his favourite single malt over ice and sat back behind the desk in his private apartment within Branxholm and scanned the TV screens of the close circuit system via which he could monitor the entire property.

He could see Romanski in the bar, and he scanned the screens monitoring the others in their suites, in various stages of preparation for dinner. His eyes lingered briefly on Susan Coltrane who was parading around in her underwear. She was certainly an attractive woman. It amused him that she must know the suites were all monitored, but she had the absolute confidence not to be fazed by the thought.

His mind went briefly back to their liaison the night before: how that cool, sophisticated and controlled demeanour had been lost in a body made for sin. He prided himself on his ability to find the weakness in anyone and with Susan it was her pure sexuality, he felt an immediate stirring of desire before his iron focus drove the thoughts quickly from him.

He sipped his whisky and smiled excitedly. Tonight was to be the culmination of all he had worked for over the passed thirty-five years or so. The excitement of seeing his mentor take his rightful place at the head of the Board of Trustees tomorrow evening was too important to allow himself to be distracted. Neither the irritating behaviour of Romanski nor the near naked beauty of Susan Coltrane could take his mind away from the job in hand.

February 14th 2007 would be the start of a new World Order, with William de Soulis at its head. Dettori would be an important part of that new order as Soulis's right-hand man. He savoured the moment, remembering how he had been nursed back to health by his mentor who had over the years entrusted him to be his representative in the world until the day came when he would take his place at its head: when gloriously all the so-called leaders of the world would bow down to him.

How Soulis had nurtured Dettori's own supernatural powers, puny compared to those possessed by his master, but nevertheless powerful enough to enable him to do Soulis's bidding in this modern unbelieving world.

How, little by little, they had built up a fighting fund of enormous proportions, initially through murder, theft, blackmail and deceit, culminating in the development and ownership of huge global corporations, banks, even countries.

But he knew the world had seen nothing yet.

He knew that starting tomorrow, all the secrecy, the pretence, the covering of tracks would be over as the most powerful man in the world openly brought it directly under his control.

Of course there would be resistance. Powerful states with nuclear weapons, armies with technical killing skills of unbelievable ferocity would resist. But who would they bomb? Who would they invade? Which armies could match the slaughter wrought by thousands of Red Caps? Supported by the almost limitless supernatural power of the only true wizard alive, once released from the bondage of Hermitage? No one existed who had such power; power refined and honed over nearly seven hundred years.

Of course he expected a little trouble: some internal political manoeuvrings from some of his colleagues in the Foundation, particularly the bombastic Romanski.

But none of them had seen the real extent of his own powers, let alone those possessed by his as yet unseen master. It might be necessary to demonstrate their power at some stage, in fact he was certain it would before the night was out, but he was not going to allow anyone, especially one drunken Russian, to jeopardise the work of thirty-five years.

He had remembered the joy Soulis had shown when he had acquired Branxholm for him. He was not sure why, but it obviously represented much to him, although Soulis had never explained and therefore he had not asked. It was enough that he had pleased his master.

He also had no idea what Soulis was planning to release himself, but he had absolute confidence that he would. He had learned a long time ago that whatever Soulis predicted invariably came to pass.

Despite expecting some challenges, he was pleased with how well the other members of the coalition had come together. Apart from incredible wealth, they also had one other thing in common. They were all totally ruthless. Nothing would ever stand in their way if money, power, or influence was at stake.

At some stage, all of them had made use of murder to achieve their ends.

Romanski and Clemenza had personally killed to advance themselves. This much they had in common with Dettori.

Coltrane, Robertson and Erikson, as far as Dettori was aware, had not personally killed anyone, but had certainly put chains of action in place that they could have no doubt would have led to the murder of several, if not hundreds, of people.

Dettori decided he needed to relax and closed his eyes, leaning back in the comfortable high backed chair. The next forty-eight hours were going to be crucial and he wanted to make sure that everything was in place for the arrival of Soulis. He thought again about Romanski, before deciding he was sure he had covered all eventualities.

His plans were complete. As complete as they could be, apart from anything that Soulis had not told him. But he was confident if he had not been told, he did not need to know.

He relaxed.

He had an hour before he was due to meet the others in the bar for drinks before dinner.

CHAPTER TWENTY

Elliot braked the car a few yards from the horrific sight. At first he saw what looked like a huge bundle of rags piled on the grass to the left of the cottage, but as the headlights lit up the scene he noticed it was rising and falling rhythmically.

A large sheep lay on its side, and certainly it was no longer moving.

Kneeling beside it and leaning over it was a hideous dwarf, its face buried in a pool of blood at the neck of the unfortunate sheep, tearing like a hyena devouring a zebra. The creature was ripping at the animal with huge yellow teeth whilst massive curved talons tore at the body of the sheep, further opening up the already gaping wound.

As the headlights hit this scene of carnage, the dwarf raised its head and glared with black, staring eyes directly into the headlights, its lower face plastered with gore, long tendrils of flesh hanging from the razor sharp teeth. Incongruously pulled tight down around the creatures head was a matted cap dripping with fresh blood.

In shock Elliot sounded the horn and the dwarf, startled by the sudden loud noise, leapt nimbly to clawed feet and darted towards the car directly into the headlights and towards Elliot who instinctively drew back holding defensive arms before his face. Leaping onto the bonnet of the car its clawed feet scraped noisily as it struggled for purchase on the slick metal, and then it jumped onto the roof and off the back of the car. Elliot turned quickly to see the back of the creature disappear into the night.

Rudely awoken, Kate and Simon struggled to shake the sleep from their eyes, looking from side to side to see what was happening. Reaching for Thomas, who was crying with fear, Kate hugged her son to her, rocking gently to comfort him.

"What the hell was that?" she said, clutching Thomas even more tightly to her.

Simon started to open the car door but Elliot reached over him slamming the door shut again.

"Did you see that?" His face was ashen and his hand trembled as he withdrew it from the door handle.

Simon looked puzzled, "I saw..." he paused, "I saw something, a shadow on the bonnet and something on the roof; but I was half asleep. I didn't see it clearly."

Elliot turned quickly to Kate, "You?" he said, a note of terror in his voice.

Kate looked at her father's face, she had seen him upset before, even angry, but never terrified and it frightened her.

"The same," she said, "I heard it more than saw it. As Simon said, it was a shadow. I was asleep."

"I don't want anyone getting out of the car until I'm sure it's gone. Kate can you give Thomas to Simon and reach over into the back of the car – there is a torch there."

"You're frightening me, Dad," Kate said as she handed Thomas to her husband and knelt up on the seat pulling coats, boots and bags to one side searching for the large, yellow hand lamp that Elliot kept in the back of the vehicle. Her hand closed around it and she pulled it out, handing it to her father.

"I want everyone to stay in the car," he said, "and keep the doors closed after me, until I say it's okay."

Simon wanted to help, but Elliot asked him to stay with Thomas and Kate. "Look after them for me – please." The comment was almost a plea, and Simon nodded, holding Thomas tight to him and reaching over the back of the seat to take Kate's hand, squeezing it reassuringly.

Taking a final look around the car, Elliot took a deep breath and composing himself, he gingerly clicked the door open, the catch sounding loud in the surrounding silence. He paused with the door slightly ajar ready to slam it closed again at the first sight of that dreadful creature. Then, hearing nothing he tentatively stepped out of the vehicle.

He swept the powerful beam of the torch firstly in the direction the creature had taken off in, moving it quickly from side to side in search of any movement of any sort. Seeing none, he did a more thorough sweep all around the car until he was satisfied that nothing was close by, before returning the beam to the ravaged body of the sheep lying motionless on the grass.

Shuddering he returned to the car. "Have you got the cottage keys?" he said to Kate, who rummaged briefly in her handbag and handed them to her father.

"Stay in the car a moment, I'll get the house opened up, check everything is okay and then we can get Thomas inside."

Kate watched as her father stepped out of the headlights of the car into the darkness at the front of the cottage. She held her breath for what seemed like an eternity until she saw the reassuring sight of the lights going on in the cottage, one by one, as her father obviously worked his way from one room to another, turning on lights as he went, until the whole place was lit up like a Christmas tree.

Minutes later Elliot returned holding a rather pathetic looking poker he had collected from the fireplace. He wasn't sure how effective it would have been against that foul creature, but it brought at least a semblance of reassurance.

"It's all fine," he said, trying to compose himself despite the fact that his heart was still pounding disconcertingly. "Take Thomas in, you go with her Simon, I'll take a quick look around the outside of the house, just to make sure it's all secure."

Elliot stood shining the torch to light the path as Simon, Kate and Thomas hurried into the house as he glanced anxiously around them.

Breathing deeply to try and calm himself, Elliot gripped the poker a little tighter and, holding the torch out in front of him, he slowly walked the perimeter of the house, checking the windows and doors for any sign of attempted entry. More often than strictly necessary he swept the beam around; particularly behind him, anxious that nothing could approach unnoticed. When he arrived back at the front porch he breathed another sigh of relief and entered the cottage, carefully closing and locking both the inner and outer doors.

In the lounge Simon had thrown more fuel on the smouldering fire. "Can I have the poker?" he said, smiling as he reached for the implement hanging loosely from Elliot's hand.

Elliot looked at it uncomprehendingly at first, and then realising, he handed it to Simon.

"Well that was exciting." Simon's comment was artificially light-hearted, hoping to reassure Kate, who had managed to stop Thomas crying and was rocking him reassuringly backwards and forwards in her arms.

Actually he seemed fine, probably his unhappiness was driven more by the apparent concern of the adults around him, rather than genuine fear.

Kate and Simon seemed to have recovered much quicker than Elliot, but then neither of them had seen exactly what he had seen.

Kate had made coffee and as they sat by the fire that Simon had now coaxed back into life, they allowed the warm liquid to soothe them. She reached over to her father who was obviously still pretty shaken, placing a gentle hand on his arm. She could still feel a tremble in his hand.

"What was it you saw exactly?" the noise and the shock had frightened her too, but clearly her father had seen something far worse than she had.

"Did neither of you see anything?" Elliot was clearly worried.

"Like I said, I heard more than I saw," Simon leaned forward to poke a little unnecessarily at the fire. "I saw something bounce off the bonnet and onto the roof, and I certainly heard it. It sounded like some kind of animal. I could hear claws or something scraping on the roof, and I felt the car lift when it jumped off the back, but by the time I'd turned around it had gone."

"Me too, I didn't see it but I certainly heard it. It frightened me to death." Kate squeezed her father's arm, "So what did you see?"

"I wish one of you had seen it as well," Elliot said quietly. "Not that I have seen one ever before to recognise it, but I am absolutely sure what I saw was a Red Cap."

Kate and Simon both looked at each other and then at Elliot.

"You mean the creature Truman was talking about? The one that Truman said helped Soulis?" Simon in particular looked a little sceptical.

Elliot went to the window in the lounge that looked out to the front and pulled back the curtains. "I really didn't want to go out there until daylight – but", he turned to Simon, "I need you to look at this."

Elliot and Simon put on jackets, raising their collars in anticipation of the blast of icy wind that was now driving sheets of rain against the window. Elliot put on his wide brimmed hat and threw the cap to Simon. Picking up the torch, he unlocked the door and with a look back at Kate, still holding Thomas in her arms he stepped out into the night, closely followed by his son-in-law.

Outside, he swept the beam of the torch backwards and forwards searching for something he dearly hoped wasn't out there. Seeing nothing, he led Simon around to the side of the cottage to where the sheep, or what was left of it, was lying.

Elliot wiped the driving rain from his eyes and shone the torch onto the carcase, "Have you ever seen anything like that before?"

Simon stared down a look of disgust on his face. The sheep's throat had been ripped out, but what was more disgusting, the stomach had been opened up. Long shreds of skin hung in tatters around the wound, as if shredded by razors, and the sheep's entrails had been drawn out, a puddle was forming around Simon's boots as rainwater and blood ran in rivulets away from the carcase and pooled around his feet.

"My God!" Simon's exclamation escaped quietly almost to himself. "What sort of creature does that to an animal?"

Elliot looked on, so anxious had he been to get his family into the cottage and safety he had not studied the sheep too hard before, but something bothered him.

"Let me look at the car." Simon held out his hand for the torch and Elliot passed it to him. Shining the torch onto the bonnet and roof of the car he ran his finger along deep scratches, cutting through the paintwork right down to the bare metal. Bits of indeterminate flesh adhered to the roof that had obviously dropped off the claws of the animal. He returned to Elliot, still standing by the dead sheep, the rain seemed to get suddenly heavier and the pair of them automatically backed up against the house, seeking some protection from the eves of the cottage.

"That will be interesting to explain to the insurance company," Simon waved his hand in the general direction of the car.

Elliot shone the torch once more onto the sheep, "I'm sure the sheep wasn't as badly mauled as that when we went into the cottage." It suddenly dawned on him what that meant. "It's been back!" he said waving the torch in wide arcs across the wild moorland. "Let's get back inside."

A few feet above their heads, squatting on the roof above them sat the Red Cap, staring down at them with dark malevolent eyes, his face and teeth still plastered with the gore from the massacred animal, his razor sharp claws slowly clenching and unclenching as rivulets of blood-soaked rain dripped from his bearded chin. The creature was twitching, frantically fighting his instinct to attack. It would be so easy, just to drop down on them, he had become very expert at despatching these humans over the years, although recently he had had to make do more and more with animals like the sheep. Two humans together was not a challenge, but he knew Soulis would be ruthless in his reprisal if the Red Cap did anything to interfere with his plans. *The child is the important one, when he is under my control, you can have the adults, but not until then.*

The two men went back into the house stripping off wet clothes and boots after having locked and re-checked the doors. They returned to the fire warming themselves in the welcoming glow.

"We need to report this to the police," Kate said after a while.

"I guess so." Elliot was not particularly enthusiastic about the idea. If Simon and Kate were sceptical, he did not particularly relish the idea of trying to convince a cynical policeman. "But there is nothing much they can do tonight and we would have to drive into Newcastleton to get them. It can wait until the morning – I could do with a drink, have we got any?"

Simon went into the kitchen and returned with a bottle of red wine and two glasses for Kate and her father and a can of lager for himself.

Thomas was stretched out asleep on the settee next to Kate; the three adults sat around the fire and poured their drinks.

"You hungry?" Kate said looking at her watch which was showing 2.00 am.

"Couldn't eat a thing," Simon replied, thinking of the slaughtered sheep outside.

Elliot stared into his wine and shook his head silently.

"I need something stronger than this," he said and he left the lounge returning a few seconds later, a pewter hip flask in his hand.

"Bowmore Legend," he explained. "Want one?" holding out the flask to Simon.

Simon took a small swig and shuddered. "God, that's peaty!" he said.

"Just how I like it," Elliot replied taking a large swallow and feeling the warm liquid slide down his throat.

CHAPTER TWENTY-ONE

Colonel Mikel Batnykov was travelling under an assumed name, as were his two colleagues when they arrived at Heathrow Airport, but despite the additional care the British immigration officials seemed to be taking with him, he was confident that they would have no trouble.

How could anyone suggest a problem with a passport and other official documentation when, rather than being forged, they had been officially created by the Russian Government?

Despite that, they were false.

But like everything else in the former Soviet Union since the collapse of the communist system, it was not necessary to go to back street forgers for false documentation, provided of course you had enough money. Gregori Romanski certainly had enough money and political influence to get anything he wanted and it was Romanski who was financing this operation.

Batnykov, at forty years of age, knew he was reaching the age where field operations would soon have to become a thing of the past.

But not yet.

At six feet tall, his weight of seventeen stone probably, in the terms of modern methods of measuring health by Body Mass Index, would have classified him as obese, but by no stretch of the imagination could Batnykov be classified as unfit.

Unless, as now, he was on a mission, he ran five miles every day in full army kit carrying a fifty-two kilogram pack on his back; a regime he could complete with little stress and this coupled with his other daily exercise and nutritional regimes meant his body was solid muscle, which accounted for his weight.

His severe crew cut hairstyle, now mostly grey, set off a strong profile, which from experience, he knew some women found hugely attractive. He was clean shaven and had strong, even, white teeth which were clearly well cared for, and the assortment of odd scars, particularly around the eyes, suggested he was not a stranger to either fighting or contact sport, he looked every inch the soldier in or out of uniform. His rank however was now honorary as he was no longer part of the once famous Red Army.

Previously a loyal and unquestioning servant of the state, he had watched corruption, murder and political chicanery destroy the blind certainty that once convinced him that he was supporting a political doctrine that would ultimately free the world.

Now like everyone else, he was working for himself selling the only skills he possessed: his ability to infiltrate, destroy and kill. He was a mercenary: a breed of man he would once have detested. His only consolation was that unlike those who would do anything for money, he would not slaughter innocent men, women and children in Third World countries.

He chose his missions very carefully and wanted to know exactly who his targets, individual and organisational, were.

He had no compunction with his current target grouping. They were representative of the type of people who had destroyed his world. They had the funds to defend themselves properly: it was not his problem if they chose not to.

His only concern was the man paying his wages. Romanski was of the same breed as the targets. But then as far as Batnykov could see it was only people like these who had the money to properly pay for his expertise.

Ultimately he was pragmatic as he knew he had little control over who he worked for, only what he was prepared to do for them, and in this case both employer and target were of a kind as far as he was concerned.

Now he waited for his two colleagues, previously non-commissioned officers in his elite Special Forces group, to meet him at the check in for the flight to Edinburgh, where he knew a hire car would be waiting for them to drive the short trip to Branxholm.

He did not need a map, he had studied the location and it was imprinted in his head.

His two colleagues arrived both with the same military bearing of Batnykov despite their smart business suits. Conversation was unnecessary. They had been over the plan many times. They fell in together and walked to the boarding gate for the Edinburgh shuttle.

CHAPTER TWENTY-TWO

"A dog!"

Elliot spoke incredulously as he sat at the table in the kitchen of the cottage with his back to the lounge door. He could see through the window that looked out to the side of the house in the direction of the road.

What looked like a couple of farm workers in dark blue well-worn overalls were clearing up the remains of the dead sheep. He watched them as they manhandled the unfortunate animal into a black plastic bag and hoisted it unceremoniously into the back of a mud splattered old Land Rover.

Simon and Kate sat side by side on one side of the table. Thomas sat on Simon's lap playing with his new favourite toy, Truman's bracelet. Simulating the game he had played with Truman he was placing it over Simon's wrist and waiting for his father to take it off and hand it back to him.

Occasionally he stopped to stare rather suspiciously at the two uniformed police officers sat on the opposite side of the table before returning to the game.

The officers looked incredibly young. Both had removed their hats which lay in front of them on the table alongside empty tea mugs. One, a Constable Scott, seemed to have an air of seniority and did most of the talking whilst the other, whose name Elliot had forgotten immediately he had been told it, sat making infrequent and Elliot felt, distinctly half-hearted notes, into a pocket book.

"You honestly think a dog did that?" Elliot waved in the general direction of the farm workers outside.

They had finally gone to bed at around 3.00 am that morning. Sleeping only fitfully they were up at 8.00 am to drive into Newcastleton to report the matter to the local police.

The police had taken details of the incident and suggested the family go back to the cottage and they would be out later that morning to have a look. They had also promised to let the farm owner know and they would get the slaughtered carcass removed.

The police had turned up around 10.00 am. The Land Rover, presumably sent by the owner of the sheep, followed the mud spattered police car as it bumped its way slowly down the track to the cottage.

From the kitchen window Elliot had watched the two policemen and the farm workers go straight to the remains of the sheep, studying it briefly and chatting amongst themselves.

Eventually, the two policemen moved off in the direction of the front door and Kate went around to let them in, leading them through to the kitchen.

The discussion had gone pretty much as Elliot feared. Perhaps he should have told them everything exactly as he saw it, but, given their reaction to his rather toned down version, he was not at all sure the full, unbridled truth would not have led to him being carted off for psychiatric assessment.

It was definitely not a dog. He had explained that. It was some kind of creature with incredibly long teeth and claws. He had left out details of the ragged clothes and the cap which was probably just as well he thought.

Living and working this close to Hermitage with the constant influx of over-imaginative tourists drawn by the haunted history of the castle, these officers had heard their fair share of stories, screaming children, faces at windows, one woman who recently claimed to have been pushed by unseen hands as she wandered near the site of the so-called 'drowning pool', close to Hermitage.

Scott had actually been the officer who took details of a sighting by a workman who had seen a hooded face at the window of the castle whilst carrying out some renovation work. A sighting remarkably similar to that experienced by Elliot himself.

He had also interviewed the apparently hysterical woman who had claimed to have been pushed.

Elliot could not help feeling Scott was treating him as just one more over-imaginative tourist.

"Those wounds were not made by a dog," Elliot tried again to convince the officers that there had to be another explanation.

126

"The way that animal's stomach was ripped apart, those strands of skin, they were done by claws, not teeth. Don't you have a 'scenes of crime officer' or someone who can look at it? I'm sure he'll tell you it was done with claws not teeth."

Scott smiled, "Mr Elliot, we are not in the centre of London, or the middle of Edinburgh for that matter. We do not call 'scenes of crime officers' all the way out here to deal with a case of sheep worrying."

"Sheep worrying? God that poor animal must have worried himself to death!"

"Look, I know it is a particularly savage attack, but this is sheep country and we see the effects of these attacks all the time. Sometimes it amounts to little more than a sheep losing a lamb because it's been frightened by some pampered cocker spaniel that the owners have failed to keep under control. It is amazing how upset they get when the local farmer shoots the dog." The little joke seemed to amuse him.

"Other times it is far worse. Dogs go wild, go feral, they will kill and eat anything if they get hungry enough, even their owners sometimes, and when they do – it is not pretty I can tell you, I've seen it many times."

Elliot wanted to tell him. Wanted to grab the idiot by the collar and say, "You stupid little sod, this was not a dog, it was a bloody Red Cap and if you do nothing he is going to kill something more important than a sheep."

Instead, he bowed his head resignedly, staring into the half empty tea mug in front of him.

"Besides," Scott continued, "we know it's a dog, there have been other attacks recently. Not quite this far out, but nearer into town. They started about ten days ago and this is the third. They all had the same wounds, the dog is obviously mad, the local farmers are out with shotguns looking for the thing. They'll find it and they'll kill it, and that will be the end of it. Until the next one."

Elliot suddenly looked up, "But how do you know it was a dog?"

"Because it has been seen in the vicinity of the other two killings. The owner of the other two sheep killed saw it on two occasions. It was a huge black dog. He was close enough at one stage to shoot at it. Unfortunately he missed. Farmers out here have lived with these stories all their lives; many generations of them.

Believe me they are not frightened by ghost stories and they do recognise a dog when they see one."

"Where were these other sheep killed?" Elliot asked.

"Back on the Jedburgh Road, down near the town by the cemetery."

"The cemetery – the one on the hill with the wall around it?"

"That's right," Scott said, "and before you read anything into that, the sheep were killed nearby. The farmer chased the dog and shot at it. It leapt the wall into the cemetery. When the farmer got there he searched the whole of the cemetery but couldn't find it – it must have gone over the back wall and across the fields.

"Obviously the dog is working its way in this direction, probably in search of easier prey. You've seen the sheep out here, it is not possible to keep an eye on them all the time and the farmer shooting at him probably drove him off in search of a safer place to eat. But sheep are these men's livelihood. Believe me they'll track the dog down and they'll kill it. If I were you I would get back to enjoying your holiday. It's highly unlikely the dog would attack a grown adult, especially when it's got nice easy sheep to kill, so, I would keep this little fellow from wandering about outside, but apart from that you'll be fine. If by any chance you do see it then stay away from it and let us know, we'll deal with it."

He tickled Thomas under the chin. In response Thomas placed his bracelet around Scott's wrist and smiled at the policeman expectantly, chuckling happily when Scott took it off his wrist again and after giving it an interested, but cursory inspection placed it back on Thomas's wrist.

"That's interesting, where did that come from?"

"Someone called Thomas Truman gave it to him. Do you know him?" Kate asked.

"Old Tom? Everyone knows Old Tom," Scott said. "Harmless old fellow but mad as a spoon. It wasn't that old fool who put this idea of wild animals in your head was it? He's quite a storyteller you know."

With an air of finality, Scott and his colleague got to their feet and Kate showed them to the door. Elliot sat quietly not even acknowledging their leaving. Scott looked at him and shook his head slightly, knowing he hadn't managed to convince him.

At the door Scott and his colleague put their caps back on. "If you keep the young lad with you, you'll be fine, and remember what I said, if you see the dog don't approach it. Just let us know. Enjoy the rest of your holiday."

Kate closed the door and returned to the kitchen to see her father standing at the window watching the farm workers leaning on the back of the Land Rover enjoying a cigarette.

He watched the two officers come around from the front door and talk briefly to the farm workers and then climb into the police car. He continued to watch as they drove slowly up the track and out onto the road, closely followed by the Land Rover.

Kate approached her father and she threw her arms around his waist from behind, hugging him and looking over his shoulder at the departing police car.

"You know the Elliots had a terrible feud with the Scotts back in the 16th century?" Elliot stared at the departing police car. "Scott of Buccleuch had several Elliots (or Ellots as they were then), executed. For a year after that they raided each other mercilessly, sometimes putting as many as four hundred men in the saddle."

He thought of the hint of condescension in the young police officer's voice.

"Maybe it's still in the genes."

"This is supposed to be a break for you," she said, "so why don't we do something you wanted to do, we seem to have got a little sidetracked."

Elliot continued staring out of the window but raised his hands to squeeze his daughter's arms that were holding him tightly.

"I want to see Truman," he said quietly.

"Does that mean I have to drink more beer?" Simon feigned annoyance in an attempt to lighten the mood a little.

CHAPTER TWENTY-THREE

As Truman was not likely to be around until early evening they decided to have an early lunch and then visit Nine Stane Rig, the place where, according to Truman and the local legends, William de Soulis was boiled in lead taken from his own roof at Hermitage.

The rain of the previous night had been replaced by a bright sunny afternoon, although the wind was still cold, so, piling warm clothes, hats and waterproofs into the back of the car, they set out for the short drive to the druid stone circle a mile or two from Hermitage Castle, having first mentally located the position on the large scale map, framed and hanging on the wall in the hall of the cottage.

It actually took two or three attempts to find the footpath, and then only after a friendly local had pointed them in the right direction.

Parking near some abandoned old buildings off the road, the three adults wrapped up against the cold wind and with young Thomas strapped to Simon's back, hiked back down the road until they found a small almost invisible brown sign, with black engraved letters, pointing up the hill indicating the direction to Nine Stane Rig.

The climb was hard going, the long moorland grass concealing small meandering burns, humps and holes that twisted them off balance and made the climb even tougher. Perhaps due to the time of year, or just the difficulty of the climb, the footpath, if it could be called such, was indistinguishable from the rest of the moor. But the occasional dilapidated gate or broken stone wall creating a path through, suggested they were going the right way.

They headed doggedly ever upwards past planted trees with their large tell-tale fire breaks.

Elliot's general state of fitness, or lack of it, coupled with a painful right knee that still hurt from his fall outside the castle, necessitated regular stops. Kate and Simon had to stop frequently to let him catch up.

Some twenty minutes later they found the circle, or what was left of it. The view from the top of the 'rig' (or ridge which was the modern translation), was quite breathtaking, but the circle itself was a bit of a disappointment.

Elliot was not quite sure what he was expecting, perhaps a smaller version of Stonehenge, but what was actually described as a circle was in fact oval in shape and consisted of eight stones most of which were broken to mere stumps. The ninth lay flat, but all the other standing stones leaned slightly inwards towards the centre. They were all well weathered and covered in moss which was unsurprising for something that dated back to the Bronze Age.

Elliot tried to picture the scene Truman had described so vividly. Imagining the dark terror, lit only by torches and the blazing fire under the cauldron as William de Soulis, screaming curses boiled to death in agony – hurling curses at his attackers until the flesh melted from his bones.

The place, despite the incredible violence of the history, did not seem to have the same brooding menace that hung over Hermitage. Perhaps it was the sunshine or the fact that little other history of a violent nature seemed to have been done here; unlike the centuries of horror that were associated with the castle.

They sat for half an hour or so sheltered from the wind in a small hollow and enjoying the warmth of the sun whilst they sipped coffee from a flask.

Then, making their way slowly back down the hill to the car, they decided to drive into Newcastleton and phone Redheugh, the seat of the Elliot Clan Society. It was out of season but they hoped, provided they rang ahead, they might be allowed to visit the clan room, which was housed amongst stables external to the main building.

As they drove back to Newcastleton, the warmth of the sun through the windscreen made the night before seem almost like a dream and apart from a persistent ache in his damaged knee, Elliot was beginning to feel quite good from the struggle up and down the hill, which, whilst uncomfortable at the time, had imbued his body with a pleasant tiredness.

They pulled into Douglas Square, parked outside the Grapes, and Elliot left the others in the car while he went to the telephone box and, searching his ever present hand-held computer for the number that he had taken from the Clan Society literature, he rang Redheugh, the home of the Elliot Clan Chief.

A few minutes later he returned. "We can go up now apparently. I spoke to a chap, must be Margaret's husband, who said it wasn't really open, and things were a bit untidy as they were reorganising things for the summer, but if we are happy with that we can go up now."

They drove the mile or so out of town turning left onto an almost hidden driveway and slowly up the long drive, alongside the burn, but this time with it on their right. The drive wound its way up to a large stone property and driving past the main house they pulled into a small stone courtyard that had obviously at one time been stables. They parked outside one that had a hand carved wooden sign hanging outside with the words 'clan room' engraved on it.

They sat for a few minutes wondering whether to go up to the house and announce their presence but not wishing to intrude, as it was, regardless of its history, somebody's home. After a few minutes Elliot decided to go up to the house, but as he was climbing out of the car a woman who Elliot recognised immediately as Margaret Elliot, the current clan chief, came around the corner and introduced herself with a broad smile.

Elliot whispered to Simon and Kate, "This is her, Margaret of Redheugh, the current clan chief. I've seen her photograph in the clan membership stuff and she was on television recently."

"That's the clan chief?" Simon smiled, looking at the attractive woman in jeans, practical high brown boots and waterproof coat looking like a working landowner, which was after all what she was.

"What were you expecting," Kate whispered back, "Rob Roy?"

"I saw you on the television recently," Elliot said, "Some Open University programme about Mary Queen of Scots' ride from Jedburgh to Hermitage to see her injured lover Bothwell."

Mary had ridden to Hermitage after hearing that her lover Bothwell lay there injured having been stabbed by a famous Border Reiver of the time called Little Jock Elliot. Bothwell had been pursuing Little Jock and in hot pursuit had shot the famous Reiver in the hip.

Unfortunately for Boswell his horse lost its footing in the rough terrain and threw him in a bog and Little Jock, seeing his opportunity returned and stabbed him leaving him for dead.

Bothwell was seriously injured but was carried to the nearest safe place, Hermitage, where he received sufficient care it would appear to survive the attack.

Mary Queen of Scots was anxious and wanted to go to her lover, and she set out to ride the forty mile round trip from her home in Jedburgh to Hermitage. She needed to return the same day as she was of course already married and it would not have been fitting for her to be seen to stay overnight in Hermitage.

Whilst forty miles would not be a particularly arduous journey now, in those days on horseback and across country it was a significant journey; particularly for a woman and ironically Mary nearly died from a fever she contracted as a result.

Such was Little Jock's reputation, (how small did someone need to be in those days to be referred to as 'Little' Elliot wondered?), that a famous border ballad was written about him. Inside above the door of the clan room was the clearly intimidating greeting of Little Jock, immortalised in that Ballad – *Wha daur meddle wi' me?*

"Who indeed?" thought Elliot, who when he had first seen the quote had immediately thought of the Robert De Nero scene from the film *Taxi Driver*

"You looking at me?" As intimidating as that scene was, it was unlikely, Elliot thought, that the film character would have lasted more than a few seconds had he confronted this little gentleman, who killed and pillaged as a profession.

Margaret jolted Elliot back from his thoughts. "So glad somebody saw the television programme," Margaret said brightly. "Everyone up here missed it," and she turned to unlock the clan room. "Excuse the mess, but we are re-organising things at the moment."

Elliot explained that he had been researching his family history for some months and had got a little stuck in the mid 1700s, so they had decided to come up and get a feel for the place.

"I'm back as far as a William Elliot. I know nothing about him except he fathered Andrew Elliot who was born out in Whitsome, near Berwick. Andrew was born in 1758, so obviously unless he fathered him at the age of twelve, William must have been alive at Culloden."

Kate smiled, it seemed she recognised the signs of the enthusiasm rising once more in her father, as he talked animatedly on his favourite subject and perhaps pleased that the concerns of last night seemed to be miles away.

"Well you're not too far away in Berwick," Margaret replied encouragingly. "I'm sure you will find a connection back to here. Have you been in touch with our genealogist, I'm sure he could help you? Unfortunately most of the clan records were lost in a fire at Stobs in the 1700s."

"No, but I intend to soon. I know it's a common fallacy that the battle was Scots against English but I know there were as many Scots against the Jacobites as for them. I'm not even sure which side we would have been on."

The use of the term 'we' rather than 'they', was interesting for relatives separated by four hundred miles and two hundred years, but clearly it was a clan thing, as Margaret slipped easily into the same way of speaking.

"Oh, we'd have definitely been on the Hanoverian side," Margaret said brightly. "We didn't like the Stuarts much; they kept hanging us!"

It might be assumed this revelation could have come as a huge disappointment to many Elliots researching their history and brought up on heroic legends of Bonnie Prince Charlie and the Jacobite revolt, but Elliot wasn't one of them. He recalled that, whilst many people started their family research looking for forgotten or overlooked aristocratic links, often the reality was even more rewarding.

He remembered how fascinated and enthusiastic he had been by the fact that he came from a long line of shepherds! Although he had often admitted that the idea of being related to the people who invented blackmail, cattle rustling and the protection racket also had a certain perverse appeal.

"Actually," Margaret continued, "when Charles passed through here with his army moving south to attack the English, all the Elliots hid rather than join up with him."

A pleasant hour passed, Simon and Kate fascinated by the various memorabilia on display, while Elliot chatted happily with Margaret.

Eventually, with a promise to attend the next 'clan gathering' which was held every four years, they said their goodbyes and left to drive back into Newcastleton.

Pulling back into the square, Kate and Elliot left Simon with little Thomas to settle in the lounge whilst they walked to the butcher's a hundred yards or so down the street to buy something for dinner.

They browsed a small antique and gift shop. Elliot bought some cards with views of the area around the river Liddel and he chatted happily to the proprietor who unsurprisingly turned out to be an Elliot.

Leaving the gift shop they crossed the road to a small butcher's shop.

"Another Elliot," Kate said noting the name above the shop. They selected three fabulous looking lamb steaks, which seemed to suggest that perhaps the trauma of the events of the night before were receding in importance.

Putting the food into the back of the car, Elliot and Kate returned to the Grapes and into the lounge bar looking for Simon and Thomas. They found them sitting on the settee playing together happily.

"Drink?" Elliot called as he walked to the bar.

"Red wine," Kate said.

"Got one." Simon raised the lager glass in a semi toast.

They sat quietly talking and waiting for Truman to arrive. The effects of the comfortable lounge and the alcohol relaxed them all and they laughed and joked happily and for a while they forgot about Truman and Elliot's insistence that they should see him again. Even he was beginning to think that maybe his mind had been playing tricks on him.

After all he had been the only person to see the Red Cap clearly and since arriving here he had hallucinated at least twice and maybe, maybe a combination of tiredness, the wine, his fascination with Truman's story...

"You have seen the Red Cap I understand?"

His sudden presence made Elliot start. Judging by Kate and Simon's reaction, they had not seen him coming either. Only Thomas, smiling happily up at Truman, seemed to have noticed.

So involved had he been with his thoughts that Elliot had not seen Truman enter the lounge and quietly come up behind him.

"Are you reading my mind?" Elliot said.

"Nothing so interesting I'm afraid," Truman smiled warmly. "I had a serious ticking off from Constable Scott. He seems to think I have been putting these ideas into your head."

Truman jabbed a thumb over his shoulder without turning, and looking over to the door Elliot saw Constable Scott coming into the hotel, obviously having just finished duty. He was wearing a civilian jacket over the top of his uniform.

Kate looked at Thomas. Generally a happy child, Thomas rarely cried when confronted by strangers. At worst he would give them a rather quizzical suspicious look. But for some reason this old man he had taken to from the start and was now fidgeting happily, no doubt hoping to play their customary game. Kate noticed the bracelet expectantly in Thomas's hand.

"Constable Scott stopped me outside and told me about your trouble last night. The poor man has very little imagination himself," he added quietly.

Simon offered Truman a drink and went off to the bar to get the half pint of bitter that he had requested.

Truman took a seat close to Thomas much to the little chap's excitement and he stared warmly down on him as they started their little game, passing the bracelet backwards and forward from wrist to wrist.

Scott had acknowledged them, but rather than coming into the lounge he passed down the corridor into one of the other bars, but not before he'd looked at Old Tom and wagged his finger, as a schoolteacher might to an errant pupil.

"I'm not sure you didn't," Elliot said quietly. "Put it into my head I mean, after all this talk of Red Caps and hauntings. This is the 21st century for God's sake!"

The old man looked up from little Thomas and deeply into Elliot's eyes, "And which god would that be? You don't believe in the supernatural but you happily call on a deity whose existence you can't possibly establish, and has almost as many faces as there are people in this world."

"It's just an expression, it is not meant to be taken literally," Elliot realised immediately the contradiction of an atheist calling on God.

"Really?" Truman was calm, "and do you touch wood, cross your fingers, avoid putting new shoes on the table, avoid ladders, salute magpies, bless people when they sneeze and all the myriad other things people do, that ostensibly they do not believe in?"

"That's different; most sensible people understand it is all nonsense."

"Many people say they do, but it doesn't stop them evoking these charms does it? 21st century, or 13th – the veneer of civilisation is very thin. These belief systems are deep in our hearts and souls, you might even say in the genes, not in the head.

"Next time you see someone cross themselves, or wish someone luck, ask yourself how far are they really from seeing Red Caps."

"Well, whatever the truth, tomorrow is our last day and I intend to spend it doing what I planned to do on the first day, before we got sidetracked. I intend to visit Hutton and Whitsome and search for my ancestors."

"Your ancestors are much closer to you than that," Truman said quietly but firmly, resuming his game with Thomas, who had become slightly irritated by the hiatus in their little ritual.

Kate had explained to Simon that she was beginning to feel a little uncomfortable with the little game Truman and Thomas were playing but could think of no good reason to stop it, her son clearly loved it and where other adults would have typically tired of the monotonous routine of these little games that children loved so much, Truman seemed to derive as much pleasure from it as the child did, or was it just part of that special relationship he spoke of between old people and children?

People spoke of the elderly going into their 'second childhood', maybe that was the source of the relationship; old people had time for these things. Perhaps literally they became more childlike in their outlook and children picked up on that.

"What of this dog that Constable Scott was telling us about? There seems to have been other sightings, other sheep; surely that is a more plausible explanation."

Despite the ferocity with which her father had disputed Scott's explanation, Kate seemed keen to put the possible solution to Truman.

She looked apologetically at her father as if realising by inference she was dismissing what he had seen, but Elliot just

137

smiled and turned to Truman, it seemed he was as interested in the answer as she.

"Oh there is a dog," Truman said, "but the dog is not responsible for the sheep – that was the Red Cap. No need to be frightened of the dog, not everything that frightens you is your enemy."

"Look," Elliot was beginning to get a little impatient with the convoluted way Truman spoke and he was a little sharper than he meant to be, "I've all but convinced myself that what I saw was a hallucination or maybe I was dozing or something, but you seem to be determined to keep us involved in this – I'm not sure what to call it – this story. But why do you not just come straight out and say what you mean? Because tomorrow we go to Berwick and the day after we go home, so if you've got something to say, I suggest you come right out and say it while you still have the chance."

Truman thought for a few moments and then said quietly, "You can't go home David, you are already home and Soulis cannot, no, will not, let you leave until he has what he wants – and if you try to pretend that this is all fantasy, then you will not have the focus or the belief to use the strengths you have to save yourself and your family."

"That's enough." Elliot was angry now, "Look, your stories were interesting, fascinating even, but now you are going too far. You are frightening or threatening my family, I'm not sure which. But either way I will not have it. I suggest you leave before I go next door and get Constable Scott, he warned us, and from what I can see, you, about these stories. The only thing I think he got wrong is that he said you were harmless. I'm not so sure. I suggest you leave."

Truman got to his feet. "I wish there was something I could say to convince you, because before you get the chance to return to where you call home, you will believe. I can assure you, you will believe. I just hope we have another opportunity to talk, but it is unlikely."

He turned to leave. "Soulis is running out of time. He has to act and act now, he will not stop until he gets what he wants."

"For God's sake man, what the hell is it you are saying he wants?" Elliot was almost shouting now, causing the barman to look up and see what was happening.

"Whatever your understanding of those two words," Truman was as quiet as Elliot was loud, "whatever you mean by 'God' and 'hell', you will experience both before the next two days are gone.

"You want to know what Soulis wants?" His voice became firm and strong, "He wants the three of you dead. But most of all – no – above all, he wants your grandson, Thomas."

The family stared in horror at Truman, temporarily unable to speak.

Truman continued determinedly, "Unless you start listening and believing, he will get him. I thought the sight of the Red Cap would convince you, but if you do not even believe your own eyes, how could I possibly expect you to believe what I need to tell you."

Simon, normally an amiable man not quick to anger was on his feet. The implicit threat to his son turning his face black with rage and he closed on Truman. Elliot grabbed him around the shoulders and upper arms; it took all his strength to hold the solidly built Simon back.

"That's not the way Simon. Kate, go get Constable Scott."

Truman shook his head sadly and turned to leave the bar. "I hope I see you again," he said as he left the room.

By the time Kate returned with Scott, Truman had disappeared into the night once more.

CHAPTER TWENTY-FOUR

Scott listened to the story the family told him quietly and attentively. "Is that it?" he said.

"That's it," Elliot said, "and before you start saying he's a harmless old man..."

Scott held up his hand cutting Elliot off. "I'm saying nothing of the sort Mr Elliot. If what you tell me is true, and I have no reason to believe that you are all lying, Old Tom has gone too far this time.

"I have kids of my own and I know how I would feel if someone made threats like that. I'll go around to his place now. What he's done is, well, unacceptable at the very least, if not criminal. I'll make sure he doesn't bother you again."

Kate was holding Thomas who was clutching the bracelet tightly as he stared at Scott suspiciously. Whatever the old man had said, and it certainly had frightened her, she seemed puzzled by the obvious affection he had for Thomas and more importantly the affection Thomas had for Truman. She had often said she believed that children like animals, were very perceptive. She couldn't believe that Thomas would feel this way about someone who meant him harm. Equally she wanted to make sure nothing could possibly happen to him.

"Look," she said, "couldn't perhaps one of us, maybe me, come with you? I really don't want to see Mr Truman get into trouble. I'm sure he's just misguided and a little lonely perhaps. His stories may be just an opportunity to be the centre of attention."

Simon was not happy with the idea. "If you are going, I'm going with you."

Kate put her hand on Simon's shoulder, "I'm not sure that's such a good idea, it all got a bit heated there for a moment. I'll be fine, I'll have Constable Scott with me and I'm sure Mr

Truman didn't mean any real harm." She looked at Thomas, in her arms and smiled when he held out the bracelet and as she reached to take it he slipped it onto her wrist laughing happily.

She smiled back and taking the bracelet from her wrist she tucked it into the chest patch pocket in Thomas's dungarees, pushing down the Velcro flap, and patting it safely.

"Well, if that's what you want, I'm happy," Constable Scott looked expectantly.

Elliot and Simon looked at each other, "OK," Simon said and Elliot nodded.

"Wait here, we won't be long. Truman lives out on Langholm Street, about five minutes in the car," Scott said and Kate kissed Simon, handing Thomas to him. She patted her father's arm as she followed Scott out of the bar.

An hour passed. Simon played with Thomas and he and Elliot made small talk, trying to pretend they were not concerned and telling themselves it hadn't been that long really.

Suddenly jumping to his feet, Simon, who could not contain himself any longer, said, "I'm going to ring the police station. They should have been back by now, I want to know what's going on."

He handed Thomas to Elliot but before he could leave, Kate walked back into the bar with Scott.

Simon hugged her and then pushing her to arms length and holding her by the upper arms said, "Alright?"

"Yes, fine," but the look on her face suggested that not everything was completely 'fine'.

Scott broke the silence, "Well, I don't think you will be having any more trouble from him. I read him the riot act. I think he realises he has gone too far this time. Being a colourful local character is one thing, but frightening our visitors is another.

"You know where I am if you need me. Just contact the police station they'll always be able to get hold of me."

He turned to leave. "Oh by the way, we've had another sighting of that mad dog. I'm just on my way up to the cemetery. If you drive by that way on your way back to the cottage, you might see us, hopefully with a very big, very dead, mad dog!" He smiled happily as he left the bar.

The three of them took their seats again. Kate took Thomas from Elliot and hugged him close.

"What's up? Did you see Truman? What did he have to say?" Simon spoke first.

"Yes, we saw him except..." Kate paused as if trying to find the right words, "...except it wasn't him. I mean it was him of course but he seemed completely different. He seemed very old."

"He is very old," Simon joked. "He must be at least eighty."

"No, I didn't mean in that way. When he spoke to us here he was old, but he seemed bright, alert, had all his faculties. When I saw him just now he looked so frail, his hands were shaking like he had Parkinson's or something. He didn't seem to be able to string a coherent sentence together."

"Perhaps he was just frightened; realised he'd gone too far and was frightened of what Scott would do to him," Elliot offered.

"No, it wasn't that. I mean it was him; unless he has a twin brother. But his eyes looked dull and disinterested. He just sat in an old armchair trembling his head bowed, mouth open, he looked like he couldn't have got himself down here to the pub without help.

"When Scott confronted him, he just kept apologising saying he hadn't meant anything by it, that he was sorry, it wouldn't happen again. I really couldn't make it out."

"Sure he hadn't had a stroke or something?"

"No. I asked Scott if he noticed anything different about him, was he ill or something, but he said he looked like he always looked as far as he could see. He was old and frail, but he could still make it down the pub before closing time if he set off early enough. He made a joke of it really; he didn't seem to think his condition was unusual."

"Well, as long as he stays away from us from now on, that's the main thing," Simon said. "How about we go back to the cottage and get something to eat, I'm starving."

As they passed the entrance to Redheugh and crossed the bridge, Simon reminded Elliot to take the Jedburgh road. "Might as well see if they've caught that dog. If we can see anything in this darkness. Better get the torch out again."

As they drove slowly by the cemetery, they saw Scott's police car parked neatly in the shingle parking area alongside a Land Rover. The emergency light on the police car was spinning;

142

the blue light illuminated the area as it swept the cemetery and surrounding fields. Orange flashers winked to front and back.

Elliot pulled up. There was just enough space alongside the Land Rover for one more car and they all got out and walked to the gate that led into the older part of the cemetery.

Swinging the powerful beam from side to side, Elliot surveyed the cemetery looking for signs of the policeman or farmer but saw no movement.

"Probably in the fields behind the cemetery. You guys stay here, I'll take a look. Don't want anyone being mistaken for a wild dog with a protective shepherd with a shotgun around."

He left Simon, Kate and Thomas standing by the gate as he set off across the cemetery the hundred yards or so to the far wall, calling as he went, "Constable Scott. You out there?"

Picking carefully through the rough grass, he called out again, "Constable Scott?"

Again no reply. Three-quarters of the way across the cemetery he stumbled as he placed his foot on some uneven ground. Falling onto his injured knee he swore under his breath as the pain shot through his leg and he struggled uncomfortably to his feet, brushing at the damp mud on his trousers.

As he recovered it suddenly occurred to him how stupid this was, crossing a cemetery in the dark with a mad dog and a trigger happy farmer on the loose. Limping painfully he started to return to the gate and to his waiting family. They could always check in with Scott tomorrow, to see if the dog had been caught.

But as he turned to go back, from the corner of his eye he saw a light – was it a torch – guttering briefly from behind a square tomb in the far right hand corner of the cemetery.

The tomb was a rectangular raised stone erection, with a pillar at each corner and a slanted roof mounted on the pillars. Looking like a kind of four poster bed, it was open on three sides. The fourth side; the back of the monument was sealed with a large block of stone, sporting a huge carved shield with weathered engraving.

Elliot approached cautiously along the side of the tomb, pausing before looking around the hidden end and calling again, "Scott, is that you?" The torch light wavered slightly but there was still no reply.

Swallowing hard and bracing himself, Elliot turned the corner quickly swinging the torch beam ahead and sighing with relief as it lit on Constable Scott, in full uniform standing at the far corner, a lit torch dangling and swinging in his right hand.

"Scott! You stupid bastard, you frightened me to death Is this your idea of a joke? Why didn't you answer me?" Elliot's anger was more from embarrassment at his own fears than genuine anger at the policeman.

Scott's head moved slightly turning towards Elliot, but still he said nothing.

Then Elliot saw the blood.

It ran down the front of Scott's shirt and tunic from the neck and the strange deadness in his eyes seemed to stare directly at him but somehow not see him. As Elliot's eyes traced the trail of blood down the front of the Officers shirt collar and tunic, he noticed Scott's legs lying awkwardly sideways and at a strange angle, and he suddenly realised he was not standing; he was hanging.

His gaze returned to Scott's neck and there, with horror he noticed for the first time, curving upwards, through Scott's neck were four yellow claws, protruding through the hapless policeman's neck and upwards towards his chin. As he watched the claws were withdrawn sharply with a sickening tearing of flesh, and Scott's body collapsed in a heap like a sack of loosely packed potatoes. He was dead before he hit the ground.

Elliot's jaw fell open in horror as there, swinging by his left claw, where he had previously been hidden by Scott's hanging body, and with his feet braced against the pillar was the Red Cap, rocking back and forth like a hideous monkey. His right claw was still extended out in front of him, dripping with Scott's blood, and the creature's dark, soulless eyes were boring directly into Elliot's, an expression of pure evil on the blood spattered face.

Elliot froze momentarily and then began slowly to back away stumbling on the uneven ground and afraid to take his eyes off the foul creature that followed his every movement, tongue flicking menacingly. As he stepped back his foot trod on something, soft and slippery and he fell backwards. Twisting as he fell he threw out his arms to break his fall and to his horror landed awkwardly on top of a mutilated body, his face inches from the hideous wound where once the man's throat had been.

Dead eyes rolled upwards, half obscured by open lids, the mouth hung open in horror. Presumably this had been the farmer. His body was in a similar state to the sheep at the cottage. Throat ripped open and stomach sliced apart with his entrails pulled out. It was this slippery mess that Elliot had fallen in.

He fought to resist the urge to retch and tried to struggle to his feet, his injured leg causing him to wince with pain as it twisted beneath him, his hands and upper body slippery with the blood of the dead farmer as he gazed down on his blood soaked hands.

His eyes returned quickly behind him to the Red Cap who still hung on the tomb, swinging back and forth, eyes fixed malevolently on his stumbling prey.

Elliot backed slowly away and then he turned and began painfully to half run, half hobble back up the slope towards the gate. He expected the Red Cap to come straight at him, but instead, with an ear piercing squeal, he swung quickly backwards and jumped off the tomb on the other side, emerging quickly from the far side, obviously intending to cut Elliot off as he headed back towards the gate.

"Get out!" Elliot screamed hoarsely as he scrabbled, stumbling back towards the gate, "Get out, get to the car!"

His desperation to save his family became paramount as his lungs burned with the effort and tears of pain or fear; he wasn't sure which; blurred his vision and rolled down his blood spattered face.

He realised as the Red Cap appeared from the other side of the tomb, he was not going to make it to the gate.

The Red Cap was fast and nimble compared with the overweight and unfit fifty-seven year old. Elliot cried out hoarsely again to his family. "Go!" he screamed. "Get Thomas out of here, Go!" and then almost to himself, "Please, for the love of God, get Thomas away from here."

He realised that nothing could help him; but perhaps his family could save themselves.

He struggled again to get to his feet but managed only to rise to his knees as once again his leg gave way beneath him on the rough, slippery grass.

"Please, get out. Get to the car," his voice was raw and he sobbed breathlessly as he waited to feel the razor sharp claws of the Red Cap that he knew would slice into him at any moment.

He turned towards his attacker resigned to his imminent death. Still kneeling he tried to raise the torch as an improvised weapon above his head. Maybe he could delay the dwarf if only for a few seconds, to give his family the smallest of chances to make it to the car.

Thankfully, feeling relatively safe in the presence of the police car, he had left the keys in the ignition. If they could just get to the car they might get away from this hideous nightmare.

Kneeling in this ridiculous position he awaited the inevitable. But instead of attacking the Red Cap was standing a few yards away snarling, claws flexing and un-flexing, his skinny body heaving as he breathed.

As Elliot watched he noticed that the Red Cap was no longer focussing on him, but over the top of him to the other side of the cemetery. Still panting and kneeling on all fours, he turned his head slowly in the direction of the Red Cap's gaze.

To his horror, standing snarling twenty yards away stood a huge black dog the size of an Irish wolfhound. The jet black creature lowered its head, the upper lips curling upwards to reveal huge yellow fangs. The animal's hackles were raised making the creature look huge and more wolf-like; but no wolf had luminous red eyes like the ones that bore into Elliot's.

Letting out a howl that froze Elliot's blood the dog bounded towards him and Elliot instinctively rolled onto his back away from the charging animal, throwing his arms across his face to protect his head as at the same time he could see the Red Cap racing towards him from the opposite side. The dog reached him first; but instead of sinking his teeth into the prostrate Elliot, the creature launched himself into the air and flying directly over Elliot's head the creature crashed with sickening force into the Red Cap, bowling the creature backwards as he sank his teeth into its side.

The Red Cap gave out an unearthly scream of agony as he slashed wildly at the dog that was now shaking him from side to side like a rag doll.

Huge red wields appeared across the flank of the animal as the Red Cap tried desperately to repel the attack of the hell hound, although the dog's jaws seemed to have clamped into the side of the dwarf and showed no signs of loosening.

As the two hellish creatures locked twisting and snarling in this savage battle Elliot, who for a moment had been mesmerised by the sight, climbed painfully to his feet and bent double he hobbled awkwardly towards the gate.

Simon was running towards him desperate to help and Kate was clutching hold of Thomas as if her life, or more importantly his, depended on it.

"Go, go..." Elliot awkwardly tried to wave back Simon who ignored him and continued on until he was able to grab Elliot's arm and hoist him to a more vertical position and pull him towards the gate.

Looking back over their shoulders, as they stumbled towards the exit from the cemetery they watched the life and death struggle happening behind them. They saw the dog swing the Red Cap violently and with a huge scream a large chunk of the Red Caps flesh came away in the dog's mouth and the dwarf cart-wheeled screaming in agony and crashed against the wall surrounding the cemetery.

The two men took Kate by the arm either side of her and pulled her, still holding tightly to Thomas, towards the car; Simon opening the back door as Kate tried to climb in with her son. Elliot ran around the back of the car towards the drivers door pulling it open desperately.

Clutching at his injured side, the Red Cap rushing to escape a further attack from the dog, leapt onto the wall above the car just as the family struggled to get their child into the relative safety of the vehicle. The Red Cap crashed onto the roof of the car and swiping out viciously he caught Simon across the back and he yelled out in pain as the blow span him around and he collapsed to the ground, huge bloody stripes appearing through his shirt.

Kate screamed.

Falling to her knees she tried to help her stricken husband with one hand, still holding Thomas in her other arm clutched to her side.

Suddenly she felt Thomas being tugged upwards by powerful arms and attempting to rip him from her grasp. Desperately she raised her other arm from Simon to try and hold onto her son with all her strength.

She screamed again as she felt her grip slipping from her son. Her strength was no match for the vicious dwarf above her on

147

the roof of the car and she watched helplessly as the creature ripped Thomas from her hands.

Elliot from his position by the driver's door, looked on in horror as he saw the Red Cap on the roof of the car his terrified grandchild slung over his shoulder, gripped in powerful talons. He threw himself forward just managing to grab the festering rags that hung from the Red Cap's back but the cloth came away in his hand and the side of his face crashed painfully against the roof of the car and he fell back stunned.

Elliot watched helplessly as the blood spattered Red Cap leapt off the back of the car still with Thomas slung over his shoulder. At the far side of the road he paused, panting, and looked back as the huge hound suddenly leapt from the cemetery onto the wall above the cowering adults.

With a look of ferocity that turned Elliot's blood cold, the dog bared its red stained fangs and stared at the cowering Red Cap on the far side of the road before throwing back its head as it issued forth an unholy howl that was enough to freeze the family in terror as the foul creature clutching Thomas turned away from the dog, ran down the bank on the far side of the road and disappeared into the night.

Instead of pursuing the Red Cap the dog slowly turned away from the road. It paused, looking back over its shoulder in the direction the Red Cap had run, before it leapt out of sight back into the cemetery.

Elliot's ears were still ringing from the howl of the dog as it was suddenly replaced by an even more terrifying sound as Kate screamed into the dark.

"Thomas!"

Elliot felt the heart being torn out of him as he heard his daughter screaming helplessly into the darkness for her lost son.

"Thomas!" she screamed again, reaching out her arms helplessly into the night.

CHAPTER TWENTY-FIVE

It took Batnykov and his two colleagues around an hour and a half to drive to the village of Branxholm, near Hawick. Approximately two miles from the edge of the grounds of Branxholm Estate they parked the hire car in a public car park where it would appear like any other tourist's vehicle left overnight.

Carrying rucksacks, the three men entered some woods at the edge of the road before pulling out night vision glasses from their bags and fitting the strange looking binoculars in place over their eyes. With a brief glance at each other, they set off in line deeper into the copse until they found a small clearing where they stopped to change into their mission gear.

Black combat trousers tucked into high soft leather boots, thin but warm, black polar-necked jumpers were covered by tight-fitting, sleeveless, stab-proof jackets which closed with Velcro. The men blackened their faces from small tins before pulling on black woollen hats that came down to cover the tips of their ears. They then each connected a short wave radio inside the vest, pushing in a small wireless ear piece and settling it comfortably in their ears.

Batnykov spoke quietly into a small microphone clipped in the sleeve of his sweater and his two colleagues nodded silently to confirm that they could hear him.

Each man carried an automatic pistol at his belt, along with a large, sheathed hunting knife, and four stun grenades.

Finally they put back on the night vision glasses and hanging a small machine pistol and a back pack over their shoulders, they set off silently through the woods again in single file and across the moors in the direction of Branxholm Estate.

Batnykov checked the luminous dial on his watch – they were exactly on time.

CHAPTER TWENTY-SIX

Elliot desperately tried to comfort Kate as he helped Simon to his feet.

"Come on darling help me with Simon," he said trying to distract her momentarily from the loss of Thomas by getting her to focus on her injured husband.

Kate, kneeling by the car, seemed almost comatose, staring helplessly into the darkness after her beloved Thomas as tears streamed silently down her face.

He pulled Kate to her feet and hugged her tightly, "Come on Kate. We'll get him back. Help me with Simon."

He really had no idea how they would get Thomas back or even where to start, but he knew they had to do something for Simon. At least that would give him time to think. Elliot opened the tailgate of the car, piling coats and clothes in the centre of the floor space.

He supported Simon to his feet and helped him remove his fleece and shirt, knowing that the razor sharp claws had sliced through both, and into his back as evidenced by the widening dark stain, as the blood seeped through the material. He tried to get him to lean forward so he could check the injury.

Simon struggled, "We need to go after him. We need to find Thomas."

Elliot tried hard to sound calm, "We will, we will, but first we have to make sure you are not bleeding to death."

"I'm fine," he said, although clearly he wasn't.

Elliot struggled to hold onto Simon who even in his weakened state was difficult to restrain.

Kate, still sobbing fitfully, climbed to her feet and walked around the side of the car to hold on to him and gently asked him to keep still.

The Red Cap had swiped out indiscriminately and the four cuts from shoulder blade to kidney were not as deadly as they could have been had the Red Cap meant to kill rather than escape with Thomas. But the wounds were still dangerously deep and hung open, clearly in need of serious medical treatment and stitching.

Elliot realised how unmatched they would have been had the Red Cap not been distracted by the power of the great hound. He scrabbled in the side of the boot for the first aid box, and ripped it open to reveal an inadequate collection of bandages, plasters, antiseptic cream and pads.

Kate bunched together cotton wool she had amongst Thomas's stuff, and they used bottles of mineral water to wash the wounds as best they could. Covering the area with antiseptic cream they taped a patchwork of bandages and antiseptic pads across the wounds.

"We need to get you to the hospital. Some of these cuts need stitching and God knows what filth and disease you could pick up from that creature."

Taking his own fleece off, he wrapped it around Simon's torso, zipping it up and sitting him in the back of the car. Obviously in pain, his face was grey and he was shaking feverishly. Slowly, perhaps mercifully he seemed to be battling unconsciousness.

Fighting to stay awake, Simon tried to pull himself forward, "I'm not going anywhere until we get Thomas back."

Elliot restrained him as best he could. He knew he would have little luck changing his mind. He turned to Kate who had sat next to Simon and was holding him, rocking him gently, but her lips were quivering and her eyes were filled with tears that burst and rolled uncontrollably down her cheeks.

"What are we going to do? What will they do to Thomas?" she said quietly and as she mentioned her son's name she began again to sob uncontrollably.

"They won't hurt him, they want him for some purpose. We just need to find them. I promise you they will not hurt him. We will get him back." He wished he believed what he was saying, but at the moment he needed to reassure his daughter.

He thought of his beautiful grandson and immediately tears welled in his own eyes and he turned away from Kate so she

151

wouldn't see how unsure he was himself. He felt weak and ineffective, guilt welling up in him, how could he allow his grandson to be taken? How could he allow his daughter to suffer like this? He must get him back; he would never be able to face his daughter again otherwise.

For the first time since his father's death nearly thirty years ago, he turned his tear stained face to the millions of bright stars and he called for help. Never before had he felt so in need of his father. It always seemed to him that his father knew what to do and his desperate need to provide that same level of reassurance to his own children led him to give assurances when deep inside he was completely unsure himself. So he called for help. Not from God, who he had long since lost faith in, but to that person who he had always believed could solve all problems.

"If you are up there, Dad," he spoke quietly, "now would be a good time to let me know."

Maybe he answered. Perhaps it was just the effects of talking to this man who had been taken far too early in Elliot's life, a man who seemed never to be afraid of anything or anyone. Elliot wasn't sure why, but suddenly he felt stronger as he turned to face his daughter and son-in-law.

"We have to see Truman, he is the key here. He knew Thomas was going to be taken. We go to Truman and if necessary I'll strangle the truth out of him."

He settled Kate back into the back seat of the car where she lay back staring forward still sobbing and rocking Simon in her arms. The strength she had found to help Elliot with Simon seemed to have left her and she was once again in a state of deep shock at the loss of her son.

Elliot reversed the car out of the parking space and swung it hard around so it was pointing back towards Newcastleton. Taking one last look in the direction the Red Cap had gone with Thomas, he hesitated momentarily, concerned he was abandoning Thomas by leaving.

Maybe he should be following the Red Cap's route? But his head was at last ruling his heart and he realised that staggering around the moors in total darkness would be useless.

Suddenly deciding that time was of the essence, he accelerated fast back down the hill towards the town.

"Kate, you need to direct me to Truman's house; be strong; we will find Thomas I promise you."

He would find him, he thought, or die trying.

CHAPTER TWENTY-SEVEN

"Shouldn't we go to the police?" Kate said from her position in the back still holding Simon whose head had fallen forward onto her chest. "They have helicopters, dogs; surely they'd be able to help."

"That was the police back there," Elliot said shuddering as he recalled the helpless Scott hanging like so much meat in a butcher's shop from the claws of that foul creature.

"We have no phone signal and if we stop to dial 999, we will spend the next five hours making statements and answering questions, as they check out everything we say and when they find Scott and that farmer up there, do you really think they are going to believe stories of hell hounds and Red Caps?"

Elliot wished he knew why he was so sure that they should go to Truman not the police. Did he really know that was the right thing to do, or was he, as so often in the past just thinking differently to others? This time however, he knew he was gambling with the life of his grandson. This time there could be no mistakes. This time he must be right, otherwise he would not be able to face his daughter, or even himself, ever again.

"If Truman is in the same state as when I saw him earlier, I'm not sure how much help he is going to be," Kate said.

Elliot knew she was right. Of course they should go to the police. They would get Simon to the hospital, he really didn't know how much blood he had lost, although it didn't look too bad. The dressings seemed to be doing their job and Simon seemed to be shaking less.

But something told him the police couldn't help. This needed belief: belief in things that he found almost impossible to imagine let alone comprehend. As if reading his mind he was shaken from his thoughts by a weak voice.

"Get to Truman," the voice was weak but determined, "he knows what is happening here. Get to Truman."

Elliot turned round to see Simon pulling himself painfully to an upright position in the back of the car. Turning his eyes back to the road he saw the long straight main road of Newcastleton stretched out before him and he put his foot down, sending the car hurtling down the quiet road.

"Up here on the right," Kate said as they swept past Douglas Square and approached the turn to Langholm Street. They came to a halt at a small unprepossessing terraced house.

Running to the house, the door swung slowly open before he had time to knock and as Kate struggled to help Simon out of the car, Elliot saw Truman standing silhouetted by a light from behind him. He stood to one side to let Elliot through and then helped Kate with Simon, guiding him through to a small, sparsely furnished front room, glowing warmly from a small open fire.

Truman sat Simon astride an upright wooden chair so he could lean forward onto the back and he could work on the injuries. "Take this off and let me look at it," he said.

Kate unzipped the fleece and Simon winced with pain as they carefully teased it away from his back. Despite their best efforts blood was seeping from around the haphazard patchwork of dressings and the fleece was adhering to it. Plaster, unable to stick to flesh smothered with antiseptic cream, hung ineffectively from the pads.

"Kate, there is a kettle out there," he pointed to a small doorway to the back of the room, "and a bowl. Boil some water and bring it here." Then expertly he started removing the pads and bandages, peering closely at the wounds as he did so.

"Sit down and tell me what happened," Truman spoke gently to Elliot and as he worked with what looked like practised efficiency on Simon's back, Elliot, occasionally stopping to compose himself, recounted the events as they had happened.

Kate returned with the bowl and placed it on a small dining table alongside Truman then, stroking Simon's head gently as she passed, she took a seat on the settee alongside her father and placed a hand on his arm as Truman worked away. Leaving the room briefly, he returned with a small box which contained bandages and ointments of various kinds. Having washed the wounds carefully with the hot water, he smothered a large pad with a green paste and laid it gently across Simon's back sealing it with tape.

Placing both hands flat on Simon's back, Truman closed his eyes for a few seconds.

Suddenly Simon sat up sharply, "God, that's hot!"

"Good," said Truman. "That means it's working."

Simon looked a lot better although he still winced painfully as he got off the chair, gingerly pulling on Elliot's fleece over his back. He went to sit next to Kate on the settee. Elliot moved to a small armchair to allow the couple to sit together. His mind was racing frantically as he tried to consider what they needed to do next. He felt the need to do something urgently but felt completely helpless.

As if reading Elliot's mind, Truman said quietly, "Perhaps you are ready to believe me now, after your experience tonight."

"I believe in Red Caps that's for sure, and now so do Kate and Simon, but I hope you are not going to say 'I told you so'. We need to find Thomas and if you can help you need to do it now, before that foul creature does him harm."

Elliot had raised his voice and he realised, he was contradicting the reassurances that Thomas would be fine for a while that he had given Kate earlier.

He looked at his daughter guiltily, tears were still rolling intermittently down her face and he realised he had not put any thoughts in her head that were not there already.

"Please Mr Truman, how do we find Thomas?" Kate's voice was imploring, quiet and tremulous, as if she was using every ounce of her strength to avoid a complete collapse into hysteria. "Please help us."

"We do not have to find Thomas," Truman said. "I know exactly where he is. He is in Hermitage Castle."

Simon jumped to his feet, "Then what are we doing here? Let's get over there now; we can drop Kate off on the way and she can bring the police. Let's go and get my son right now!"

Elliot also climbed to his feet, "I'm with Simon, why are we not on our way now?"

Truman shook his head slowly. "Please sit down. I know you want to help Thomas but rushing up to Hermitage unarmed is not the way." He seemed to pause a moment as if choosing his words very carefully.

"Look, I will not pretend that Thomas is not in serious danger, but I am sure he has not been harmed yet. There is

156

something much bigger at stake here than the uncontrolled blood lust of a Red Cap."

"What do you mean unarmed?" Elliot said. "You mean guns? Where do we get guns from?"

"You don't kill someone who is already dead with guns." Truman leaned forward.

"I mean armed with knowledge. Only your complete understanding of what you are up against will help you here."

Kate was torn with indecision. Half of her just wanted to jump into the car and go get her precious son, but something inside her, perhaps instinct, told her that they should listen to this man. Her mind kept returning to the times she had seen Thomas and this old man together and how they were with each other. Somehow she trusted her son's instincts above her own. But one major doubt nagged at her. What if he suddenly returned to that near-autistic state she had seen him in when she had visited with Constable Scott?

"What was wrong with you earlier when I was here with Constable Scott? You seemed... so different."

"I have to live amongst these people and if they suspected I was anything other than a senile old fool then there would be just too many questions about me that couldn't be explained. There are some practical problems about being over seven hundred years old you know."

Kate's heart sank. Her son was lost to them and at the mercy of some vile, wild monster that could kill animals and humans in the same depraved way, and rather than looking for him or going straight to the authorities for help, here they were in some small terraced house talking to a lunatic who believed he was the re-incarnation of some long-dead wizard.

Despite having said Ercildoune was still alive and the correlation with the name – this was the first time Truman had explicitly confirmed the inference that he was the adept.

"You believe you are the reincarnation of Thomas of Ercildoune?" she needed one last confirmation that all hope was lost before rushing out of that place with her husband and father to call the police and search for her child.

Truman seemed calm and unfazed by their obvious disbelief. A man it would seem who was used to being taken as either a fool or a lunatic, or both, on a regular basis.

157

"My belief is not important. It is what you believe that will guide you through this; nothing else.

"And to answer your question directly, no I do not believe I am Thomas of Ercildoune reincarnated." He paused momentarily, "I am Thomas of Ercildoune – I unfortunately have not been allowed to die so I cannot be reincarnated. Because of what happened here 686 years ago, I am forced to live in a world to which I do not belong. Have you any idea what that is like?"

Elliot had sat quietly unsure of what to do. He did not want to interrupt Kate who he knew, along with Simon, must have the last say in what they did. He could not force them into a decision that they were unhappy with. Frankly also he did not want to – he was as unsure as everyone else and was terrified of the consequences of being wrong.

"Look," he said at last, "we are wasting time here. I cannot believe we are sitting here actually discussing the possibility that you might be centuries old, we must do something."

"No," said Truman, "you need to do the *right* thing – not *some*thing. Have I said one thing to you so far that has not proven to be true? About the Red Cap, the taking of Thomas, the 'barguest'?"

"The bar what?" Simon, whilst still looking drawn and grey, was now looking slightly more comfortable. Whatever the old man had done to him seemed to be working.

"Barguest," Truman said. "Sometimes called a 'Kirk Grim', or 'Church Grim'." He paused seeing their confusion. "The dog!" he said. "The dog that protected you in the cemetery, David. Did I not tell you there was a dog but he wasn't responsible for these killings and that he was not your enemy?"

"What in heaven's name is a barguest?" Simon demanded.

"Strictly speaking it was not protecting you, it was protecting the cemetery. Humans are not typically a threat to a cemetery, but evil supernatural creatures like the Red Caps are. That is why the barguest did not pursue the Red Cap after it left the cemetery; he had done his job by driving it away."

"Sorry, I don't understand," Elliot said.

"The barguest is a spirit that was once a dog."

Still seeing the puzzlement on their faces, Truman continued with his explanation.

"In ancient times it was believed that the spirit of the first person laid to rest in a new cemetery was destined to guard all the other occupants of the cemetery for all time. No one of course wished their ancestor to be damned to haunt a cemetery for eternity, so it was commonplace for a dog to be buried in the cemetery before the first human was interred The dog took on the responsibility of guarding the cemetery, rather than a human.

"The creature you saw, the barguest, was protecting the occupants of the cemetery from evil; in this case the Red Cap. Because of the recent activity of the Red Cap, the barguest has also been active. They are frightening looking creatures; it is not surprising that the locals would hold it responsible for the sheep killings.

"As so many of those occupants are your ancestors, David, he was protecting your kin along with all the others. Fortunately a barguest is usually more than a match for a Red Cap, although this particular one is not a normal Red Cap.

"Red Caps are usually fairly stupid creatures. They typically kill by pushing rocks down onto their victims. Sometimes they kill face to face with claws. This one actually has a name, which is unusual in itself. He is Robin Red Cap and is Soulis's familiar, sent by the Dark Spirits. He has served him for centuries."

Kate shuddered at the thought that there were more of these creatures somewhere.

Simon, Kate and Elliot looked at each other. They wanted to argue. Their heads told them that none of this supernatural nonsense could be true, but once again everything that Truman said seemed to be borne out by what they had seen with their own eyes.

"So tell me why you think Thomas is safe, at least for the moment?" Kate needed a hope, a single straw to hold onto; to believe that despite everything, somehow Thomas was alright.

"Because the Red Cap is under the control of Soulis. His fear of Soulis is greater even than his lust for blood. He will take Thomas to Soulis because Thomas is key to Soulis's purpose; to cross him would be to certainly condemn itself to an eternity of pain and agony.

"His punishment would not just come from Soulis, but from the Dark Spirits too, who sent him to aid Soulis. There is no room for disobedience in their realm."

"So what is this purpose you say Soulis has for Thomas and why has he not already done it? Even on foot that creature would be back at Hermitage by now at the speed it moves." Kate was clearly hoping she could believe the answer.

"Because there are rules: rituals and rites that must be obeyed. What Soulis has to do, he will do tomorrow, February 14th, exactly 686 years after he was boiled in lead on Nine Stane Rig. The 14th February, is the last day he can call on the Dark Spirits for another seven years.

"And if he leaves it for another seven years he cannot guarantee that there will be you and your family and, most importantly, Thomas available to him. Thomas is important. Soulis would not be able to allow him to leave. He would need to hide him away for that length of time. Thomas is key to this whole cosmic conjunction, keeping him for seven years is risky. He would much rather complete the process tomorrow."

Elliot said, "Then if we have until tomorrow why can we not just go up there with the police and get Thomas back?"

"Because," Truman explained, "if the ritual is under threat they will abort it and they will not be there."

He continued, realising further explanation was required, "Let us suppose for one moment that you can convince the police of all this and that is of itself a huge assumption. That you can also convince them to look in Hermitage at the right time, then you might stop the ritual, but you will lose Thomas.

"Soulis has waited 686 years. He will not baulk at hiding Thomas away for another seven years if he has to. He will prefer to do it tomorrow but given the choice between waiting seven years and losing the opportunity to come back at all, he will wait seven years."

"What do you mean, 'come back'?" Elliot asked. "From what you are saying he has already come back from the dead once. You say you were responsible for his death seven centuries ago, but now he has taken Thomas for some ritual. How can he do that if he is not already 'back' as you call it?"

"Soulis and I are not the same. He is spirit; I am flesh. He wants to come back in the same way as I have. He wants to be human, to use his powers to give him complete control in this unbelieving world. Nobody would be able to stop him with the unique powers he has been given for mayhem.

"For me, living forever is a curse. To him it is the whole purpose of his being."

Simon was listening intently, hoping to hear something that he could do rather than just talk about. He needed action to stop him thinking of what might be happening to Thomas.

"Surely everyone wants to live forever. Isn't that what everyone is striving for, with plastic surgery, cryogenics, gene therapy, medical research in general – we all want to live forever don't we?"

"Think for a moment, Simon. Imagine you could live forever. How would you feel when you watched Kate die and then one by one your children? Everyone you know, everyone you care for: friends, family – everyone. Can you imagine the pain of that? The loneliness? Would you want to go through that?"

Truman continued, "Then you make new friends, new acquaintances, even a new wife, new children and then watch them die as well. Could you face that generation after generation? Century after century? Forever reinventing yourself, constantly moving before people around you realise that as they grow old you don't?

"Never being able to form relationships, even pretending as you saw earlier that you are a little simple, a harmless old fool, to avoid awkward questions?"

The three visitors looked at each other realising what it would be like. Kate looked at the pain in this old man's eyes and felt it like a knife in her heart.

"It must have been terrible," she said, her voice cracking with emotion.

"But that is not the worst of it."

The old man for the first time since they met him seemed to show real emotion. Never angry, never loud, the closest they had ever seen to a display of emotion was a sort of vague disappointment when he felt they stubbornly refused to believe what should have been obvious to them.

"The worst of it," he said as his bright blue eyes filled suddenly with tears, "is knowing that you will never ever meet your loved ones again."

Elliot didn't understand.

161

"Surely when your loved one dies you never see them again? That is the nature of things. Unless you mean we all meet up later in heaven. Not sure I can believe that."

"Your concepts of heaven and hell are preconditioned by your early upbringing. These places are not elsewhere; they are here and now. Energy is neither created nor destroyed, it can only change state."

"Thermodynamics," Simon said.

Truman nodded, "If you want to think of it like that, yes. When we die we change state. We don't *go* anywhere. We change to a different plane or state. In that state we meet up with everyone who went before us and who were important to us.

"Naturally there is a predominance of love, kindness and well-being on that plane, That is what you would call heaven."

"And hell?" Elliot asked.

"Hell is different. Firstly there is not one of them; they are legion. Simply put it is the opposite of heaven. It is where there is the absence of love and kindness. They are opposites, Yin and Yang if you like."

"Who decides who goes where?" Kate said. "God?"

"No. We decide for ourselves by the way we are and what we do. Most people are fundamentally good. We all make mistakes in life and they are redeemable, correctable. If we accept the nature of things then typically we all end up in heaven. That means we see our loved ones again, albeit that we may take different times to get there. Just because someone 'died' in your terms before you, does not necessarily mean they get to the spirit state ahead of you."

"What about those who are not as you say, 'fundamentally good'? What happens to them?" Elliot asked.

"No one is irredeemable. Life is a test. A trial if you like, which is the preparation for 'real life'."

He saw the puzzlement in their eyes.

"Death is not a light going out," he said, "it is the turning off of the lamp at dawn. Those who are not ready or those who cannot, or, as in the case of Soulis, will not, accept a life in the spirit, either return to another life to complete their training, you would call it reincarnation…"

"Or?" Elliot asked.

"Or some others, good and bad, get stuck. Some of these you call ghosts. Others like me get stuck for different reasons. You see, the world as we know it is transient. Remember energy is not created or destroyed, therefore it is logical that all energy in the world was here from the beginning.

"At any given time there are people 'living' as you would know it, usually through multiple reincarnations, as they hopefully progress towards their real existence in spirit. Others, a far greater number, are in their 'spirit state', having achieved the purpose of their lives. This imbalance, the fact that there are more of us in spirit than in body, is the reason why 'good' is inherently more powerful than 'evil', if those two human constructs are useful."

"What do you mean by getting 'stuck'?" Kate asked.

"Some souls get stuck between the two states. Some by choice like Soulis, some like me as a punishment for disrupting the natural state of things. Others, the innocents, can get trapped by the evil that others do. Many innocent spirits for example are trapped in Hermitage. They are the predominantly innocent victims of Soulis's evil. They are held by the same power that holds Soulis and keeps him out of this world."

Elliot had far too many questions and was not sure which to ask first. He settled for, "So why are you so desperate to get out of this world, when Soulis is so determined to get in?"

"'Power corrupts and absolute power corrupts absolutely'. You are familiar with that saying?"

Elliot nodded.

"The lust for power, for lust is what it is, is the complete antithesis of the objective of our lives. Those who seek to advance through power over others are damaging their progress to the ultimate state.

"In the spirit, each is no more and no less valuable than the next. Power only exists in this world, not the next. Become too obsessed with power and you are lengthening your stay in this world, not necessarily for one lifetime but ultimately over many.

"Soulis is stuck. He has incredible power but it can only currently be invoked within the immediate confines of Hermitage. 'Goodness' if you like, confines him. He seeks to get out into a world of pygmies, as he sees it, where his power will be unlimited. He can rule unchallenged forever; or at least for a period so long that to all intents and purposes it will seem like forever.

"Soulis, when he was alive, had no love or regard for anyone but himself. The ultimate selfishness, power was, and is, his total aim. He will not miss loved ones or kin as he has no love for anyone but himself. He will therefore not miss what you and I miss: the love of people we care for."

"And you? Where do you stand in all this?"

"Six hundred and eighty-six years ago I was seduced by a lust for power. I was, under the pretext of helping the world rid itself of an evil, drawn into a battle that was not mine to fight.

"I took someone's place in this world, in order to pit my power against Soulis. It was sheer vanity and I have paid a very high price for it."

"I don't understand," Kate said, seeing the sadness in the old man's eyes.

He paused, as if trying to find the right words to explain in terms they would understand.

"Although I died in human terms some twenty-five years before the battle with Soulis, I had not completely passed over into spirit nor was I marked for reincarnation. In certain circumstances, people who have developed a great understanding sometimes are held in a different state: neither reincarnated nor passed into spirit.

"Human involvement in what is commonly known as magic, whether so called 'black' or 'white', is anathema to the balance of the universe.

"Although I had used my power for what might be termed 'good', I still needed to atone for it and rather than being reincarnated again, I was held in this world for a period to consider and repent. This was what had happened to me. I was not quite ready to pass into spirit but had sufficient learning or knowledge to redeem myself without being returned for another life through reincarnation.

"It was during this period when I made the fateful decision that destroyed the natural balance and put me in the position I am now in. Worse than this, I, albeit unwittingly, showed Soulis the way to achieve his aims.

"You remember the young man I spoke of, Walter of Branxholm, who, with his betrothed was imprisoned by Soulis?"

Truman acknowledged their nods of agreement. "Walter was mortally wounded in the battle with Soulis. In order to ensure his beloved Marion was saved from Soulis he agreed to take my place so that I could come back and do battle with him.

"This was a unique set of circumstances. Walter was special. He was ready to move into the final state – the opportunity was there. His punishment for agreeing to the ritual I conducted was to lose his place in the spirit world that his goodness had clearly earned him.

"He was put back for reincarnation. It took him another three hundred and fifty years and many new lives before he could be allowed to 'die' and to be reunited with his beloved Marion.

"My punishment, on the other hand, continues. I cannot move on until I have restored the balance and undone the damage I wrought by interfering in the natural order of things."

Kate was beginning to understand what this man must have been through and how the pain of loss over and over again must have cut deep into his heart. "It seems so cruel," she said. "Surely you have paid enough?"

"For what I have done in disturbing the balance; but most of all for, albeit unknowingly, showing Soulis how to come back; for all the evil he has wrought which otherwise would never have happened, I deserve it all," he said quietly.

"But you meant well." Kate wanted to reassure him, "You saved that couple and destroyed an evil monster."

"The road to hell is paved with good intentions," Truman replied. "It was not my place to battle Soulis in the human world. Life is cruel at times but it is part of the test that conditions humans for transition into spirit. For thousands of years people have wondered why cruel things happen, why children die, why innocence is destroyed, why evil is allowed to prevail. People call for supernatural intervention, they pray to a God to save them, and their faith is challenged when those prayers seem to go unanswered.

"The order of things is that the challenges facing people in life are to be endured and fought by them, not by others on their behalf. Whether God or wizard, the natural order cannot and must not be circumvented."

"So you are saying that prayer is a waste of time?" Elliot suspected as much.

"Never!" Truman said firmly. "Prayer is for guidance, for strength, not for a solution or some champion to fight your battles for you. I can give you guidance, I can give you hope and if you are strong enough to take it, I can give you belief."

"But you defeated him before; you can do it again." Simon spoke anxiously.

Truman lowered his head and shook it slowly.

Whilst Simon and Elliot struggled to make sense of what Truman was saying, Kate lowered her head. When she raised it again her eyes were once more full of tears as she came to understanding.

"You're not coming with us to get Thomas are you?" she looked into the blue eyes of the old man, in whose strength and knowledge she had placed all her final hopes.

Truman looked at her sadly.

"I'm sorry."

The words cut like a knife.

"I cannot," he said quietly.

CHAPTER TWENTY-EIGHT

Dettori entered the bar at exactly 7.00 pm to find he was the first to arrive except for Romanski who had gone nowhere and was sitting on a high stool at the bar still clutching his ice cold vodka in the small shot glass and expounding his theory on everything to a patient, smiling barman. He had made no move to go to his room to dress for dinner and was still drinking heavily.

Dettori took a deep breath and then putting on a broad smile he marched forward, hand outstretched.

"Gregori my dear friend, it is wonderful to see you again!"

Romanski turned his substantial bulk with some difficulty on the stool and swayed slightly. For a moment Dettori thought he might fall drunk from the stool that Romanski's huge backside seemed to be absorbing rather than sitting on.

"Andrea!" Gregori shouted, "My good little Italian friend." He staggered to his feet and clutched the proffered hand.

Dettori had slipped his thumb into the palm of Romanski's hand to protect his fingers from the unnecessarily violent crush of Romanski's handshake; it disappeared inside the vice like grip, looking like a child's hand inside Romanski's fist.

Romanski yanked him forward and into a huge crushing bear-hug. Dettori held his breath as he was pulled unceremoniously into the huge Russian's chest; his face pressed against the sweaty bulk which he knew would smell sickeningly of a combination of vodka, cheap tobacco and stale sweat.

Swaying backwards and forwards in this iron embrace, Dettori felt like a small child in the arms of an over-exuberant grandfather.

"Another drink?" Dettori gasped slightly. He knew the last thing Romanski needed was more vodka, but he needed to bring this crushing embrace to an end before he lost the ability to breathe altogether.

Thankfully Romanski released him and eased his huge bulk back onto the stool. "Vodka!" he shouted at the barman, emphasising the demand with a violent slap of his hand on the top of the bar, "And whatever my little friend is having."

The barman didn't need to ask. He poured a fine malt whisky over ice. He worked for Dettori and knew exactly what he liked.

"In honour of you, Gregori, we are having finest Russian caviar tonight. Are you dressing for dinner?"

"Of course," Romanski spoke through an alcoholic belch. "I may be a simple Russian peasant but I know how to behave in polite society." The answer contained an undisguised sneer at what he obviously felt to be a Western bourgeois affectation.

"We must not let the great William Soulis think that we do not know how to behave must we? When do we finally get to meet the great man?"

"As I told you all, Mr Soulis will join us tomorrow to outline his plans for the Trust. You will all meet him then."

Romanski cast a look at Dettori which in the army would have been interpreted as dumb insolence. "I am expecting great things," he said sarcastically.

"Andrea my dear chap!" The unmistakeable upper class English voice of Sir Ronald Robertson sounded from behind Dettori and he turned to see the tall, slim Englishman entering the room with Clemenza and Erikson. He gestured to his colleagues, "We met in the lift." He smiled graciously.

"Gregori, how are you?" Robertson waved from a distance; he clearly was not going to get close enough to the Russian to risk his over boisterous greeting. "So hear we all are – except for the delightful Susan. Woman's prerogative I suppose."

"No special treatment for me gentlemen, please."

The men turned towards the source of the soft, Boston-American accent to see the stunning vision of Susan Coltrane in a dark blue, long, figure-hugging, evening dress which sparkled as brightly as her smile. The plunging neckline finished just above her navel, her large breasts held beneath the material by some form of ingenuity unknown to man.

Dettori walked briskly to take her hand and kiss her gently on both cheeks, Susan having to bend to accommodate the much shorter Italian.

"You look delightful as usual. Let me get you a drink. Gin and tonic, lime not lemon?"

"Thank you," Susan smiled warmly.

With the initial pleasantries over they settled in comfortable leather chairs and settees, with the exception of Romanski, who preferred to remain on the barstool, presenting his huge bear-like back to them and to shout across the room at the others.

Discreet waiters appeared with silver trays of assorted canapés and glided silently between the members of the group.

"So we all wait for Soulis like a bunch of lackeys do we?" Romanski slurred. "Too important to dine with us is he?" There was a worrying hint of drunken aggression growing in the booming voice.

Dettori smiled politely holding his hands out to the group as a whole. "I can assure you Mr Soulis holds you all in the greatest esteem, which is why he has given you all the opportunity to be part of this marvellous enterprise. It is merely timing, he cannot make it until tomorrow."

"I do not need the esteem of some unknown Scotsman. I have made my money through my own guts and brains, I am known throughout the world by anyone who matters. Who has ever heard of this Soulis?"

Perhaps, Dettori thought, he had underestimated the trouble he might have with Romanski whose usual belligerence seemed to be accentuated tonight by his constant drinking.

"My dear Gregori," Dettori smiled quietly, "we should discuss this after dinner when the staff have left. I assure you, you will have ample opportunity to express your concerns."

He was relieved that Romanski seemed to accept the point, albeit grudgingly and he returned to his vodka muttering under his breath.

"When do we eat?" Susan spoke, obviously trying to move the conversation on from the dangerous line it was beginning to take. She also had her concerns about this unknown Scot, but she realised the necessity to be discreet in the presence of the waiters.

"In half an hour. I think you will find a bottle in the freezer in your room Gregori, whilst you change."

Fortunately Romanski seemed to miss the rather unsubtle hint and grunted heavily as he levered himself off the barstool,

"Time to pretty myself up," he said and staggering slightly, headed towards the door.

CHAPTER TWENTY-NINE

The realisation that the three of them were ultimately and completely alone suddenly seemed to knock all of the resistance out of them and for long moments they sat without speaking, deep in the realisation that whilst they all knew they would go to Hermitage anyway, and they would fight for Thomas, the possibility that they could face up to Soulis without Truman was hopeless.

Elliot spoke, breaking the frightened silence between them, "So you are prepared to watch us go and face this alone?" He realised his rather unsubtle attempt to instil guilt was hardly likely to change Truman's mind, but he could think of nothing else to challenge him with.

"The three of us with the help of that dog, the barguest or whatever you called it, could not keep Thomas safe from the Red Cap. Yet alone you expect us to face the Red Cap and Soulis who from what you say is hugely more powerful than that foul creature that took Thomas?"

"There will be more for you to face there than Soulis and the Red Cap. Believe me Soulis can conjure many more demons if he feels the need. Hopefully his vanity will stop him doing that. He is arrogant, he will probably feel you are incapable of hurting him."

"With good justification as far as I can see," Elliot said. "Without you we will die up there."

Kate looked disbelieving. "You are prepared to send us alone to our death?"

"There are things far worse than death," Truman said looking distracted momentarily and then continued, "And who said you would be alone?"

Truman was again calm and thoughtful, "You are not alone."

Elliot once again was filled with anger as Truman continued to talk in riddles as far as he was concerned.

"You can't help us but you continue to taunt us. Who do we have but you? Who can possibly help us, the police? The army? God? Angels? Who on earth can help us?"

Truman thought for a moment, obviously trying to explain why his words were so measured.

"I cannot give you the solution or tell you precisely what to do. That vanity is what caused me to be here for all these centuries. You must work this out for yourself."

They still looked confused as he continued, "Why did you come here, David?"

"To see you. To get your help to save Thomas. What a waste of time that has turned out to be."

"Your anger is blinding you, David. Why did you come here, to Scotland? Who did you call on earlier when the Red Cap took Thomas? Think, David, you must think. Who could possibly help you?"

"You know why I came here. You saw us that first night. I came here to follow up on my family history research..." Elliot suddenly stopped.

He looked at Kate and then at Simon as realisation dawned on him, "I called on my father for help," he said as he recalled his desperate prayer on the road by the cemetery. "But how could you possibly have known that?"

"I told you prayers are not a waste of time." Truman paused as if ensuring that Elliot's racing brain was fully comprehending what he was saying.

"You came here looking for your family, your kin, your clan," he said, emphasising each point deliberately. "You called on your father, the last of your immediate family to pass on. How many more of them are there here to help?

"I told you I needed to arm you with belief. The belief that the three of you are not alone. You have your family with you. You have your clan.

"Believe, David. You above all must believe in clan."

Tears welled in Elliot's eyes as he thought of his father and it was all he could do to keep from sobbing uncontrollably.

"And you have one other thing with which to battle this monster. One thing that is more powerful than you, your family or me."

The three of them stared uncomprehending at Truman who was standing before them looking from one to the other as if willing them to understand.

"I don't understand," Elliot said.

"I think I do," Kate said quietly, "You mean..."

Truman cut her off. Somehow he knew she understood.

"Yes, Kate, you have the most powerful weapon that could possibly be used against Soulis."

Kate wiped the tears from her eyes

"We have Thomas," she said quietly.

"You have Thomas," Truman confirmed.

CHAPTER THIRTY

The three of them sat for a long time, silently considering what Truman was telling them and desperately trying to work out how any of this would help them get their beloved Thomas back.

Leaving them with their thoughts for a while, Truman went to the kitchen and returned after a few minutes with tea for them all.

"Drink this," he said handing the tray around.

Kate broke the silence. "Thomas is a child. How can he possibly cope with Soulis?"

"Look for the answer in your own experience, Kate. Remember your own childhood, fairy stories, nursery rhymes.

"And you, David, you have studied your family name, your history, look for answers there."

Elliot felt his brain going over and over these strange circumstances and one thing kept nagging at him like a thought not quite fully formed. When he approached it, it scurried away like a startled animal as if frightened by examination.

He had kept asking himself over and over since this all began, 'Why me?', 'Why us?', but he kept driving it away because it seemed weak, like a child feeling sorry for himself.

But somehow he realised that it was not just that.

He couldn't understand why they were so much the focus of Soulis's hatred. It didn't make sense to him.

Then he asked the question that he had been afraid to ask because he didn't want to appear weak and pathetic in the eyes of his daughter.

"Why does Soulis hate us so much? What makes us special in his mind? I thought it was because the Elliots occupied his lands and defended them, so it is logical he should dislike the clan.

"But why not others? The Bruce and his descendants. The Bruce kept him from the Crown and confiscated his lands. His son who occupied them. The Douglas Clan who really controlled Hermitage as far as I can see. The Elliots were just the militia. What about Wallace and his descendants? Wallace nearly killed him and kept him from the Crown by refusing to support him against Robert the Bruce. There are so many more important people far more worthy of his hatred."

Truman smiled as if encouraging Elliot with his line of thought.

"Even you and your descendants. Yes you," Elliot's mind was racing now. "You killed him, or at least you showed the Elliots and the young Walter of Branxholm how to kill him. He has far more reason to hate you than my clan. Why is he not pursuing your family? Why...", he broke off as if a sudden realisation had hit him.

He looked down, putting his hands to his head trying to force his thoughts into some kind of order.

After a few seconds he looked up at Truman, "But he is pursuing your family isn't he?"

Truman smiled.

"This is not about us is it? This is about you," Elliot looked at Truman for some sign that he was right, but something told him that it was not the whole story.

"No – not you alone," he continued, "Both of us. No all of us. There is something bigger here. Something connecting us and it culminates in Thomas. What happened in the 13th century that ties the Elliots to your family?" he struggled, searching for some fragment of information from his research that tied them together.

"History didn't start in the 13th century, David," Truman encouraged.

"Nine Stane Rig!" Elliot said his mind racing. "It is from the Bronze Age. The Bronze Age ended seven hundred and fifty years before Christ was born. You took Soulis to Nine Stane Rig. This is older, much older. We are going back nearly three thousand years not just seven hundred – maybe even further than that!

"The name Elliot came from Elwald, literally 'Ruler of the Elves'. We were magicians too?" he looked for confirmation from Truman who said nothing.

"The Elwalds and the Ercildounes were both magicians involved with each other. Or was it more than that? Not just involved, related. We have the same ancestors.

"We are," his eyes widened, "we are the same Clan!"

175

Truman smiled again.

Simon was listening fascinated. Then something seemed to strike him and he asked Kate if she had a pen. Fishing around in her bag she found her small note book with pen attached and he took it and started scribbling furiously.

After studying his jottings as if reassuring himself, he looked up and spoke to Elliot, "What did you say the modern name for Ercildoune was?"

"Earlston," Elliot replied.

"That's what I thought," he said. "Look at this."

He handed Elliot the pad he had been scribbling on. At the top was the name 'EARLSTON' with each letter crossed through and underneath was a series of dashes over which was written another word.

Elliot realised Simon had been solving an anagram, under 'EARLSTON' and above the dashes was written 'RALSTONE'.

"My name, Thomas's name, Ralstone, is an anagram of your family name, Earlston," Simon said.

As if wishing to complete the thought process Elliot added, "So Thomas is not only Simon and Kate's child, he is not only my grandson, but we started in the same place in pre-history and we have come back together again – Kate through the Elliot line and Simon through yours."

"You are not the only ones who want Thomas safe," Truman nodded and tears filled his eyes. "I need you to save him from Soulis. I need you to save my great grandson. I am Thomas's 18th great grandfather.

"That is what makes him special," Elliot said.

Simon and Kate looked at each other and then at Elliot. "I'm not sure I understand, what do you mean by 'special'?"

"You remember Truman here said when he 'came back' to fight Soulis it was a unique time. He needed someone special to take his place and that person was Walter of Branxholm. If he had not been 'special', by virtue of his closeness to the spirit world, Truman would not have been able to come back."

"The Balance needs to be maintained," Truman said encouragingly. "The replacement must be someone worthy, someone at least as far advanced in their journey to spirit as they are."

"And," Elliot continued slowly, "as Walter was a worthy replacement for you, special in that regard..."

Kate completed it for him, "Thomas is a worthy replacement for Soulis, by virtue of his ancestry."

"His ancestry and his inherent goodness. Thomas has no need for further incarnations. He is ready for spirit when he comes to his natural end in this life. He is, like Walter was, uniquely 'special'."

Elliot studied Truman closely, "But that means the danger he is in is far greater than the end of his life."

"Death is not the end for any of us," Truman said quietly. "Being trapped for eternity in Hermitage is. We must – *you* must – save him."

Elliot shuddered as if someone had walked over his grave again. Never had that expression held such resonance for him before.

Turning to Kate, he hugged her to him, "I think it is time," he said quietly, "I think it is time we went and got Thomas back."

CHAPTER THIRTY-ONE

Batnykov was concerned.

Every instinct in his body told him that something was wrong.

This was too easy.

He, and his two colleagues had approached the runway silently, their objective to secure the landing strip for the rest of his team that would fly in to the private runway in fifteen minutes.

Romanski had told him that Dettori had no concept of security; there were no guards, no dogs, no firearms or alarms. Frankly, Batnykov had not believed him. He had done his research and Dettori did not seem to be the kind of man who would leave things to chance.

He had assumed that Romanski was wrong, that there would be professional security – Romanski had just not seen it, which of itself attested to the professionalism of what they would be up against.

Batnykov knew that Romanski would have flaunted his security, armed guards, baying dogs, patrolling the grounds behind razor wire – but this was the United Kingdom, not Russia, and such obvious shows of force would have been unacceptable.

He was convinced that Dettori would have a team of highly professional guards, probably ex-SAS, now working freelance. He had encountered the SAS many times in his career. They were good, very good, and could not be taken for granted.

This of itself did not overly concern him. Of course they were good, but he was better: confidence borne of experience, not conceit.

But there had been one man 'guarding' the control tower for the private runway, and the ease with which Batnykov had approached him and despatched him showed he was no professional soldier. The man was dead on the floor of the control tower with a broken neck before he had even realised someone had entered the tower behind him.

Apart from a mobile phone, there seemed nothing to suggest any early warning system and if they were reliant on this 'guard' checking in at regular intervals, it would be too late by the time anyone checked to find out why he had not called.

Still concerned, he checked in with his two colleagues, positioned strategically at either end of the runway. Both acknowledged that all was well.

Batnykov had complete confidence that no one could approach these two professionals or the tower without them seeing and warning him of their coming. A single click on the radio would suffice, something that could be done in a split second even under immediate attack.

It seemed Romanski was right. There were no guards, at least in the near vicinity. It still bothered him though as he turned his eyes to the night sky and saw, exactly on time, the black shape of the jet dropping silently against the moon, approaching the runway like a bird of prey.

Soon a further twenty of Batnykov's crack team would be with him on the ground.

CHAPTER THIRTY-TWO

It was 1.00 am on February the 14th as the three left Truman's house in silence and climbed wearily into the car. Truman stood in the doorway watching as they drove away. Kate watched from the rear window as he slowly closed the door. It seemed an indication of how alone they were.

As they passed the small police station in the main street it was obvious that Scott and the farmer had been found. Unusually, it was lit up like a Christmas tree and several police cars, an ambulance and other less obviously identifiable vehicles were parked. Police officers both in uniform and plain clothes milled around and passed urgently in and out of the building.

"Maybe we should stop," Simon said. "Try and get some help."

Elliot considered for a moment, "Maybe. But I would not even begin to know how to explain all this. We don't know how much time we have to find Thomas. Supposing they don't believe us? Which I would have thought is going to be their first reaction. They will probably think we are responsible for Scott's death. Either way they will keep us from going to Thomas straight away.

"And remember what Truman said, they could go up to Hermitage and stop the ritual; then we might lose Thomas forever."

Kate said, "I want to be with Thomas. I can't bear to think of him up at that castle alone. I don't care what happens to me. I don't want him to be alone for one second longer than he needs to be. If we can't rescue Thomas we can come back later and try to explain to the police."

"If we are able to." Elliot thought but did not feel the need to verbalise the probability that was obvious to them all.

On the basis that they did not want to get tied up with the police, he decided to take the Hawick road rather than the Jedburgh road that passed the cemetery. He was sure the police would be all over the cemetery and frankly he was happy to avoid the area that held so much horror for him.

Simon was surprised when Elliot turned off the road and down the track towards the cottage. "Why are we going to the cottage? We are wasting time. We need to get to the castle as soon as possible."

"I thought we might be able to find some kind of weapon at the cottage," Elliot said but not convinced. "A knife or something," he added, realising how pathetic it sounded.

"We are not going to save Thomas with knives," Kate seemed stronger now than any of them. It seemed her protective instincts for her son were stronger than her fear. Nothing was going to keep her from her child any longer than she could avoid.

As it transpired, they could not have got back to the cottage anyway; at least not without getting tangled up with the police. Elliot pulled up a few hundred yards away from the entrance to the drive and turned off the headlights as he looked across the moor to the cottage which should have been in darkness.

All the lights were on and two police cars and a Land Rover stood outside. He could see the shadows of people moving around in the house. Presumably the Land Rover belonged to the owners who must have brought a spare key to the cottage, unless of course the police had broken in.

Elliot backed up gingerly, without putting the lights back on until he was confident that they could not be seen from the cottage. Bumping on the grass verge he turned the vehicle around and they set off back up the track towards the Hawick road and to Hermitage Castle.

"Why are they looking for us?" Kate said looking back in the direction of the cottage.

"They must know Scott had been with us earlier. They are probably trying to trace his last movements. We are the last people to see him alive apart from that farmer, and he was probably waiting up at the cemetery for him. In any event the farmer was in no condition to give them any help."

Elliot shuddered as he remembered the slaughtered farmer in the cemetery, whose blood was still staining his face and clothing.

181

"We'd have been there all night if they had got hold of us," he said trying to convince himself as much as the others, that going up to Hermitage alone was the best thing for Thomas.

In a few more minutes they saw the sign off to the left indicating the direction to Hermitage Castle.

They turned and Elliot slowed as they took the final bend, seeing the frightening edifice silhouetted ahead, black and brooding in the dark against the night sky and lit only by the moon.

The stars glinted brightly from gaps in the wispy clouds that scudded across the face of the moon, little sparks of hope in a grim and oppressive nightmare.

Elliot shuddered again; not for the first time that evening he wondered what the hell he was doing as he approached this evil looking place in the dark.

"Look!" Simon shouted suddenly, "The police!"

Ahead of them in the lay-by that served as a car park for visitors stood two police cars, both parked by the small bridge that crossed the burn to the castle grounds.

Elliot noticed that the gate at the entrance to the castle grounds was swung wide. The driver's door on one of the police cars was open and a police radio crackled intermittently but there was no sign of any of the police officers.

"They must be in the castle," he said pulling up alongside them and climbing out of the car.

"Maybe they've got Thomas," Kate cried hopefully rushing to get out of the back of the car.

"Or maybe they've frightened Soulis off like Truman warned. We'd better get in there." Simon clutched at the torch that he had grabbed from the back of the car and leaping out, started hurrying across the bridge.

"Wait, wait for me," Elliot shouted after Simon as he tried to keep up with the younger couple who at the thought of being so close to their son were running towards the huge entrance at the northern end of the castle.

Elliot was running with a painful gait favouring his uninjured left leg as he tried to keep up. He stumbled and fell heavily. Unable to see clearly the path in front of him and cursing under his breath, he struggled again to his feet, distraught that he was so physically incapable of helping his own grandson.

Simon, on the other hand, ignoring his injured back completely was running full tilt stumbling occasionally on the uneven tufts of moor grass; closely followed by Kate. The torch beam swayed erratically ahead of Simon as he ran.

Elliot struggled after them. "Wait!" he called again as his son-in-law, closely followed by his daughter, disappeared into the darkness of the huge gate leading into the castle.

Panting, he finally arrived at the entrance and followed them through into the castle. He found Simon with Kate beside him, sweeping the torch from side to side across the gutted interior walls and random ragged blocks of fallen stone.

"Nothing," Simon was frantic. "There is nothing here," he fell to his knees in disappointment. "They've gone. They've gone and Thomas has gone with them."

Elliot pushed himself up from the wall he had been leaning against trying to catch his breath. Lungs burning with the effort and breathing loudly he walked forward and laid a hand on Simon's shoulder.

"They must be here," he said more in hope than belief. "If they are not here, where are those policemen?"

He took the torch from Simon and gave another despairing sweep of the ruins that were the inside of the huge building.

"Think, we must think. No more rushing about." He put his hand to his head, running his hands through his matted hair and massaging his scalp roughly in a familiar mannerism he had when trying to think things through: trying to force data into some logical sequence.

This time however, it was more an attempt to drive his tired brain to work properly.

"Think," he said to himself. "Belief is important here, belief is the key. Think!"

Kate crouched beside Simon and took her desolate husband into her arms holding him close.

"Underneath!" Elliot said under his breath, almost to himself. "They must be underneath the castle."

The couple looked up at Elliot.

"Remember the side of the castle, where I collapsed?" Elliot looked at Simon who was trying to recall the scene.

"I don't really remember," he said, "I was more concerned with what had happened to you."

"There was a small door and an arch that looked as if the whole castle had sunken into the ground. I noticed it because I remembered the story of the castle sinking beneath the weight of its own iniquity.

"It is the only place they can be. They are under the castle! Come on."

He raised Simon and Kate up and led the pair back out of the door and around the side of the building nearest to the burn and the road, staying close to the ancient stone walls. He felt along it as it indented and then straightened out as they followed along the mid-section of the building.

Suddenly the torch lit on a small door. "It's open," he said quietly.

The door was indeed open, or more accurately, ajar rather than open. An arc of mud and slime on the ground had been swept away by the door and showed that it had recently been opened after a very long time, presumably by the police officers.

Elliot pushed against it to try and open it completely, but the pile of mud that had built up behind the door as it had been pushed back had jammed it solid, leaving an opening of around twelve inches. Placing the torch on the floor, Elliot placed both hands around the edge of the door and pushed and pulled, but the door was jammed fast, he could neither open it further nor close it.

Realising he was not going to budge the door he picked up the torch and leaned round it into the space beyond, tentatively shining the torch through into the dark void behind the door. The torch lit an old damp corridor barely wide enough for two people to walk side-by-side. The walls and floor were damp and running with water and the corridor headed down for around three metres, where the corridor turned left continuing on a downward slope.

He turned to Kate and Simon, "I can't see very far, it turns a corner just ahead, but it does seem to head downwards."

"Let's go," Simon said pushing forward passed Elliot and squeezing past the door into the corridor. Kate followed.

"Take the torch," Elliot said passing it through to Simon. Briefly turning from the door in trepidation he looked up at the sky through the leafless trees waving gently in the wind. He looked through patchy cloud at the reassuring stars and wondered if he would ever look at the sky again. Taking a last deep breath of the cold fresh air he turned and squeezed with difficult through the gap into the corridor to join his daughter and son-in-law.

The tight squeeze and the oppressive closeness of the dark corridor triggered familiar feelings of claustrophobia and he tried to fight back the rising panic in his heart as he felt his breath shortening in the familiar onset of a panic attack. He swallowed hard, managing for the time being at least to submerge his panic beneath the fear for the safety of his grandson.

Inside the corridor it took a few minutes for his eyes to adjust. Simon was standing a couple of yards ahead, Kate holding his arm and slightly behind. The torch beam was focussed down the corridor to the bend ahead.

Coming up behind his daughter Elliot placed an arm around her shoulder and squeezed gently. He turned again to look at the rectangle of light from the moonlit sky outside.

As he watched, the door slammed shut with a huge crash that echoed loudly in the stone corridor and plunged the corridor into complete darkness save for the light from the torch behind him.

With a start, Simon swung the torch back towards the door, to see that it had indeed slammed shut, and standing between them and it, blocking any possibility of retreat, they saw the black soulless eyes of the Red Cap. The hideous face stared at them, the lower half of which was smothered with blood, as were the razor sharp teeth that hung from the open mouth.

The creature's black eyes glinted malignantly in the light from the torch.

The three froze for a few seconds as the Red Cap stood staring at them and then snarling, the creature moved slowly forward. Not for a moment did those evil eyes divert from the three prey ahead of it.

"Go, go!" Elliot pushed Kate and Simon ahead of him as he turned to run blindly down the corridor after them desperately trying to keep his footing as he tried to follow the bouncing torch light that danced erratically as Simon ran ahead.

As he ran, the strength that the creature must possess to have slammed the tightly jammed door closed did not escape him. As he stumbled down the corridor he braced himself for the pain of those vicious claws he expected to plunge into his back at any second.

For some unaccountable reason the pain did not come.

The corridor continued steeply down and they ran on until gasping, they burst into a large stone chamber lit by burning wooden torches around the walls. Elliot, still trying to run in one direction and look behind him at the same time, crashed into Simon who had stopped ahead, knocking the torch from his hand as he did so. The torch landed with a clatter at his feet, and he grabbed hold of it to shine it back to the corridor expecting to see the Red Cap closing on him.

The creature was nowhere to be seen.

They stood huddled together and as Elliot turned back from the corridor, he saw Simon and Kate standing staring straight ahead, their faces transfixed with horror.

Following their gaze to the centre of the dank dungeon he saw a large wooden chest bound with rusty iron bands. A large church candle burning at each end of it gave the chest the look of a makeshift altar. Standing behind the chest and dressed in a huge black robe stood a hooded giant. He looked close to seven feet tall and the hood of the cloak came so far forward that his face was obscured in darkness. His left arm extended forward horizontally without effort or strain, as he stood holding onto the dangling body of Elliot's grandson, Thomas, by the straps at the back of the small dark blue dungarees he was wearing.

The child's head was slumped forward chin on chest and the dangling body looked completely lifeless.

Kate screamed, "Thomas!" as she saw her young son hanging motionless in the grasp of this hooded giant. Tears welled in her eyes as she screamed again, "Thomas!" sobbing uncontrollably.

Elliot stared. His mouth was open and he seemed frozen to the spot and incapable of any coherent thought. He felt completely impotent in the presence of this giant.

"What have you done you bastard?" Simon was the first to move. Hurling himself forward he ran towards the giant as he held Thomas effortlessly before him.

Without moving from the spot on which he was standing, the giant swung Thomas easily to one side and lashed out with the back of his right hand as if cuffing a recalcitrant school child.

Catching the blow high on the cheekbone, Simon yelled in pain as he felt his cheekbone crack and he was hurled like a rag doll tumbling backwards landing heavily on his back near the feet of Kate. Pain like a knife shot through him as the wounds on his back re-opened and he felt the unmistakable feeling of blood trickling down his spine. He lay at Kate's feet groaning and semi-conscious as Kate dropped to her knees and tended to him, cupping his head into her lap as his face swelled around the damaged cheekbone, causing the right eye to close, the white bloodied from ruptured capillaries.

Elliot took two steps forward as if he too was going to launch himself at the giant. Then looking at the far fitter and far stronger Simon laying prostrate at his feet, he realised the futility of it. Whatever action he took he realised that he could not out fight this giant.

As he stood there frozen with indecision the giant reached up and pulled back the hood, revealing shoulder length red hair and a full red beard. A huge scar disfigured the grey-white pallor of his face, the vicious-looking wound ran diagonally across from forehead to chin. Hollow hooded eyes stared pitilessly from a face covered by countless other smaller scars, confirming that this was the face of a warrior.

"Welcome to Hermitage, I have been waiting for you." The guttural voice imbued with so much threat, seemed ethereal. "You are privileged to witness my rightful return to power in this world."

Elliot realised he was looking at seven hundred years of history as he stared into the face of William de Soulis, Lord of Hermitage in 1321, until his clan, on the authority of Robert the Bruce, King of Scotland and with the help of an ancient wizard called Thomas the Rhymer, had dispossessed him.

His blood chilled as he also realised that in this year almost seven hundred years later, he, his beloved daughter and grandson and his son-in-law, were about to suffer the revenge of this long-dead lord in the name of all his ancestors.

"Thomas," Kate suddenly shook Elliot from his thoughts, "Thomas is alright!"

Looking at Thomas still dangling from the hand of Soulis, Elliot realised that Kate was right. Thomas was moving!

Little legs kicked as he struggled against Soulis. Seeing his mother before him, he began to cry, his face red with the effort and large tears welled in his eyes and burst from them, rolling down his cheeks.

Kate's heart was breaking and she laid her husband's head gently onto the ground and climbed slowly to her feet reaching out towards her son and moving towards him instinctively, only to feel the restraining pull of her father's hand on her arm.

"Don't," Elliot said to his daughter. "Look after Simon. Soulis is too strong for us. We must think. We must use what we know. What was Truman trying to tell us?"

Kate sobbed as she watched her son crying and struggling in the arms of this monster. "I can't. I can't leave him. I must go to him."

Elliot held her tightly, "No, wait. You can't help him that way. Think...think." He pulled his daughter to him and pulled her to a sitting position alongside Simon, rocking her gently in his arms.

"The police!" he said suddenly "Where are the police?"

Soulis laughed. "There is your help," indicating a damp corner of the chamber. Elliot squinted into the darkness just making out an indeterminate shape in the corner, moving slowly. Shining the torch at it, he stared with horror as he saw the Red Cap astride the mutilated bodies of what had obviously been two policemen piled one upon the other and so mutilated it was hard to distinguish them as anything more than a pile of butchered flesh.

Elliot realised that their concerns that the police might frighten off Soulis were illusory. It would take more than a couple of policemen to stop this madman in his own environment.

Ripping and feeding with powerful jaws, the Red Cap stopped as the light from the torch hit him and he glared menacingly at Elliot, its jaws slowly working.

As if to terrify them further, as they watched he pulled off his matted cap and slowly and deliberately dipped it into the blood pooling in the body cavity where one of the policeman's stomach had been.

Happy that he had completely soaked the cap in the gore, he pulled it tightly back over his head.

They watched in horror as rivulets of the policeman's blood ran down the creatures face and dripped onto the blood-matted rags he was wearing. The foul dwarf snarled triumphantly.

Soulis seemed to feed off the horror on the faces of the humans and laughed loudly.

Kate buried her face into Elliot's chest unable to look any further upon the horror before her. He hugged her close, feeling her tears soaking through his shirt.

He then saw something that shook him to his very core. As Soulis laughed, Thomas stopped crying and looking at Soulis he gurgled happily and began to laugh along with him.

Hearing her son laughing, Kate raised her head from her father's chest and looked towards him horrified.

"What has he done to Thomas?" she looked distraught. "How can Thomas be laughing at that?" she waved her hand in the general direction of the mutilated corpses without wishing to gaze upon it further herself.

Elliot was as shocked as his daughter. Had somehow the evil within Soulis been transferred into his chuckling grandson? As he watched he saw Thomas reach out a chubby little hand trying to grasp hold of the wild red beard of Soulis, whose reaction triggered something in Elliot's mind.

Soulis pulled his head away from the child's hand sharply and immediately pushed the child straight out before him again at arms length in the same way he had held him when they first entered the chamber. As he had taunted the humans with the sight of the dead officers he had allowed the arm holding Thomas to drop slightly and as his elbow bent, Soulis's face had come within the reach of the child's arms.

Kate was still wondering why Thomas was laughing, more concerned that somehow he had been 'contaminated' by the evil that he had been exposed to since he had been taken, or somehow was in some kind of shock brought about by the trauma of it.

Elliot whispered quietly into Kate's ear, "That monster is uncomfortable with Thomas. He does not like him close."

Kate looked at Soulis who had stopped laughing and was staring at Thomas in disgust, but it was apparent to her that he could kill Thomas any time he wanted, in any one of a number of ways that she was desperately trying to avoid thinking about. It seemed impossible that her small helpless son could cause any discomfort to the evil giant who held him.

"What are we going to *do*?" she pleaded with her father as she turned to Simon who was stirring painfully, struggling to raise himself with a massive effort onto one elbow as he tried to focus his one good eye on Soulis and Thomas.

"He is laughing because Soulis was," Elliot said. "He can't possibly understand all that," he pointed at the mutilated bodies of the police officers and the Red Cap feeding on them. "He is laughing because he recognises happiness, just as he laughs when he sees you, Simon or I laugh, it is his inherent goodness, his pleasure at seeing people happy. He wants people to be happy."

Kate was not sure how that helped. She still had an almost uncontrollable urge to rush to Thomas and take him out of the arms of that monster but she realised it would be useless.

"What did Truman say to you earlier about childhood and fairies?"

Kate thought back, "He said I should examine my own childhood, nursery rhymes and fairy stories."

"I think I understand what he meant." Elliot paused before continuing, "Why in all children's stories and fairy tales do the witches, the wizards, the monsters always hate children?"

Kate looked puzzled.

"Because," Elliot continued, "they are good. They hate them for being their very antithesis, for being good. Soulis hates Thomas because his goodness is painful to him. That is why he avoids his touch. That is why Truman said he was our best weapon. Thomas can hurt Soulis much more than we can."

As if to reinforce what he was saying, Soulis dumped Thomas unceremoniously onto the chest before him, laying him on his back and holding him there with one hand. His other hand disappeared beneath his cloak and emerged again with a long thin glistening blade.

Too long to be a dirk, this looked like some kind of ceremonial knife or parrying dagger that might have been carried by a medieval lord to indicate his status. The long, thin blade glistened in the candle light, the hand guard was narrow and the handle looked to be gold with silver filigree woven intricately around it. He held the point to Thomas's neck, pointing up under his chin.

"I tire of you and your spawn of Ercildoune. It is time: time for me to take my place in your world and for this creature to take mine in Hermitage." He closed his eyes and began an almost unintelligible muttering under his breath as he performed some well-practised mantra.

Kate looked at Thomas who seemed mesmerised by the muttering of Soulis, just as he had been on that first night she had seen him with Truman. He stared upwards into Soulis's eyes, not frightened, not happy, as if he were in a trance.

"Stop!" Kate screamed, "Stop!" She struggled to her feet but Elliot pulled her down again. Leaning on her he raised himself to his feet.

"No," his voice had an air of finality. "Thomas needs you. Let me."

Elliot had no clear idea of what he was going to do as he walked slowly towards Soulis, but he had to stop him somehow. He tried to seek some help from what Truman had said to him, 'You are not alone. What did you come here for? Who did you call upon? Thomas is special.' It made no sense to him as he moved relentlessly forward towards the giant.

As he approached to within a few yards of the muttering giant, Soulis opened those cold soulless eyes and stared deeply into Elliot's. His cruel smile chilled Elliot to the core.

"It is time," Soulis said raising the dagger high above his head over the small defenceless body of Thomas. "And now my little foul friend," he looked across at the Red Cap, "your reward, the adults are yours."

Like a trained guard dog the Red Cap raised his head slowly from the corpses with which he had been toying like a cat with a mouse and turned his vile head towards where the prostrate Simon and the kneeling Kate were.

He leaped nimbly to his feet, the razor claws clicking on the stone floor and, snarling, approached them slowly.

"No!" Elliot lunged forward in terror. His effort to hide his terror and his inherent feeling of weakness left him and he screamed for help.

"No! Leave them! Leave them! God help me! Someone, please? Dad, where are you! Help me! If you are there, please help me!"

The cry came from deep within his terrified soul, as for the second time that night he called like a helpless child on his father for help.

His eyes were blinded with tears as he grasped despairingly at Soulis trying to block the downward arc of the knife. It sliced through his upper arm and Soulis grasped Elliot by the throat. He felt the life being choked out of him as Soulis raised him bodily from the ground and then the sharp pain as the dagger pressed against his lower abdomen as Soulis slowly and deliberately pushed it into his stomach.

As the knife entered like a hot poker deep into him he heard a voice behind him; a voice he had not heard for a long time.

"I'm here David," the voice said quietly, "I'm here, son."

CHAPTER THIRTY-THREE

"Perhaps you will serve coffee and drinks in the lounge and then you and the rest may leave. Thank you for an excellent meal."

Dettori spoke quietly to the head waiter who nodded politely and clapped his hands sharply at the waiters who stood hands clasped behind their backs along the far wall awaiting further instructions.

They scurried away quickly as the six colleagues made their way out of the dining room into the lounge and sat again in the comfortable leather seats.

Coffee was brought and laid on a low table and the head waiter poured one for each of them. Bowing formally to Dettori he acknowledged with a nod of his head Dettori's dismissal and he and the waiters silently left the room.

Dettori waited thirty minutes, giving the staff time to collect their belongings and leave. Ensuring that they would be alone.

"I suppose I need to serve myself," Romanski said aggressively, climbing clumsily out of the deep armchair and heading for the bar. Walking behind it he removed the bottle of vodka from the freezer and returned to his seat carrying the frost covered bottle and a shot glass.

"My people are trustworthy. I do not have to send them away to ensure discretion," he smiled malevolently. "The last man who spoke out of turn in my presence never spoke again. I cut his tongue out with scissors in front of my key employees. No one would ever dare cross me."

Dettori for once let his gentle smile slip, the menace in his voice seemed to be accentuated by the quietness of his reply.

"I am sure you are an excellent disciplinarian, Gregori. Let me assure you, so am I.

"I want to go through the details for tomorrow." Dettori's eyes left Romanski's and he looked at each of his guests in turn.

"Mr Soulis will arrive tomorrow afternoon. I will go to meet him. He has not informed me of exactly what time we will return, but you will be ready for him. We will all be ready to take our instructions."

Romanski exploded with anger his face almost purple with rage, "I take instructions from no one. Who the hell does this Soulis think he is to presume to instruct me?"

Susan Coltrane, Robertson, Clemenza and Erikson looked towards Dettori wondering how he would handle the Russian giant.

No one liked Romanski particularly, but Susan at least felt he had a point. None of them apart from Dettori, she assumed, had met Soulis and yet they had all to some degree gone along with the opportunities that had presented themselves.

However business was business and there was no room for sentiment. Challenges to run any consortium were frequent and often bloody. There was no reason why the Soulis Foundation should be any different.

Dettori looked at each of the delegates in turn apparently assessing their position before returning his gaze to Romanski. No longer was there the pretence of a smile. He stared coldly, directly into the eyes of the Russian who was still shaking with rage.

"I trust this is the vodka talking, Gregori," he spoke softly. "I expect your unconditional loyalty to our mentor, William Soulis. There is no question of a challenge to his authority from you," he turned to the others, "or any of you."

Susan Coltrane smiled brightly at Dettori. She was no fan of Romanski but she also knew that he had a point.

"Dear Andrea," her voice was as sweet as the smile she cast in Dettori's direction, soft and reassuring in direct contrast to Romanski's aggressive tone, "I'm sure Gregori like the rest of us is extremely pleased with how our association has worked out, and it is not the time for us to fall out with each other. But businesses must be run by the right person. Blind obedience is simply not good business, surely?"

Dettori was quiet for a moment, considering his words carefully before speaking.

"This is not a normal situation," he answered. "Tomorrow William Soulis will be here and he will take responsibility for the direction we all take. This is not negotiable. I expect your loyalty. If I cannot rely on it then we must resolve this now."

He looked at them all in turn before continuing.

"Five years ago I came to you all with a business opportunity. To build a foundation that would become the most powerful in the world. You were all hand-picked for what you brought to the Foundation. You, Susan, with your financial expertise and contacts, Clemenza with your unparalleled network in human frailty, Erikson your global communications empire, you, Robertson with your political contacts and finally you, Gregori with your access to oil and gas resources and armaments.

"We have a unique grouping through which power can be exercised," he continued.

"Everyone knows what we bring to the party," Romanski replied. "The question is: what does this unknown Soulis bring? No one has ever heard of him! What gives him the right to run this foundation?"

Dettori sighed, "Gregori, have you forgotten the 250 million dollars I transferred to your personal bank account as a sign of my good faith? The same amount was deposited in each of your accounts. William Soulis spent 1.25 billion dollars as a sign of his commitment. I heard no one questioning him then."

Romanski waved a dismissive hand. "I am worth at least $10 billion – your 250 million is peanuts."

"I think you will find you are worth around $8 billion, Gregori, and at least fifty percent of that as a direct result of the mergers, acquisitions and partnerships we have organised for you. You have all benefited in exactly the same way."

Dettori was gratified to see that Clemenza, Erikson and Robertson were nodding in agreement. Only Romanski and Susan Coltrane remained uncertain.

Romanski's tone became slightly more conciliatory. "Look, I am not saying we have done badly, we have not. We are in a good position to make more money than any organisation has ever made, to be more powerful than any one grouping has ever been. We need to ensure that the person who leads this foundation has the balls and the track record to cope when the going gets tough."

"And that person would be you of course?" Dettori replied starkly.

"I have the armaments, the experience and most of all, I have the balls." Romanski was beginning to raise his voice again.

Dettori sighed.

"I will not debate this, we are too close to completion. I want the personal assurance from all of you that William Soulis has your unquestioned loyalty and I want that assurance right now."

Romanski started to speak, but Dettori held up his hand to cut him off. "Let me hear from the others first," he said quietly looking towards Erikson.

The quiet Swedish/American answered in his pedantic tone.

"I still own a controlling interest in a media business that has doubled in size since we joined forces. Mr Soulis has proved his worth to me as a businessman and his commitment by the investment he made unquestioningly, of $250 million. I am happy with the arrangement."

Dettori turned his gaze to Robertson.

The tall Englishman took a large swallow of brandy. "I am not as rich as you gentlemen – and lady," he added bowing graciously towards Susan, "but I am richer now than I was five years ago by some considerable margin. I have no reason to question the mysterious Mr Soulis."

Clemenza looked up to see Dettori looking at him expectantly. He struck a large match and lit a huge Havana cigar, blowing out a large cloud of blue/grey smoke towards the ceiling before answering.

"Me too," he said eventually. "I see no reason to change something that is working well."

"That leaves you, Susan," Dettori spoke gently, "Where do you stand?"

Susan leaned forward to place her drink on the low table, conscious of the eyes that immediately went to her cleavage as she bent.

"I agree we have all done well and I am not suggesting we should change anything for the sake of it. But I do believe we should hear Gregori out. After all, things change. Who is to say that what is right for us now might not be what is right in the future?"

"I will take that as a 'don't know', Susan. Very well, I think I already have your view, Gregori."

The Russian scanned them all briefly before replying, "We do not need to change very much," he said eventually, "but I am not a follower. I believe I am the right person to head this foundation and that is what I propose."

Dettori rose from his seat and walked to the bar where he lifted a telephone, pressing a single internal button.

"Please come in," he said into the telephone before replacing the receiver.

He turned to the five who sat watching him expectantly.

"As of this moment my dear Gregori," he said, directing his gaze at Romanski, "you are relieved from your position on the Soulis board. I have sent for your replacement, he will be with us shortly."

Once again, Romanski's face went purple with rage and he heaved his considerable bulk from the armchair lunging awkwardly in the direction of the small Italian.

"Who the hell do you think you are talking to you little Italian faggot? I will rip your head off. You think you can talk that way to me?"

He surged towards Dettori, his arms outstretched aiming to close around his throat.

Dettori made no attempt to move as the huge Russian closed on him. He merely turned his head towards the door which had quietly swung open.

In the doorway stood a tall, thin young man dressed in an expensive but still ill-fitting suit. Some people could not look smart regardless of how much they spent on clothing.

A thin neck poked out from an over-large collar, and a badly tied knot on an unironed tie made him look like a student dressed unwillingly for a family wedding.

The young man had a greasy complexion with serious acne, and his hair looked as if it needed a good wash and comb. He stared nervously out into the room through thick horn-rimmed glasses.

"Come in Vladimir; join us please," Dettori said smiling warmly.

Romanski stopped in his tracks as he stared at the young man standing in the doorway. His jaw fell open and he looked as if he had seen a ghost.

"No need to introduce you Gregori I'm sure."

He turned to the others who were sitting staring unsure of what exactly was happening.

"Let me introduce you to your new colleague and Gregori's replacement." He returned his gaze to Romanski who was still staring in disbelief at the young man.

"Meet Vladimir Romanski, Gregori's only son."

The seated party were not sure they understood what was going on, so Dettori continued.

"Vladimir is Gregori's only son, but more importantly, sole heir to Gregori's holdings in STATOL. We no longer need you my dear Gregori," he said quietly.

Suddenly the lounge that had plunged into complete shocked silence was raked by an explosion that shook the room and the twin doors separating the lounge from the main hall, blew inwards, both doors coming off their hinges completely and collapsing on the floor inside the room.

CHAPTER THIRTY-FOUR

Blood erupted into Elliot's mouth as Soulis withdrew the knife from his stomach and let him fall helpless at his feet. A huge sigh escaped Elliot's lips as the air seemed to escape his body. With an enormous effort he rolled away from the feet of his attacker, clutching at the wound in his stomach and stared in the direction that the voice had come from.

There, standing quietly at the entrance to the corridor that they had entered the chamber from, stood a figure. Not tall, but a stocky defiant figure he had not seen for almost thirty years.

He recognised immediately his father standing, staring directly and with purpose straight ahead into the eyes of Soulis.

"I'm here, son," he said again and Elliot, sobbing from his position lying on the dank floor, reached a blood-soaked arm towards the comforting figure of his father.

Walking forward, Elliot's father knelt and despite being physically considerably smaller than his son, he picked him up effortlessly and carried him back to where Kate and Simon sat. He laid him gently on the ground beside them.

"Look after him Kate," he said quietly.

For the first time since they had entered the chamber, Soulis looked concerned. Not by this one figure, but what he knew it represented.

Elliot's father spoke deliberately and slowly, "Yes, you let us in Soulis. Your vanity once again. You let us in."

He knelt by his stricken son and Elliot felt his head taken into strong cool hands. Looking down at his stricken son, he stroked his forehead. "I'm here," he said again soothingly.

Kate was staring at this figure kneeling and holding onto her father. She had been three years old when her grandfather died, but somehow she recognised him. Holding his son's head in one hand he beckoned to Kate with the other. "Kate," he said softly, "Simon."

Simon rose painfully to his feet leaning heavily on Kate.

"Look after your father and your husband," he said touching Kate's arm gently, but never once taking his eyes off the tall figure of the wizard.

As Kate knelt and took her father's head again in her lap she watched as her grandfather stood and faced Soulis.

"You fool, Soulis. You could not resist tormenting these people who have done nothing to you except to be born to the wrong ancestors. You had to bring them here to witness your slaughter of their child."

Kate was desperately trying to staunch the flow of blood from her father's stomach. Removing her fleece and bunching it tightly against the wound, she applied as much pressure as she could to try and stem the flow, but she knew the wound was bad and her father was losing blood dangerously quickly.

At the same time she kept her eyes on her grandfather, stood before Soulis and on her son who was lying prostrate and vulnerable on top of the chest and under the blade of the weapon in Soulis's, hand which was still dripping with her father's blood.

Simon hobbled alongside Kate's grandfather determined that he would do whatever he could to help.

"I don't understand," he said looking at this complete stranger who obviously meant so much to his father-in-law.

"He disturbed the balance," the senior Elliot said. "There is a natural barrier around this place, around all places of evil, it is what keeps this creature in here," he said looking at Soulis with disdain. "It is created by the totality of evil that builds up in one place."

"Multiple hells," Simon said almost to himself as he recalled Truman's explanation of heaven and hell.

"Anything trapped in here is prevented from leaving. Soulis wants to get out by leaving a suitable replacement here retaining the balance, that replacement he intends to be Thomas.

"But he overlooked or ignored in his vanity one thing, the trap can be weakened by disturbing the balance in here between good and evil."

Simon looked confused.

"By bringing Thomas and three people who love him deeply into this place he has weakened the barrier between the two worlds. The barrier can be breached."

Simon was still confused, "But surely that just means it is easier for him to get out of this place."

"Yes," came the reply. "Yes it makes it easier for him to get out. But the barrier operates both ways. It also keeps those in spirit from coming in. By weakening the barrier he makes it easier for him to get out, but it also means we can get in."

Soulis had recovered from his shock of seeing the older Elliot and recovered his composure. "Do you really think you alone, a thirty-year-dead nobody can really face up to a seven hundred year old adept?" he mocked. Turning to the Red Cap who had stopped unsure and uncomfortable by this sudden unexpected appearance, he ordered him forward.

"Kill this nobody," he ordered.

"Alone?" came the reply. "Oh, but I didn't come alone..." and turning towards the charging Red Cap he waved a hand as if beckoning someone or something from behind him.

With a howl that echoed around the chamber a huge black shape careered headlong from out of the tunnel. Red eyes burning and yellow fangs exposed came the frightening apparition they had seen in the cemetery. Snarling and howling, the barguest threw itself headlong at the Red Cap.

The Red Cap fought back viciously rolling on his back. Like a cat it presented the barguest with four sets of razor sharp talons. Blood sprayed across the chamber as a vicious kick slashed open the barguest's stomach, but the weight of the charging dog pinned the Red Cap to the ground and he locked powerful jaws around the Red Cap's left shoulder. Bone cracked as the jaws locked and ripped.

As they watched these two strange creatures locked in this life and death struggle, Kate, Elliot and Simon failed to notice Soulis pull Thomas from the top of the chest and dump him unceremoniously at his feet as he threw back the lid.

Their eyes were drawn once again to the wizard as an ear-piercing scream emanated from the chest and they watched in horror as another Red Cap leapt out of it, followed by another and another. Soon a seemingly endless stream of vile dwarves surrounded Soulis, a heaving, seething, mass of snarling, foul-smelling death.

"Welcome to my hell!" Soulis screamed as he stood in the midst of his gruesome army.

Elliot's father stood defiantly in the face of the overwhelming forces railed against him. Simon was trying to hold himself together as he took his side but obviously still in serious pain. Kate sat holding her father's head in her lap. His breathing was shallow and his face a deathly white.

"And welcome to my family, Soulis," came the reply as stepping from the corridor behind him appeared a young man. He looked around nineteen and he was wearing a First World War army uniform.

"Meet my father, Walter Kerr Elliot."

The young man in the uniform smiled and Elliot, through tear hazed eyes looked into the face of his grandfather who had died in 1930 – almost twenty years before Elliot himself was born and when his own father was just five years of age.

"And my uncles, Andrew James Elliot and Adam Sherlaw Elliot also of the Northumberland Fusiliers. You think that your hell holds any fears for them?"

The two brothers stood turned towards each other as Adam leaned to light a cigarette from a proffered match held by his brother.

Elliot knew that these young men had died aged twenty and nineteen, just a few months apart in the slaughter that was the Somme in 1916 where 72,000 died in a pointless and unimaginable hell of mud, artillery and machine gun fire, that started in July 1916 and was only stopped in November of that year by the onset of winter.

The strange clan roll call continued.

"Their father, Walter, his father, Andrew, his father, John..." The procession of ancestors poured into the room, each family head, surrounded by his sons as they ranged before Soulis and his army of snarling Red Caps.

Simon backed up staring open mouthed at the incredible sight before him. He dropped to his knees next to Kate, who was still cradling the head of her father in her lap, and holding his arm which was clamped across the fleece pressed against his stomach.

She looked into her father's ashen face and saw tears welling in his eyes as he stared upon the father and the family that meant so much to him, arrayed defiantly before the Soulis army. She could only imagine what it must feel like for him to see again the father he had missed every day for close to thirty years.

The cacophony of noise from the life and death struggle between Soulis's familiar, Robin Red Cap and the barguest and the animal snarling of the Soulis legion of Red Caps was suddenly added to by the sound of horses from a distance but growing louder.

Suddenly with a crescendo of noise a stream of small, stocky horses crashed into the chamber peeling off alternately circling from left and right. Upon the back of each horse was a rider, dressed in the classic garb of the 'Best light cavalry in Europe', the Elliot Clan, the Border Reivers. Some carried long spears; others brandished short swords or axes and wore steel bonnets and light quilted jackets embedded with small steel plates to protect them.

Elliot knew that each of these men had met, unflinching, some kind of personal hell. Some at the end of a rope, beheaded or drowned in a drowning pool. Others had been imprisoned and starved to death, or faced death by disease and famine.

The lucky ones had died at the end of a sword or battleaxe, either as they raided, or fighting like men possessed at the many blood-soaked battlefields of Scotland or the North of England.

This irregular cavalry lined up before the legions of Soulis. Horses rearing and snorting, their hot breath steaming from flared nostrils as they shook long, untamed manes, their hooves clattering noisily on the stone floor and stirring the centuries of mud and slime that covered it, in an almost unbearable cacophony of war.

Suddenly the horses parted at the centre and a gap appeared in the middle as a small, stocky man strode purposely to the fore standing alongside Elliot's father.

At a little over five feet tall, he was also dressed in a steel bonnet and quilted sleeveless jacket over a long sleeved, dark red shirt. Brown trousers were tucked into knee-high boots turned over at the top.

His scarred face was framed by dark brown collar length hair and a full moustache covered his upper lip and drooped around the side of his thin mouth to his chin. His hand rested on a large sword at his waist.

He glared at Soulis with cold brown eyes.

Elliot knew instinctively who he was before the small stocky figure announced himself in a voice that belied his small stature.

"My name is Little Jock Elliot," he roared. "*Wha daur meddle wi' me?*"

CHAPTER THIRTY-FIVE

Batnykov's feeling that something was seriously wrong was undiminished.

The jet containing the rest of his assault team had landed and his men had disembarked in seconds, the jet taxiing to the end of the runway and turning so it was ready for immediate take off at the end of the mission.

Leaving three men to guard the runway and jet, the rest of the team had advanced on the building. They lay off some twenty metres away from the building, invisible amongst the shadows, trees and bushes and watched as the staff climbed into an assortment of vans and elderly cars and drove away down the main drive.

Any possible external communications including telephones and satellite dishes were disabled speedily.

Batnykov had deployed seven men around the perimeter of the property watching all possible exits from the building as well as positioning them so as to be able to detect any possible approach from outside.

An external sweep of the castle, using scanners to search for body heat, showed no trace of a single person in the entire building other than the six people he was expecting to find and one other. The six were congregated together in the front of the house in a single room that Batnykov knew was the lounge and bar. The seventh person was a mystery and was unexpected but he also was easily containable, being located in a small anti room directly off the bar area where the others were.

There was not a single trace of any other personnel anywhere within the building or in the grounds.

Perhaps Romanski was right after all – maybe Dettori didn't think he needed security. If he believed that, then he was shortly to find out his error.

Batnykov made one last radio sweep of all his men including those back at the runway. Each response confirmed that everything was fine.

It was time to go in.

Slowly the ten remaining men approached the front door. Batnykov tried the handle and the door swung open silently onto a large entrance hall. Fully lit, there was no sign of any activity of any kind.

"Colonel," a soldier at Batnykov's side touched his shoulder and positioned the heat scanner before him. Batnykov noted that the seventh figure had now moved into the bar lounge and was with the others.

He nodded acknowledgement. This made life even easier as there was now a single group to be contained.

Batnykov pulled a stun grenade from his belt. The noise and shock would terrorise and disorientate the targets, making them incapable of any coherent combined action.

"Go," he said and seven of the men swept silently into the hall passing without a glance the lounge where all the targets were located. They all had predetermined points in the building to secure to ensure no approach to the lounge could be made from any internal location without meeting one of Batnykov's men.

Batnykov watched as the seven men disappeared from view en route to their posts leaving just Batnykov and the two soldiers, his most trusted comrades, who had travelled with him.

Whilst Batnykov covered them his two colleagues slipped into the hall and placed small explosive charges at each hinge point on the double doors to the lounge and one at the lock.

The complete lack of proper security suggested to Batnykov that the doors were probably open anyway, but he wanted no possible delay entering the room, so he was taking no chances. In any event the explosion was part of the plan of attack. The deafening noise which he knew from experience was painful to the ears, coupled with the stun grenade would further disorientate the targets, ensuring Batnykov and his men could secure the targets in seconds.

As the two soldiers returned to his side Batnykov rolled in the stun grenade into the empty corridor and the men flattened themselves against the external walls to protect themselves from the blast, triggering the small charges at the doors at the same time.

The hall was filled with noise and smoke and before the sound of the blast had died away the three soldiers burst into the hall, crashing through the gap where the lounge doors had once stood but now lay flat on the floor of the lounge having been taken completely off their hinges.

The three men rushed in spreading out. One went left the other right with Batnykov himself taking centre ground. Before the final echo of the explosion had died away, machine pistols were aimed directly at the seven people in the room.

As the noise and smoke subsided Batnykov checked that none of the captives had bolted or hidden behind furniture and was satisfied that each was accounted for and covered by the three machine pistols.

"Put your hands on your heads and kneel down. Keep very still," Batnykov barked in perfect English.

With a look of terror, Erikson, Robertson, Clemenza, Coltrane and Vladimir Romanski complied, falling awkwardly to their knees with their hands already interlaced above their heads.

Only Romanski and Dettori remained standing.

Romanski laughed loudly and approached the nearest of the three soldiers reaching for the automatic pistol at the soldiers side. Only to feel the vice like grip of the soldier's hand grasp his wrist and thumb and bend it painfully back against the joint, holding it just at the point where, with one further twist, it would snap like a twig.

Romanski squealed with pain as the soldier looked across at Batnykov for instructions.

Batnykov nodded at the soldier, "Let him have it," he said.

The soldier let go of Romanski's wrist and pulled out the sidearm, spinning it around to pass it, hand-grip first to Romanski.

Ignoring the pain in his wrist, Romanski took the pistol and walked across to where Dettori was still standing defiantly, pressing the cold steel under the chin of the small Italian.

"I warned you many times about your lack of security, Dettori. You should have listened," the Russian was inches from the smaller man's face and Dettori could smell the foul odour of Romanski's breath.

"What is my son doing here?" he continued, looking across at the skinny youth kneeling in terror a few feet away.

"I explained to you, Gregori," Dettori's calm demeanour did not seem to have wavered, "you are no longer required by the Foundation. Your stupidity and arrogance has made you surplus to requirements."

Romanski stared in surprise at the sheer confidence that Dettori exuded. "You have balls my little Italian cocksucker, I'll give you that, but you will not have them for much longer I assure you."

Dettori continued unfazed. "When you are dead your son will inherit. He has already agreed to release a controlling interest in STATOL to the Foundation, and he will take your place on the board."

Romanski's face coloured and his eyes blazed in the direction of his kneeling son, "You little bastard..."

Dettori interrupted him, "Gregori, you should be proud of him. He is even more ruthless than you. He has made the right decision, when he takes over from you – even with his reduced shareholding – his net worth will be at least twice what yours is now."

"As he will now die with you Dettori, he will not have the opportunity to benefit from his inheritance."

Romanski turned to the others in the Foundation who were still kneeling, terrified, not sure what was going to happen next.

Romanski spoke to the kneeling directors. "Dettori and my son will die, as will this William Soulis, if and when he actually arrives tomorrow. You on the other hand have a choice."

Romanski walked over to where he had left his bottle of vodka. "My vodka is warm now," he threw the three-quarters full bottle violently against the far wall and walked behind the bar to retrieve another from the freezer. He placed the automatic pistol on the bar while he opened the fresh bottle, poured himself a shot and knocked it back in one, immediately pouring out another. Picking up the pistol again in one hand and his drink in the other, he returned to the kneeling board members.

"You have a choice. You will submit to my chairmanship and you will follow me as the new head of the Foundation. I expect you all to assign a controlling interest in your companies to me tomorrow. Don't worry, you will still run your individual businesses, but they will all become subsidiaries of STATOL."

He swallowed back the vodka. "You will have a shareholding in STATOL, it will be small, but you will all still be rich."

Susan was the first to speak. "You say we have a choice," she said. "What choice?"

Romanski smiled broadly as if amused by his own joke. "You have the choice to die instead. Now wouldn't that be a terrible waste of such beauty, my lovely Susan?"

He lurched lecherously towards her and then checked himself, before smiling. There would be plenty of time for the delectable Susan later.

The smile disappeared from the Russian's face as he turned to Dettori. "Unfortunately my arrogant Italian, I have had enough of you and your secret master. You and that disloyal wretch that once I called a son will die here and now."

Romanski strode purposefully towards his kneeling son, pressing the cold barrel of the pistol to the youth's temple. The gathering saw a dark patch appear at the crotch of the youth's trousers as the terrified boy soiled himself, terrified and shaking the tears streaming down his face as the Russian cocked the automatic deliberately and slowly.

CHAPTER THIRTY-SIX

Soulis, his face filled with hatred, screamed at his army of Red Caps, "Destroy them, destroy them all!" and with a roar the two facing forces tore into each other.

Swords and spears slashed and stabbed as the dark army of vile dwarves leapt into the fray, slashing with tooth and claw, to be met by the tough Reiver warriors, slashing and stabbing with sword, axe and pike.

The cacophony of the hand-to-hand warfare was deafening, whinnying horses reared and bucked and steel clashed with claw.

Kate and Simon could only watch the incredible sight and sound. The war cries of these single-minded warriors battled fearlessly. Blood and screams of pain, mixed with the snarling and screeching of the Red Caps, as they clashed without quarter.

In the midst of this battle Soulis scooped up Thomas and started backing towards the far wall, keeping the damp stones to his back and the battle raging ahead, he placed Thomas on the floor and withdrew the dagger once more.

Kate screamed her voice almost inaudible in the noise of battle around her, "He is going to kill Thomas, he is going to complete the ritual! He is going to kill Thomas!"

Simon leapt to his feet, driving any thoughts of pain from his mind. He pushed his way forward, struggling through the battle raging around him, forcing his way through the heaving mass of bodies towards Soulis who had dropped to one knee and recommenced the muttering under his breath. Then like a javelin thrower he reached out one hand towards Thomas whilst raising the dagger high above his head.

Simon screamed, "No!" as he realised he was not going to get through the tangle of battling bodies in time, his outstretched arm reaching helplessly above the shoulders of the battling clansmen and Red Caps towards his son.

Soulis turned to Simon and smiled. A chilling smile, as if relishing the fact that this human was going to witness the death of his child. He revelled in the familiar elation and surge of energy that the pain he was causing to these weak humans always brought.

As he turned back to Thomas he paused, looking quizzically as the child was holding out to him the Ellot bracelet that he had pulled from the patch pocket on the front of his dungarees.

Simon's heart broke, as he saw his son, moments from death but hopelessly trying to present this evil murderer with his most precious gift.

"Keep your toys," Soulis said, "you will need them for the eternity you will be here."

Simon cried out as he saw his son attempting to play out the repetitive game he had played with Truman and at different times with all of them.

"No!" he screamed again as he struggled hopelessly, unable to reach Thomas.

At least it seemed Thomas was unaware of the extreme danger he was in; he smiled expectantly as he slipped the bracelet onto the outstretched wrist of the wizard.

Soulis looked at it in puzzlement as if distracted momentarily as Simon, with an almost superhuman effort, pushed aside several fighting bodies between him and his son. But to no avail, he was still too far away to really help Thomas.

Suddenly the chamber was split with a roar of anger that rose high above the sounds of the battle. So ear-splitting was the noise that the crash of sword and claw silenced, and the life and death battle was suspended instantly as the combatants turned towards the source of the scream. All eyes turned to Soulis who, staring at the band on his wrist had risen to his feet holding his arm out before him.

He staggered and fell back against the wall and as the strange audience watched in wonder, the bracelet began to tighten around Soulis's wrist so viciously that the wizard screamed out in pain. He looked on in disbelief as slowly the interwoven snakes on the bracelet began to move. One slithered, lengthening and widening as it did so, coiling anti-clockwise around Soulis's outstretched arm, it travelled up his arm towards his head.

Reaching Soulis's neck, it travelled on across his shoulders, encircling the other arm and travelling on down towards the wrist, pausing as it circled his arm from shoulder to wrist.

The second snake was travelling clockwise around his arm following the path of the first snake but this time clockwise until it reached Soulis's neck.

With both arms completely wrapped, the second snake coiled around Soulis's neck, and clamped its mouth onto the tail of the first.

Soulis's arms were stretched cruciform, and he fell back against the damp stone of the wall, as the coils tightened in a vice-like embrace. His head cracked hard against the stone as the huge wizard battled violently against the snakes, but each struggle seemed to tighten their grip.

Simon fought desperately, shoving and pulling the combatants to one side as he fought his way through the mass of bodies that were now standing, watching in wonder as Soulis struggled, screaming in fury against his bonds.

Simon managed to struggle through the remaining bodies and sweeping up Thomas from the floor he hugged him too his neck as he backed away from the writhing Soulis.

As Soulis screamed curses, to the right of his ear appeared a chubby child's hand no bigger than Thomas's, that slipped through the wall as if the stone were a sheet of water and grasped his long red hair pulling back violently so that his head cracked again hard against the wall.

This was followed by another equally tiny hand to his left which also grabbed his hair and clamped his head back from the other side.

Soulis's eyes rolled in terror as he tried to move his head to see what was gripping him.

Without taking his eyes off Soulis, Simon clasped Thomas protectively deep in his arms and backed cautiously through the staring combatants, desperate that at any moment one of the Red Caps would attempt to snatch his son back or turn its savage blood-lust towards him, but they all seemed totally focussed on the struggling warrior.

Further small hands appeared, each grasping, clawing and pulling at the body and cloak of Soulis. Hands pulled back on the hood, while others ripped at the cloak, pulling it open to expose his scar covered body, his muscular frame flexing and glistening with sweat as he tried to free himself. The hands continued to appear until finally dozens of them clamped tightly onto Soulis's head, arms, torso and legs.

Small pools of blood appeared around the fingers as they sunk deep into his flesh, the blood running in small rivulets down his body as the wizard was held motionless, flat against the cold stone wall; only his eyes and mouth able to move.

Once Soulis was no longer able to struggle, the two snakes pinning his arms and neck uncoiled partially and swung their heads towards the face of the trapped warrior and swayed before his terrified eyes which were wide with horror. His mouth was pulled wide open by the grasping hands, and seemed to be frozen in a silent scream, as the snakes opened their mouths wide and flattened out as if to strike at his eyes. Three-inch inward-curving fangs glistened against the pink, ribbed roof of the open mouths.

But the snakes did not strike, instead a movement could be seen inside the gaping jaws as small creatures began to appear from deep within and scrabble out of the snakes and drop onto the pinned body of Soulis.

The creatures were like black centipedes with multi-sectioned bodies and rows of legs that flowed, wavelike as they scurried, in all directions, across Soulis's body. Each creature was around three inches long and sported barbed horns on their heads above tiny red eyes. The tails turned up at the end and sported a scorpion like sting. Slowly at first, the creatures scurried out of the mouth of the snakes, the trickle growing into a steady swarm until Soulis's body seemed to shimmer and writhe with a black sheen.

Simon eventually backed up to where Kate was kneeling and she reached out, eyes flooding with tears as she clasped Thomas tightly to her, rocking him and burying his face into her breast as if to protect him from the horrific sight before them.

Suddenly, Soulis, who had been silenced briefly by the tightness of his binding, screamed in pain as the small centipedes began to clamp themselves like leeches to his body, firstly stabbing the flesh with the stinging tail and then sinking in the barbed horns.

So tightly did they attach themselves that any attempt to pull them away would certainly have ripped chunks of flesh from his body, but no such opportunity existed, and all Soulis could do was scream as one after another the thousands of creatures ripped into his flesh.

After a few seconds the clamped centipedes, one at a time, seemed to harden and lighten in colour, until they crumbled into light, golden sand and cascaded off Soulis's body to the floor around his feet, leaving behind a vicious open cut a few inches long. The wounds, though insignificant individually, criss-crossed and merged until Soulis's body began to look like raw meat.

The sand pile around Soulis's feet grew inexorably. Then terrifyingly, the creatures, who until now had attached themselves exclusively to the outside of his body, began to invade his mouth and nose, shuffling swiftly into him, silencing his screams as he began to gag as a constant stream of the horrific little creatures poured into his body.

The family watched in horror as they noticed Soulis's stomach begin to distend and Kate felt the bile rising in her throat as she realised the centipedes were turning to sand inside his body and slowly filling and choking him.

Soulis began to choke, spraying fine sand and blood out across the chamber, but the attack continued remorselessly until horrifyingly, the creatures turned their attention to his eyes and ears. The vicious horns burrowed into the corners of his eyes and through his eardrums causing trickles of blood to run from both ears and the corners of his eyes.

The distended stomach of their victim could take no more and split along the fault lines caused by the external cuts around his abdomen, and fine sand began to flow like small waterfalls from multiple exit wounds.

The creatures did not slow until Soulis's head slumped forward as he succumbed to the choking sand that filled his body and poured out of him, burying him to the waist. Slow streams of sand flowed from his hollow eyes, his mouth and his ears.

Soulis's body, encased from the waist down in sand, hung lifeless as the flow of centipedes ceased and the snakes closed their mouths. In a complete reverse of their original attack they slowly unwound shrinking back as they went, uncoiling back across his body until they reverted back into the bracelet that now hung from the limp wrist of the dead wizard before falling from the lifeless hand into the sand below.

The army of Red Caps, stood staring at their dead master, buried to the waist with fine sand still flowing with a faint sound slowly from empty eye sockets, open mouth and both ears. They stood unsure what to do, until a small stocky figure wielding a blood spattered sword, pushed forward to where a large black dog lay on it's side, body striped with vicious wounds, breath shallow.

Sitting astride it was Robin Red Cap, face coated with gore, body rising and falling, claws still embedded in the side of the barguest, his eyes fixed on Soulis until he sensed the presence of his enemy. The Red Cap stared with hatred into the eyes of Little Jock Elliot, as he raised his sword and with a practised and powerful stroke, swung the sword at the Red Cap, severing the head completely.

The remaining Red Caps, seemed disorientated as they looked first at Soulis and then at the body of their decapitated brother, Robin. Slowly at first, one or two backed away from the clan, then others followed until they formed a tight group around the wooden chest. Then still snarling defiantly, one at a time they stepped into the chest and crouching down, they disappeared one by one, as the family watched in wonder.

As the final Red Cap disappeared into the box, the small Reiver kicked the lid shut contemptuously.

Simon turned to Kate who was still rocking Thomas in one arm, whilst she stroked the head of her father cradled in her lap. He knelt alongside her and wrapped his arms around his wife and son as he felt tears begin to burn in his eyes as it began to dawn on him that they had somehow survived.

As the family sat there, still unsure of exactly what was happening, they watched as several of the clan began to pile wood and rags around the old wooden chest. When they had finished, Elliot's father, carrying two torches from the walls, approached the makeshift pyre and slowly and deliberately pushed them under the kindling and for a few seconds, watched as the fire grew, slowly enveloping the chest.

When he was sure that the chest was burning he turned and moved slowly to the family.

"We've got to get Dad to hospital," Kate looked into the bloodless face of her father, who stared up at her and Thomas. His eyes were filled with tears and he was attempting to smile.

Crouching down by his stricken son, her grandfather turned and smiled gently at Kate. "No hospitals, my son has come home. Look after your son, Kate," and taking Elliot's head into his hands once more, "let me take care of mine."

Kate cried out, "No! No, I can't leave him here, I won't leave him here!" She hugged her father's neck.

Her grandfather took her face in his hands, and looked deep into her eyes. "He is not staying here I promise you. It is his time."

Quietly, eight clansmen, including Andrew and Adam, his grandfather and great grandfather and others surrounded the stricken Elliot, and with practised hands, lifted him to their shoulders and carried him gently towards the corridor, his father leading this strange cortège slowly and quietly out of the castle.

Outside they lay him gently on the turf and backed away respectfully as Kate, clutching Thomas to her and Simon and Elliot's father knelt beside him again, Elliot's father taking his son's head in his lap.

Kate looked at her father. "No, we need to get Dad to hospital. Simon, maybe you can call from the radio in one of those police cars?"

Elliot's father looked at the couple gently, "Kate, your father is home. It is his time, he is with me and he will never lose me again."

Kate looked at her father and wept, "But I can't leave him here alone," she said the tears streaming down her face.

She looked into the ashen face of her father. As she watched he opened his eyes, looking at her, he struggled to raise his hand to her and he seemed to be trying to speak, but the effort seemed too much for him. Taking his blood-soaked hand, she clasped it to her cheek as she leaned closely in until her ear was inches from his mouth. Almost inaudibly he whispered to his daughter:

"Be happy Kate. I am. How many people get to really know they will see the people they love again, you will see me again...we will all be together again, look after Thomas and..."

His voice tailed away and he closed his eyes, his head rolling to one side in the embrace of his father's hands.

Kate wept.

Simon took his wife into his arms and he held her and his son, rocking gently and not speaking for several minutes.

Eventually he turned to Kate's grandfather, "I really don't understand what happened back there," he said.

"Your son saved you," came the reply, and seeing the continuing puzzlement on his face he continued. "Soulis broke the rules seven hundred years ago," he said quietly. "When he first called on the Red Cap for power he was granted virtual invulnerability and having been granted it he was warned not to call on the dark forces again for seven years."

Simon remembered how Truman had described it, "Steel shall not wound thee, cords bind thee, hemp hang thee or water drown thee."

"But he wanted more and he called him again before the seven years had passed. He was punished with a curse."

"Something about 'a coming wood'." Simon re-called the picture Truman had painted of the Elliots arriving to confront Soulis with staves of rowan wood.

"'Beware a coming wood and triple binds of sifted sand'," Elliot's father reminded him of the full curse.

"Soulis was destroyed the first time by the first part of the curse. Thomas destroyed him today by the second. The bracelet consisted of three bands, the twin snakes and the underlying bracelet."

"Sifted sand? I'm not sure..." Simon started.

"The three bands were hollow, each was filled with sifted sand, Thomas the Rhymer made it and gave it to your son."

"So somehow, Thomas knew how to destroy Soulis? Truman taught him?"

"No, Thomas knew nothing. He was just playing. That is what children do."

Simon recalled how Truman had continually played the repetitive game with Thomas, passing the bracelet backwards and forwards wrist to wrist, and how the three of them had played the game with him as well.

"Truman taught him how to destroy Soulis," Simon said.

"No, Thomas did not know how to destroy Soulis he was just trying to play with him. What killed Soulis was what ultimately destroys all evil. Soulis was destroyed by Thomas's natural goodness."

Simon and Kate looked at their son realising at last why Truman had set such store by him.

"Truman would not deliberately teach a child to kill, he just reinforced his instinct to be kind. Soulis died as a result of his own antipathy to good."

"One thing," Kate said, "who were those people who held Soulis to the wall, were they clan?"

Elliot's father rose to his feet. "No, they were the spirits of Soulis's young victims, the ones he sacrificed over the years.

"Thomas not only destroyed Soulis but he released those poor trapped children; they can now move on and be reunited with their loved ones. Thomas has done a great deal here, he is a very special child."

Laying the head of his son softly on the ground, he got to his feet.

"Take your son home Kate, Simon, and be happy, we will all meet again I promise you."

Simon and Kate watched as Elliot's father walked slowly back into the corridor, without turning back, disappearing into the darkness of Hermitage Castle, slowly followed by the ancestors who had carried her father's body.

Kate looked at Thomas who was watching his great grandfather, smiling and waving a chubby little hand to him.

CHAPTER THIRTY-SEVEN

Romanski's finger slowly tightened on the trigger of the pistol, pressed hard against the temple of his kneeling son who was now sobbing and begging for forgiveness.

"Shut up and be a man Vladimir," the voice was stern with a hint of disgust at the sight of this grovelling youth, kneeling terrified in a pool of his own urine which spread out around his knees, staining the expensive beige carpet on the floor of the lounge.

The group turned to Dettori who, still standing defiantly, had berated the youth for his lack of control.

Romanski turned to Dettori his face black with rage as he realised that the Italian was still defying him despite the fact that he must be aware that the Russian was about to kill him. He slowly raised the pistol from his son's temple and pointed it towards Dettori, aiming directly at the head of the small Italian. He paced slowly and deliberately towards him until the barrel was a couple of inches from Dettori's right eye.

"Kneel, you arrogant little bastard, kneel and I will end you quickly. Defy me and you will be a long time dying."

Dettori's eyes bore directly into Romanski's.

"I always detested you, you ignorant Russian peasant," all trace of Dettori's usual easy smile and careful politeness was gone, "but you were useful. Now your usefulness is at an end. I subjugate myself to no one but William Soulis. My one regret is that I have no time to take pleasure in watching you bow before him. You are unimportant and your time is at an end."

Romanski screamed with rage as he turned to Batnykov and his two colleagues as they stood pointing their machine pistols at the assembled group.

"Put this bastard on his knees!" flecks of saliva flew from Romanski's mouth as he bellowed at the soldiers.

Batnykov frowned. He hated this kind of sadistic nonsense, but he was realistic enough to know that this was as much a show to keep the others in line in the future, as inherent sadism. He nodded to the soldier to his right who was looking at him awaiting instructions.

At the signal the soldier walked forward purposefully, he had defeated countless trained soldiers in close contact, with or without weapons. This small, skinny businessman was almost an embarrassment to his dignity. He approached, transferring his weight to his left leg, intending to aim a downward kick at the Italian's knee. The damage to the knee joint and ligaments would force the man to his knees and it was unlikely that he would ever stand on it properly again.

As he raised his leg to kick, the small Italian shot his arm out in front of him, palm flat and pointed towards the soldier. His hand snapped six inches short of the soldier's chest but, nevertheless, the soldier expelled air as if he had been hit directly in the sternum and a searing pain shot through him as he was driven backwards, crashing awkwardly at the feet of Batnykov.

"Colonel Batnykov, you are an honourable man and a good soldier, you should not be working for this ignorant peasant." Dettori's natural charm and quiet voice had returned to normal. "Lay down your arms and I will let you live. You should not die with this Russian fool, you are an honourable man and you are good at your job, it will be a shame to kill you for the sake of this worthless thug. Will you accept my offer?"

All Batnykov's instincts told him this would end badly, but he also realised that he would never be trusted again if he were to change allegiances in the middle of a contract, his only course was to continue.

Romanski was still confused as to how this skinny little Italian had disabled the ex-special forces soldier, apparently without touching him, but as if suddenly realising the fact that he had a complete force of mercenaries at his disposal, he shook the doubts from his mind and turned again to Dettori.

"Enough talk," he said, and raising the pistol once more to within an inch of his adversary's eye, he cocked the gun and pulled the trigger.

The hammer clicked harmlessly as he re-cocked and fired once again, and again, the hammer seemed to be hitting on an empty chamber.

"You fool, you cannot fire your guns in here. Would you like to try, Colonel?"

Batnykov raised his machine pistol towards the ceiling and pulled the trigger. Nothing happened.

He slipped his pistol from his belt. Aiming at the ceiling he pulled the trigger, again nothing.

As Romanski stared uncomprehending at Batnykov, Dettori raised his hand and grabbed the barrel of the pistol Romanski was holding and twisted violently. Romanski had to release his grip or have his finger, trapped in the trigger guard, broken.

Batnykov tensed his muscles preparatory to launching himself at Dettori.

Dettori turned the gun around and pointed it directly at Romanski's eye. "Please stay where you are, Colonel. You cannot possibly reach me before I have killed both this Russian peasant and you."

Romanski was beginning to sweat profusely as he stared directly down the barrel of the automatic. "But you said the gun would not fire in here." Despite his terror he was trying to give the impression he was still in control.

"You see Romanski, this is why you will never amount to anything. You don't listen. I said YOU cannot fire your guns in here. I, on the other hand, can."

Romanski sighed briefly with relief as Dettori pulled the gun away from his eye then watched in horror as the small man aimed the pistol quite deliberately at the head of the soldier still lying at Batnykov's feet. The shot echoed around the room and a small, dark hole appeared directly between the eyes of the prostrate soldier. He was dead even before the exit of the bullet removed a good portion of the back of his skull, a dark crimson puddle pooling rapidly at the back of his head on the carpet.

He immediately swung the pistol in the direction of Batnykov, "I am sorry your men must die, but you of all people know it is an occupational hazard."

Batnykov expected his men to burst in, in approximately fifteen seconds. Having clicked the pre-arranged signal through his microphone, he analysed the distance between him and Dettori, estimating exactly how he would disable Dettori once he was distracted by his team's attack.

Batnykov counted the seconds in his mind, not wanting to tip Dettori off by looking at his watch, one thousand and one, one thousand and two, one thousand and three...

Dettori returned his attention to Romanski.

"Now, Romanski, it is time for you to kneel and to apologise to your colleagues for your lack of manners and causing them all of this distress."

One thousand and ten, one thousand and eleven...

"On your knees!" Dettori's raised voice, so out of character, shocked the kneeling Erikson, Robertson, Coltrane and Vladimir Romanski. Dettori turned quietly to them and smiled, "You my friends, please take a seat and make yourselves comfortable whilst I deal with this little annoyance."

The four paused for a moment, not sure they understood who was in control here, and they looked at each other in confusion, each of them seemed to be unwilling to be the one to make the first move.

"Please my friends, please, you are in no danger here," Dettori's voice was quiet and comforting.

Susan Coltrane slowly dropped her hands first and gently climbed to her feet. The others followed nervously, settling themselves into the chairs.

One thousand and fifteen, one thousand and sixteen, Batnykov braced himself, expecting imminently the explosion of stun grenades and the crashing of glass as his team poured in though the doors and windows. He needed to ensure they used knives rather than guns, he was still unsure as to what kind of technology Dettori had, which seemed to protect the room, selectively, from the use of firearms.

One thousand and nineteen, one thousand and twenty...they were late.

Romanski looked to Batnykov for help, he could not bring himself to kneel before the Italian.

"Ah, I had forgotten you, Colonel," Dettori spoke without turning away from Romanski. Viciously he kicked Romanski in the side of his right knee, causing the huge Russian to collapse clumsily on the floor, pitching forward he landed painfully on his arms as he braced to break his fall.

"You are of course expecting your men to come to your aid. I am sorry to tell you that will not be happening. Please go to the window." He waved Batnykov, with the barrel of the pistol, in the direction of the large front windows which were covered by floor length, heavy red drapes.

"Allow me," Dettori said as he walked towards the blasted doorway of the room and pressed a small, white switch on the wall. A gentle hum from a hidden electric motor started and the drapes slid silently open.

Batnykov, now standing directly before the window struggled to see out of the brightly lit room to the darkness outside. His vision was further obscured by the reflections of the internal lights on the glass.

Dettori pressed a small switch and the lighting in the room dimmed significantly, he then pressed yet another switch and the manicured lawn separated from the house by a wide gravel path was immediately illuminated by powerful floodlights mounted on the building.

Batnykov blinked and the first thing he saw was a large stone column about three feet tall, with a square slab bowl mounted on top like a largish birdbath, in the exact centre of the oval lawn. On top of the ornament was what looked like an oversized gargoyle, squatting and staring out across the grounds. When it moved as Batnykov watched, he suddenly realised this was no statue or gargoyle.

Turning to look over its shoulder, dark eyes staring malevolently directly at Batnykov, was a creature the like of which he had never seen before, or even imagined in his darkest nightmares. The creature had wide jaws with rows of razor sharp, yellow teeth, the lower face was matted, blood soaked beard, and bizarrely, pulled tight on its head was a gore encrusted red bonnet. The chest rose and fell, in short sharp breaths.

"Meet my security, Colonel. I am sure you will have encountered nothing like them before. They are known as Red Caps."

It was then that Batnykov's eyes were drawn ten metres or so to the right of this vile creature.

Batnykov had seen the horrors of many wars in Afghanistan, Africa, the Middle East and many other campaigns. He had seen great evidence of man's inhumanity to his fellow man.

But he had seen nothing like this.

Tears filled his eyes as he saw his men. Horribly mutilated, and piled like the carcases of dead animals. So hideously dismembered were the bodies that it was impossible to count them accurately, or even recognise men he had called colleagues and friends through many dark moments.

But he knew instinctively that they were all there, the seven who had been guarding the perimeter outside, the three whom he had left guarding the runway and the seven from inside the house.

Some still appeared to be twitching, but they were not alive, the movement was caused by a dozen or so of the vile creatures Dettori had called Red Caps, who were tearing and feasting on the bodies of his men.

"My God!" he choked as he fell to his knees and dropped his head into his hands.

"God has very little to do with it, Colonel." Dettori smiled as he admired the pure savagery of these creatures sent to guard him by his all powerful mentor.

Dettori turned to the remaining soldier, who was still standing his machine pistol aiming hopelessly into the room.

"I'm afraid I can leave you with no one, Colonel, but I will honour your courage by giving the last of your men an easy death." He pulled the trigger, killing the soldier outright.

"I am sorry I could not get you to change to the right side in this battle, but I admire your loyalty, even if this scum doesn't deserve it."

He turned to Romanski, who was physically shaking as he stared out of the window, still in his kneeling position, mouth hanging open in horror as he looked out onto the lawn.

Dettori seemed to think for a few seconds before speaking, "I am going to let you go, Colonel. You may leave now. This is a reward not only for your loyalty to your employer, I admire that, but for the good work you did in saving our distinguished colleague, Mr Clemenza, in Columbia."

He waved the weapon in the direction of the door, indicating Batnykov should leave.

"But I counsel you, Colonel, most earnestly. Never seek to go up against me again. We have repaid Clemenza's debt to you with your life, the books are balanced. If we meet again you will surely die."

"You expect me to go out there with those creatures? Why do you not just shoot me, have you not seen enough horror?"

"You have little faith, Colonel. I said you may leave, and that you will live. I am a man of my word, but if you stay here you will surely die. Please go now."

Batnykov got to his feet realising he had little choice. He took a last look at his fallen colleagues and then walked slowly out of the room, followed by Dettori to ensure he left by the front door and did not seek to escape through the house.

Seconds later the group saw him appear on the gravel drive outside and slowly walk towards the steps that led down to the grounds. Clearly he saw no point in trying to run from these creatures.

The Red Caps looked up at the approaching Russian and slowly moved towards him until he was completely surrounded. Batnykov stared directly ahead as the Red Caps who were now within a metre of him, snarled about him. He continued walking towards the steps, knowing that any second they would leap on him and tear him apart.

As he approached ever closer to the two directly in front of him he almost gagged as the foul breath of the creatures hit his face.

Then miraculously the creatures stepped aside and let him pass, he continued walking slowly and steadily, still expecting them to pursue and overpower him.

But they did not come.

The Russian colonel slipped into the trees surrounding the grounds and headed, tears streaming down his cheeks, through the woods to the village where he and his colleagues had left the hire car what seemed to be a lifetime ago.

CHAPTER THIRTY-EIGHT

Romanski climbed awkwardly to his feet and watched with the others as Batnykov passed remarkably through the hideous creatures that surrounded him. They had all braced themselves for the inevitable attack which never came and they kept watching until the colonel had disappeared into the woods.

"We have just one issue left to resolve." Dettori had returned to his position by the window and the waiting group.

"Our foundation is now complete with Vladimir taking the place on the board of his father. We shall be ready tomorrow for the arrival of our chairman, William Soulis, and you will have the privilege of meeting him for the first time."

He turned to Romanski, "Let us see if you have the same dignity and courage as the colonel. It is time for you to follow him."

"I thought you intended to shoot me," the large Russian said.

"You are finished with the Foundation, Romanski. Get out! Perhaps if you hurry you can catch up with the colonel and he will guide you through the woods."

Romanski looked out of the window at the huddle of Red Caps, a terrified look on his face.

He tried to smile, opening his hands in a gesture of friendship he stepped towards Dettori. "Look this has all gotten out of hand. We have all done well out of our relationship. Vladimir does not have the experience. I will honour the deal he has made with you and of course I will accept Mr Soulis's chairmanship. We can do great things together."

Dettori raised the pistol and smashed it viciously across the bridge of the nose of the huge Russian. "I told you to leave, Gregori, unless you would like me to shoot you in the knee and leave you to my friends outside. Go, catch up with the colonel."

Romanski looked from one to another, searching for any small indication that one of them might speak up for him. It was a hopeless wish.

Seeing there was nothing more he could achieve, he walked slowly towards the door, pausing to look at them once more. Seeing that further conversation was useless, he turned and left.

In the hall outside he considered running to the stairs, or down the hall away from the front door and the waiting Red Caps, but as he briefly moved in that direction he saw several Red Caps approaching him from the hall and down the stairs, blocking his escape. He backed away from them in terror as he realised he had no choice but to move to the front door and step outside into the night.

Dettori called all of his guests to the window and they assembled around, watching as Romanski appeared on the gravel near the front door. He paused and then set off in the direction that the colonel had gone minutes earlier, but unlike the colonel, he looked nervously from one Red Cap to another as he walked.

As had happened with Batnykov, the Red Caps closed around him and Romanski stopped. Then taking a huge breath he resumed his walk towards the Red Caps directly in front of him, looking for a sign that they would step to one side as had happened with the colonel.

He too gagged on the foul breath of the nearest Red Cap, he took one further step but the Red Cap did not give way. Snarling viciously he held up a claw in front of the terrified Russian's face.

Romanski could see fresh blood on the razor sharp claw just inches from his eye as he suddenly realised he had to die, otherwise Vladimir would not inherit.

For one brief moment he had imagined that he too might have been reprieved. His terror had allowed him to fool himself that he might survive. As the realisation hit him, he turned on the spot, looking from one snarling creature to another, unsure as to whether he should try to run back to the house, which was closer, or to the woods after the colonel. As he realised the futility of it, a loud scream of terror started in his throat as he covered his face to block out the horror around him.

Dettori turned to his colleagues in the room and spoke quietly, "You will remember this. I trust none of you will ever be foolish enough to question William Soulis's position again."

He returned his gaze to the window and nodded almost imperceptibly.

A loud scream of pain emanated from the Russian as one of the Red Caps slashed the back of his ankle, severing the Achilles tendon. His leg collapsed beneath him.

He then screamed again as the Red Caps tore into him, ripping open his stomach exposing his entrails, slashing and biting. The audience watched in horror as they realised the creatures were deliberately not killing the Russian, but purposefully inflicting the maximum pain.

As the slaughter continued, Vladimir threw up and collapsed to his knees, and Susan Coltrane turned her back, unable to look any more on the horror before her.

Dettori grasped a handful of the young Romanski's hair and roughly pulled him to a standing position, he took hold of Susan Coltrane's hair with his other hand and turned her around to face the window once more.

"You will watch; you will remember," he said coldly.

The young Russian was ashen as he stood with his mouth open, paralysed with fear as he watched the Red Caps playing sickeningly with the bloody mess that had once been his father.

Dettori turned his head towards Susan who was staring, eyes wide with horror, at the scene of carnage outside. His lips pressed close to her ear as he whispered quietly to her, "You questioned us Susan, and normally that is enough for you to die. But our master remembers our beautiful encounter in London the other night. He will forgive you – this time – you will be his when he comes, you will have the great honour of ruling with him. But never question us again. *Never*," his eyes suddenly became as cold and hard as flint.

Susan looked at Dettori in shock, confused by his words, but remembering the rough hands, the powerful body she had felt but not seen as she had been clamped to the bed.

She began to speak, "But that was you Andrea, surely I..."

Dettori cut her off, "Our master knows all and he experiences all. I have the honour to be his conduit to this world until he can return in person."

Susan's mind raced, torn between the horror she could see before her eyes and the almost more horrifying implications of Dettori's words.

Not for the first time that evening, she struggled to resist the urge to vomit.

The vicious attack seemed to continue for an eternity, until the Russian stopped screaming and it was apparent he had also stopped breathing.

"Our work for the night is complete. We can now concentrate on making ready for tomorrow. It has been an interesting evening. Perhaps you all need a drink?"

Dettori walked to the bar and started pouring drinks for everyone. He looked like any thoughtful host serving drinks to his dinner guests. His quiet politeness had returned and there was a gentle smile in his eyes again.

"Perhaps you would close the drapes, Vladimir, and turn off the floodlights. I think we have seen quite enough tonight, don't you?"

CHAPTER THIRTY-NINE

Kate and Simon sat hugging each other and Thomas for long minutes, watching as the morning sun began to rise slowly behind the distant hills, not knowing what they should do next.

The castle was silent, and the lifeless body of Kate's father lay on the grass beside them. "We can't leave him here any longer," she said stroking his forehead.

"I suppose we will need to call the police," Simon replied, "but God knows what we are going to tell them. You wait here I'll go to the police car and see if I can radio somebody."

He did not need to bother. As he rose to his feet he looked across the burn to the road and saw a procession of three marked police cars and a van, blue lights flashing, and one unmarked car, speed around the bend and pull to a halt by their car and the abandoned cars of the dead officers.

Simon sat again and waited as the police officers disgorged from the cars. Fifteen or so officers poured over the bridge, most running, followed at a more sedate pace by a man in his forties, balding and wearing a dark suit. He was accompanied by another slightly older and shorter man similarly dressed.

Officers peeled off in different directions some heading around the far side of the castle out of sight of them, presumably entering through the main entrance, others hurried in through the small door from which the family had exited.

Four of the officers stood around the seated couple awaiting the arrival of the plain clothes officers. One knelt to examine the lifeless body of Elliot.

The bald plain clothes officer introduced himself as Detective Superintendent Munroe and his colleague as Detective Inspector Armstrong.

"Would you like to tell me what the hell has been going on around here since you arrived?"

The use of the word 'hell' amused Simon and he smiled ironically. "I'll tell you about hell shall I?" he said as he started to tell the story, holding nothing back. He decided that anything he tried to modify or tone down in some way, would just create more questions than answers and, frankly, he was resigned to being thought insane.

As Simon told his story with the occasional confirmation or comment from Kate, the officers listened incredulously. As he spoke officers began to arrive and stand around presumably having established that there were no other suspects in the area or evidence that needed preserving.

About three-quarters of the way through his story, a uniformed officer who had emerged from the corridor behind the small door interrupted them, "You had better come and see this," he said.

The superintendent broke off to follow the officer into the corridor closely followed by his shadow, leaving the family being eyed suspiciously by the surrounding uniformed officers.

"Like to see him explain all that in there," Simon said to Kate quietly.

After ten minutes or so they returned. Superintendent Munroe looked ashen and he stared uncompromisingly at Simon.

"I have two more dead officers in there," he said, "I thought when I saw the bodies of Constable Scott and the farmer earlier, that I had never seen anything so...", he seemed to pause struggling to find the right words, "so depraved," he said finally. "Are you going to continue with this ridiculous story. Are you already hoping for an insanity plea?"

Simon looked at the officer with a surprised look on his face. He had of course anticipated that his story would sound incredible, but it genuinely hadn't occurred to him that he would have been a suspect in the killings.

Deciding it was too late to go back, he continued, more determined to tell the story accurately, completing his account as he had started.

The officer stared at him apparently deciding on his next course of action. "Can you explain to me, how any of that could have happened without a single trace of evidence remaining? All I have here is three dead officers and a farmer, all mutilated horribly, plus another dead body out here, and two adults and a child with some ridiculous story about wizards, Border Reivers, clans and ghosts," he was now raising his voice angrily.

Simon seemed unperturbed. The disbelief of this police officer seemed relatively unimportant after what they had been through over the last few hours.

"How much evidence do you want?" he shouted defiantly. "There is a dead wizard and decapitated Red Cap in there, a dead barguest, a burnt wooden chest, even Soulis's dagger must be where he dropped it. There was a huge battle in there, how much more do you want?"

"Come with me," the officer said, taking Simon by the arm and pulling him unceremoniously towards the corridor. Loathed to re-enter that hell hole, Simon baulked, and then resignedly walked into the corridor and down into the chamber ahead of Munroe.

Officers had dragged portable floodlights into the chamber driven by a portable generator that worked away noisily. The chamber was lit up as bright as day with the exception of a few dark corners, where stone pillars and walls blocked the powerful beams of light.

Simon stared around the chamber in disbelief.

Apart from the pile of mutilated flesh in the corner that had once been the police officers and was now being photographed and poured over by people shrouded from head to foot in white overalls, hoods and footwear, there was not one single sign of anything to suggest a pitched battle had taken place.

There was no dead barguest or Red Cap, no sign of Soulis or his dagger, no sign of the remains of a fire, let alone the chest.

Even the mud covered surface of the floor showed no disturbance except the tracks of the feet of officers, who were religiously sticking to a single pathway through the mud on the floor of the chamber to preserve as far as possible any evidence that might be destroyed by a careless boot.

The floor showed no other signs of intrusion.

"Can you explain to me how all that nonsense you gave me could have happened without leaving even a single footprint?"

Pulling Simon unceremoniously back out of the chamber he led him by the arm, back to where Kate and Thomas were sitting.

Munroe, stood looking at Simon and began to speak formerly and precisely, "Simon Ralstone, I am arresting you on suspicion of...", his sentence was cut off by a loud shout:

"Sir, look!" and he turned in anger towards the voice that had interrupted him at such a crucial moment.

What Munroe saw, caused his mouth to drop open and the whole shifting mass of officers froze staring uncomprehendingly.

Coming slowly from the walls around the corridor and door, not from the corridor itself, snaked a column of horses. Two astride they walked slowly across the grass and down the bank towards the burn.

The horses horse carried riders, dressed in steel bonnets with quilted sleeveless jackets and carrying long spears, swords at their side. Some had small crossbows strapped to the backs of their saddles.

Others on foot walked alongside or behind the horses. Each of the walking Reivers held the hand of a small child who toddled alongside looking up at his protector. Others carried younger babies, crooked in powerful forearms.

The procession continued past Munroe who estimated it as being two to three hundred strong. It passed within a few feet of the staring officers, those on horseback stared down contemptuously at the police as they passed.

One officer approached the procession and attempted to catch the bridle of one of the horses. A leather booted foot crashed into his chest from the rider and the officer fell backwards scrabbling for his footing and being caught by his colleagues as he fell.

The procession passed sedately down the bank, across the burn. It turned left onto the road and, after about ten minutes, disappeared around the bend in the road.

Munroe looked from Simon to Kate to the child and then back to Simon.

"I think we'd better get back to the police station," he said.

CHAPTER FORTY

Dettori woke early in the morning on the 14th February 2007.

Something was wrong – he felt it, but he could not identify what it was.

The rest of the evening had gone well and he had retired to his bed confident that Vladimir and the other executives would be suitably compliant from now onwards. He had reassured them using all his confident charm that they were all valuable and important links in the chain of command. But he had left them in no doubt that further disobedience would not be tolerated. The vision of Romanski's demise would no doubt haunt their dreams for years to come.

But this morning something was definitely wrong and he climbed out of bed urgently to check the cameras to reassure himself.

He checked the guests' rooms first. Everyone was still sleeping, albeit fitfully, but sleeping nonetheless. It was not surprising as they would have been awake most of the night, and that was good. It meant his message had been fully understood.

But as he passed from one to another there seemed nothing to concern him.

An examination of the front lawn showed not a trace of the carnage from the night before. The bodies had been dragged away by the Red Caps, he knew not where, but from many such experiences, he knew they would never be seen again and he noticed with satisfaction that staff had already arrived and were busy clearing the damage in the hall.

His staff was hand picked and well paid. They did not need instructions, nor would they ever show any interest in an explanation for this strange damage. They would simply put it to rights, and in a day or two no trace of the explosions, blood and urine stains and gun shots would remain.

No, nothing appeared to be wrong as far as he could see, but still he felt uncomfortable.

He then realised, it was nothing external – it was coming from within himself.

Finally he decided it was just the prospect of all the planning and hard work of the last few years in bringing to fruition the plan of his master.

He decided to have breakfast in his room.

He had explained to his guests that he would be leaving after breakfast to collect William Soulis and that they should make use of the extensive facilities whilst he was gone.

He would return early in the evening, no later, and they would meet their new chairman and they could celebrate the dawning of a new era, a new beginning for the world.

CHAPTER FORTY-ONE

The police drove them back to the cottage to get a change of clothes, because they wanted to keep theirs for forensics, before bringing them back to the police station for further questioning which really just went over the same ground.

It was several hours before Simon and Kate were allowed to leave, with promises that they would be contacted either for more information or to be advised of the final outcome of the investigation.

Frankly however, Simon felt that Munroe was really more concerned about how he was going to explain the mass hallucination, for that was the only conclusion that made any sense to Munroe, that he and the other officers had seen.

Given the circumstances, the evidence of himself and his own officers was no less incredible than that of Simon and Kate.

What had been, or had appeared to be, a particularly brutal, but nonetheless believable, set of serial killings had turned into... well, Munroe had no description or explanation for what he and twenty other officers had seen.

Elliot's car had been brought back by one of the officers to the police station but they had been told that it would be needed for forensic examination.

Unwilling to try and explain the problem and the damage to his father-in-law's ex-employer, he decided to leave that to the police.

He would hire a car at his own expense.

The hire company agreed to deliver the car to the cottage and they returned themselves by taxi to pack their belongings. They really did not want to spend another minute in the company of these openly hostile police officers.

Four hours later they were driving slowly back through Newcastleton heading towards Carlisle and the M6 for the journey home.

"We should stop and see Truman," Kate said as they passed Douglas Square and the Grapes on their right.

Simon nodded and turning into Langholm Street, he pulled up outside Truman's small house. "It will be nice to talk to someone who doesn't think we are lying or insane," he said ruefully.

They knocked several times on the door, but there was no reply and as they turned to leave a little old lady came out of her front door in the adjoining house, and looked over the fence at the young family.

"We're looking for Mr Truman," Kate said to the old lady.

"Are you family?" she said.

"Not really, well yes I suppose we are, distant relatives," Kate was not quite sure how to explain the relationship. "Probably more friends I suppose," she answered.

"I'm sorry," the old lady said kindly, "I'm afraid I have some bad news for you. Old Tom died this morning. The police arrived very early this morning and when they couldn't raise him they climbed in through a window, found him peacefully in bed. They thought he was asleep at first. Seems he went off to sleep and just didn't wake up."

Seeing the look that the young couple gave each other she obviously felt she needed to explain more. "I'm sure it is the way most of us would like to go, peacefully and happy in our sleep. They say he wasn't in any pain, he was just very old."

The old lady looked strangely at the young woman, who smiled at the news. She would never understand young people, how could she possibly smile at such tragic news? She shook her head in puzzlement and went back in doors closing the door behind her.

"You have no idea how old," Kate said to the closing door. Smiling she kissed Simon and Thomas who gurgled happily.

"Looks like Dad and Old Tom have both gone home," she said. "Maybe we should do the same."

CHAPTER FORTY-TWO

Dettori drove himself to Hermitage arriving at midday. This was a moment for William Soulis and himself to share alone but he was horrified to find several police cars and vans and police officers, some in uniform, some plain clothes and some carrying mysterious boxes and dressed from head to toe in white protective clothing. Yards of blue and white tape flapped in the strong February wind as the officers hurried about their business.

Alarmed by the activity he immediately left and drove to Newcastleton. He had no desire to explain his arrival to some over inquisitive policeman.

From there he phoned Robertson at Branxholm to use his contacts to find out what was happening. He told him to get back to him at a hotel called the Grapes, he would wait there until he heard from the politician.

He booked a room in the small hotel to provide himself with the privacy to wait and make confidential calls, ordered lunch and sat impatiently awaiting Robertson's call.

Robertson called back inside half an hour with preliminary information.

He explained that an incident had occurred. Initial reports were sketchy but two policemen had been killed along with a civilian called David Paul Elliot, the man's daughter and son-in-law, a Kate and Simon Ralstone, were currently in custody being questioned about the incident.

The names meant nothing to Dettori. "Do we know anything about them?" he asked.

"There appears to be nothing special about them. I am having them checked out now but so far it seems they are nobodies."

"Nobodies who are interfering in the plans of the soon-to-be most powerful man in the world. Keep checking," Dettori answered coldly.

"Apparently there were some extremely strange stories of ghosts and the supernatural, but no one seemed to be clear on the details. Not surprisingly they want to get their facts right before the press gets hold of it. I'll let you know as soon as I have more."

"The press *will not* get hold of it. Who is in charge?" Dettori demanded.

"A Detective Superintendent Munroe. He is there in Newcastleton leading the questioning."

"Get him to me now," Dettori said. "I don't care what he is doing, I want him here in an hour. I don't care who you have to call, but get him here and make sure he is ready to cooperate," Dettori slammed the receiver down angrily.

Forty-five minutes later the phone in his room went and the receptionist explained there was a Mr Munroe in reception for him.

At least by not using his rank, Munroe had indicated his ability to act with discretion. "Send him up," he said quietly.

Dettori was waiting with the door open when Munroe arrived at the room. He looked puzzled as the small, smartly dressed businessman let him in.

"Who sent you here?" Dettori said abruptly.

Munroe still looked slightly shell-shocked; he had never been ordered to leave in the middle of an interrogation of a murder suspect before.

"I had a call from the Chief Constable, he told me to leave what I was doing and come and see you. Apparently there is an issue of state security. I am to cooperate with you."

Dettori knew this was Robertson's work. Munroe would know not to ask too many questions.

"I want all of your officers, and I mean *everyone*, away from Hermitage Castle right now. I need to go there and I need to examine the place alone. You will come with me but you will wait for me by the bridge. You will not come in and you will stop anyone else entering. Is that clear?"

"But it is a murder scene, I can't..."

Dettori waved an irritated hand at him, "I do not have time to discuss this with you. You will return to the police station and get me copies of all the witness statements taken so far. Bring them

239

back to me here and then drive me out to Hermitage. I will read them on the way. Alternatively you can finish your career as a uniformed beat officer, is that also clear?"

Munroe started to protest then thought better of it. The Chief Constable had sounded intimidated when he called and it was quite rare for him to call directly. Usually he would have left a message. These people were obviously very important.

"I am sure you are a good efficient officer. If you feel you need to clear this with your Chief Constable please feel free, as long as you do so whilst you are on your way to get the statements. I will expect you back here in thirty minutes."

Munroe lowered his head. "I am sure that will not be necessary," he said quietly.

"Then I suggest you go now. Time is pressing."

CHAPTER FORTY-THREE

Dettori sat in the back seat of his car outside Hermitage Castle, silently reading the witness statements. Munroe sat in the driving seat occasionally looking at Dettori in the rear view mirror.

Dettori was gratified to find his orders had been obeyed to the letter, there was no longer any sign of anyone in or around the building.

"Is this all?" Dettori said waving the pages before him.

"That is all the statements so far," Munroe said.

"Tell me of these horsemen. Leave nothing out."

Munroe looked embarrassed, "I am sure it was some kind of hallucination or mass hypnosis, it is not...", he started.

"I did not ask for your opinion, just tell me what you saw," Dettori was clearly irritated.

Munroe thought of modifying his story. It seemed lunatic to him. He could not but believe this man would think him mad, but something told him that Dettori would know if he tried to conceal anything.

He told his story exactly as it had happened. When he had finished he looked at Dettori expecting to be berated as a lunatic, but his passenger's face remained totally impassive.

"Stay here. Let no one in and stay out yourself. I will be back."

With that Dettori climbed out of the car, walked across the bridge and headed around the perimeter of the building to the small door which he had entered so many times. Without so much as a glance back, he walked into the dark corridor.

The huge chamber was empty, apart from the generators running the huge floodlights that were illuminating the entire chamber, save one or two dark corners, where jagged outcrops of stone had crumbled over the years to form shadowed alcoves.

He had been here many times and the powerful presence of Soulis was always there. But now he felt nothing.

He walked around the perimeter until, reaching a particularly dark corner, he heard the sound of water running down the dank walls and also a familiar shuffling.

"Come out," he commanded, knowing exactly what was hiding there.

The foul shape of a Red Cap slowly emerged, cautiously, sniffing at the air, head swinging from side to side. He had expected Robin Red Cap, but this was not Soulis's familiar.

"Where is my Lord Soulis?" he demanded of the cringing figure.

"He is with our masters," the Red Cap hissed.

"I am in a hurry Red Cap. We have great plans. I have no time for your riddles. What do you mean?"

"We all have masters, even the most powerful Lord Soulis. You served your Lord; Soulis served his. The Dark Spirits are all powerful. He has gone to explain his failure. You cannot comprehend the hell that your Lord is going through now. Failure is not tolerated by our masters."

Dettori's anger was growing. "No one is more powerful than my Lord Soulis. I am tired of your stupidity, where is Robin Red Cap? Perhaps he can tell me what is happening?"

The Red Cap dropped his head, "Ah, my brother Robin. I too have lost my brother and teacher. He is no more. Destroyed by the clan."

"The clan? Who are the clan? Explain yourself."

"I have been sent to explain," the Red Cap whined. "The Dark Forces have sent me to serve you, you are my master as Soulis was Robin's. I am yours to command in all that the Dark Forces will allow."

"Then explain," Dettori demanded.

"The Dark Forces have chosen you. Soulis failed in his quest, you must now replace him and spread the power of our masters to the world. Soulis allowed his arrogance to underestimate the love of these humans for each other. He was defeated by love."

The Red Cap continued his story, "The battle between the dark and the light is eternal. Soulis is but one battlefront, his failure is a small delay in an ongoing battle. You are to continue his work."

Dettori listened, not fully comprehending.

"In the mists of time, the dark and light forces chose their weapons to fight their battle for the souls of man. The Dark Spirits weapons were many. They knew the frailty of the human spirit: they use the weaknesses of men, greed, sloth, anger, avarice, gluttony, lust, pride."

"The seven deadly sins," Dettori said.

"Precisely. But the light chose but one, love, and they chose wisely for love to these humans is as powerful alone as all their weaknesses together. This has led to the balance. The battle to own the souls of men has raged ever since."

"So how does this affect my Lord Soulis?" Dettori asked.

"He promised much. He was to release himself from Hermitage, and through the empire you were building for him he would move the balance in favour of the dark side, eventually giving them domain over the hearts of men.

"He sought to release himself by trapping the soul of a worthy replacement. The soul of a child, a direct descendent of the wizard who destroyed him in 1321."

"What happened?" Dettori asked.

"Soulis did not content himself with taking revenge on the descendent of his enemy. He sought to take vengeance on the entire clan that helped in his destruction."

"You keep talking of this clan. What is it you mean?" Dettori was struggling to follow. "Who or what is the clan?"

"The Elliots," the Red Cap replied. "The Elliots are the hated clan who occupied Soulis's land at the behest of Robert the Bruce. They held this castle and they slaughtered your Lord under the instructions of the wizard, Thomas of Ercildoune.

"The wizard and the Elliots shared the same history, they are one family. Fatefully, they came together again when the direct descendent of the clan married the direct descendent of Ercildoune. The child of this union was uniquely qualified to replace Soulis in Hermitage."

"So these people being held by the police are the clan?" Dettori asked.

"Kate Ralstone is the daughter of the dead man David Elliot. Simon Ralstone is the descendent of Ercildoune. But the real power is in the child of that union. Thomas Ralstone."

"So what happened?" Dettori could not understand how his mentor could have been overturned by these nonentities.

"Soulis wanted to take vengeance on the Elliots. Instead of just taking the child he wanted to see the suffering of the child's family when he took his life.

"He underestimated the power of love. By bringing them together within these walls he weakened the barriers keeping the forces of light out. Those members of the clan that had gone before were allowed in and the sacrifice failed."

Dettori began to understand why he had awoken that morning feeling the absence of his mentor.

He turned to the Red Cap. "Still, everything is in place, the Soulis Foundation sits in Branxholm, we are ready to proceed with the new World Order."

The Red Cap turned and shuffled into the dark shadows and soon Dettori heard a scraping as the creature returned, dragging behind him a huge wooden chest, bound with iron bands into the centre of the chamber.

"You are now Master of Hermitage, my Lord Dettori," the Red cap grovelled at the feet of the small Italian.

"I am your familiar sent to serve you by the Dark Spirits. This chest is the source of your power. You can call me by knocking on it nine times, three times over."

Dettori smiled. He may have lost his mentor, Lord Soulis, but now he had the opportunity to increase his powers to the levels of his passed master.

"Then this is just a small hiatus," his excitement was growing as he began to comprehend the possibilities. "The organisation is in place, we can continue with our plans."

"You have been granted a great honour by the Dark Forces my Lord Dettori. You are now Master of Hermitage in place of Lord Soulis, and I have the honour to be able to serve you."

Dettori could hardly contain his excitement. "I will not fail," he said. "Our masters will not be disappointed."

CHAPTER FORTY-FOUR

Dettori spoke with the Red Cap for a further hour and his excitement grew as he realised that he would have sole control of the Soulis Foundation and he was set, in place of his erstwhile mentor, to become the most powerful man in the world.

His mind raced as he considered the possibilities. He was anxious to return to Branxholm, to inform the executives of his new position, that he would be leading the Foundation in place of William Soulis.

Suddenly he recalled the fact that Munroe must still be sitting outside in the car. It had been two hours since he had left him there. Despite his warnings to stay outside he was sure the policeman would by now be concerned. After all, as far as he was concerned, the castle was empty. What could Dettori possibly be doing in an empty building for that length of time?

He turned to the Red Cap who was squatting quietly on the chest. "I must dismiss the policeman outside before he becomes inquisitive. I will then return to Branxholm and give orders to the executive team. There is no time to lose. You, Red Cap, keep my castle safe until I return."

The Red Cap stared at Dettori, uncomprehending, a quizzical look on the creature's face.

Dettori turned and walked towards the corridor leading out of the chamber. Passing into the corridor he saw ahead of him the open door and the warmth of the daylight and sunshine was welcoming. The air inside the castle was dank and musty, he was looking forward to filling his lungs with the crisp fresh air outside.

As his mind raced, planning, prioritising, he considered the best way to explain the change of circumstances to the others.

Suddenly, as he approached within a yard or so of the open doorway, he felt a blow like an iron bar smashing into his chest, and he was driven back into the tunnel, scrabbling in the slime and mud on the floor of the corridor. He gasped in the dank air, the pain in his chest was excruciating, and he scanned the corridor ahead, not sure what had hit him.

He saw nothing and as the pain in his chest slowly lessened, he climbed uncomfortably to his feet, looking in disgust at the foul slime that matted his fine Italian suit and his manicured hands.

Slowly, one hand tentatively stretched before him, he stepped cautiously forward towards the doorway. The dampness and narrowness of the corridor was beginning to feel oppressive and he felt a feeling of claustrophobia rising in him; he fought to avoid a feeling of panic. All he wanted was to step outside and fill his lungs with the fresh cleansing air promised by the open doorway.

Then, as his hand reached to within a yard of the doorway again, he saw a flash of blue light and a pain, as if he had touched a high voltage electrical source, shot through his arm, again throwing him back to fall painfully to the slime coated floor.

The effects of the second blast combined with the first had weakened him appreciatively and he began to crawl back towards the chamber. He would order the Red Cap to explain, to get him out of this foul dungeon.

As he made it on hands and knees into the chamber he had regained sufficient strength to climb painfully to his feet.

The Red Cap was sitting on top of the chest, watching him strangely.

"What the hell is happening to me?" Dettori demanded. "Why can I not get out?"

The Red Cap looked puzzled, "But I explained to you, about the balance."

Dettori looked confused as the Red Cap continued, "You are the Master of Hermitage now, in place of Lord Soulis. This place belongs to the Dark Spirits. You cannot leave until you find a suitable replacement to maintain the balance, just as our Lord Soulis was seeking to do."

"But the Foundation? You said you were sent to help me, to serve me?" Dettori was beginning to panic again.

"And so I shall," replied the Red Cap. "Just as my brother, Robin served Lord Soulis." He lifted the lid of the chest and climbed in.

"It is time for me to leave. You know how to call me. But remember the error of Lord Soulis, punishment awaits if you try to call me before seven years has elapsed."

"But how do I find a replacement?" Dettori's voice was filled with terror.

The Red Cap paused holding onto the lid as he stood inside the chest, "Just as your Lord Soulis did. You must take time to develop your powers. You are far too inexperienced as yet to conjure such a difficult task. Call me and I will help you. It will not take long."

"But you said I cannot call you for seven years?"

The Red Cap wiped his hand across his salivating jaws. "Seven years is the blinking of an eye. The battle between the light and the dark is as old as time. You have a good start already, It will not take you longer than your master took to build his powers to the requisite level."

"How long did it take William de Soulis to reach the necessary level?"

"No time at all," the Red Cap replied, "just a little over five hundred years."

Dettori watched in terror as the Red Cap closed the lid above him.

Dettori rushed to the box unsure as to whether he should open it or signal as he had been told to, but the warning of an early recall was fresh in his mind and he stood undecided, horrified at the prospect of making the wrong decision.

Suddenly, hearing a noise he looked towards the corridor and his heart leapt hopefully as he saw Detective Superintendent Munroe standing at the entrance to the chamber calling his name, "Mr Dettori are you there?"

"Thank God you are here, Superintendent," Dettori was desperate. "I need your help, you need to get me out of here."

Munroe seemed not to hear. Stepping further into the chamber he shouted, louder this time "Mr Dettori, are you alright?"

"No I am not, you fool. Get me out of here. I am right here in front of you, are you blind?"

Dettori stepped towards the policeman who was now walking towards him. Dettori went to meet him, but instead of stopping when Dettori was directly in front of him he continued forward as Dettori raised his hands to stop the policeman crashing into him.

Dettori felt a huge coldness go through his body as he felt the policeman pass directly through him as if he was a shadow.

Munroe shuddered. "God this is an evil place," he muttered to himself as he briefly looked around in the shadows for any trace of Dettori. "Where the hell did you go to, you arrogant bastard?" he whispered almost inaudibly, although Dettori was standing so close, he heard every word.

Munroe decided to give one last call, "I must leave Mr Dettori, I'm needed back in Newcastleton. If you can hear me, let me know, otherwise I must leave."

He waited listening for any response and despite the fact that Dettori was standing in front of him screaming directly into his face he heard nothing. Giving a final shrug and one last look around, he turned to leave.

"Don't go, I need your help!" Dettori struggled after the departing policeman following him into the corridor.

He continued to shout trying to grab Munroe by the arm, but his hand seemed to pass directly through him.

Munroe reached the door and passed out into the sunshine. Dettori tried to follow, but again felt a massive pain and blast in his chest as he was driven backwards falling painfully to the muddy floor.

He climbed to his knees, staring out of the open door into the daylight.

He felt as if the walls were closing in on him and he began to hyperventilate as the panic of claustrophobia overtook him. Panic, like steel bands, gripped his chest and the tears streamed down his muddy face as he realised that soon, the darkness would come.

He had no idea for how long the floodlights in the chamber would continue but in any event he knew they would be removed eventually by the police.

He collapsed to his knees, holding out his mud spattered fingers towards the light of the sun before dropping his face into his hands and sobbing, contemplating in horror, an eternity in the dark.

EPILOGUE

It was six weeks before the coroner eventually released her father's body and Kate and Simon could arrange the funeral.

Initially the body was to be returned to Oxfordshire for burial, but Kate had made enquiries and she had managed to get permission to have him buried in the cemetery on the Jedburgh Road, outside Newcastleton.

It was not particularly difficult given his name. Somehow she had the feeling that her father would have wanted that.

The enquiry had gone nowhere and in the absence of any forensic evidence that could not be explained away by a clever lawyer, they had eventually been told that the official version was that the officers and the farmer had been killed by a particularly vicious wild dog, suspected of many sheep killings in the area.

A couple of weeks after they had left Newcastleton, a large black dog was discovered, shot, near the cemetery. Kate and Simon were unimpressed.

The photograph displayed in the local Newcastleton paper looked nothing like the barguest and they assumed that the dead dog had been 'arranged' to help put the enquiry to rest. It seemed the police wanted this story to go away and as the killings had stopped, it was argued that a farmer had probably killed it without further report to avoid getting involved in the paperwork.

This of course did not explain how David Elliot had died.

It was clear the fatal wound had been a single, deep trauma to his stomach, and although no vital organs had been damaged, he had bled to death internally.

Other injuries, including a defensive wound on the forearm, probably caused by the same weapon that had struck the fatal blow, a damaged knee, and a fractured cheek bone were inconclusive.

The most puzzling of the injuries however, were signs of strangulation. Not fatal, but consistent with an incredibly strong grip with a single hand from which could clearly be seen a thumb and finger marks.

Both Kate and Simon were covered with Elliot's blood, but nothing that could not be explained away by their attempts to help or comfort him.

Most telling though, was that the span of the hand that had gripped Elliot's neck was huge. Far too large for either Simon or Kate to have done it.

This effectively eliminated them as possible suspects. Clearly some person of huge strength and stature had held Elliot by the throat. The evidence could be used as an excellent defence for the couple, if the police felt inclined to press charges.

They showed no such inclination.

This coupled with the lack of the murder weapon suggested that the coroner's verdict would be murder, by person or persons unknown.

Of course the file would stay open and the police would pretend to continue to investigate it for a decent period, until they could quietly put the case to rest.

Actually, Simon believed the story suited the police who really wanted the whole incident to just go away. None of them were actually very keen to discuss what they had seen with their own eyes.

So it was that two months after the events of the 14th February Kate, Simon and Thomas stood in the Newcastleton cemetery by the side of two freshly erected headstones, side by side. Both graves were covered with flowers.

The actual funeral had taken place the day before. Elliot's family, his mother, brothers and sister and, of course, his other children, David and Emily along with assorted other relatives had attended.

No one apart from Kate, Simon and little Thomas, attended the earlier internment of Thomas Truman that had been scheduled for two hours before Elliot's.

The only flowers for Truman had been sent by them.

Kate and Simon with Thomas wanted to say a private farewell to both Elliot and Truman so the couple and their son stayed at the Grapes that night and returned the following morning for a private goodbye.

The additional flowers on Truman's grave had been placed there by Kate, who had taken some from her father's.

She was confident he would not have minded, after all he was family and Kate knew how important family was to her father. In any event the single bouquet they had sent seemed an inadequate token for a seven hundred year-old life.

Kate read the inscriptions on the headstones.

One bore the words:

David Paul Elliot
Born 12th February 1950
Died 14th February 2007
Fortiter et Recte

The other, even simpler read:

Thomas Truman
"Old Tom"
Date of Birth Unknown
Died 14th February 2007

Simon hugged Kate and Thomas to him.

"Are you sure we are doing the right thing leaving him here?" he said.

Kate raised tear-filled eyes to her husband and smiled gently at him, not answering.

Turning away from the graves she looked across the cemetery to the corner which overlooked the defensive mounds in the valley beyond.

Watching them at the graveside and sat with mouth open, tongue lolling and panting, was a huge black dog.

As she stared into the soft dark eyes of the animal she seemed to see a brief flash of red which disappeared instantly.

"He'll be safe here," she said quietly.